HIDDEN NO MORE

Includes a special bonus short story,
LOVED EVER MORE

USA TODAY Bestselling Author
Christina McKnight

La Loma Elite
PUBLISHING

Books By Christina McKnight

A Lady Forsaken Series
Shunned No More
Forgotten No More
Scorned Ever More
Christmas Ever More
Hidden No More

The Undaunted Debutantes Series
The Disappearance of Lady Edith
The Misfortune of Lady Lucianna
The Misadventures of Lady Ophelia
The Season of Lady Chastity
The Desires of Lady Prudence

Lady Archer's Creed Series
Written with Amanda Mariel
Theodora
Georgina
Adeline
Josephine

Craven House Series
The Thief Steals Her Earl
The Mistress Enchants Her Marquis
The Madame Catches Her Duke
The Gambler Wagers Her Baron

Standalone Titles
A Kiss at Christmastide
For the Love of a Widow
The Earl of St. Seville
The Lady Loves a Scandal
Bedded Under the Christmastide Moon
Bound by the Christmastide Moon
Fated for the Duke

DEDICATION

To My Readers~

Hidden No More brings the end of a great three years in my writing career. I am heartbroken to be letting these characters go,but I know you will keep their stories alive.

Onward and upward!

ACKNOWLEDGMENTS

There are several people I'd like to thank for staying with me through the emotional journey of writing this book.

To Marc, my amazing boyfriend, who continues to stand by my side through the utter chaos that is my creative process. Thank you...your love and dedication never ceases to amaze me. I hope to one day be as selfless and compassionate as you are.

To Lauren Stewart, my critique partner and best friend, you pushed me to explore new avenues of thought that I never dreamed possible. If we were in a true relationship, it would be one based on co-dependency, but in a good way. My writing would not be what it is without your comments, criticism, suggestions, and guidance.

I'd also like to thank the wonderful women who've supported me in both my writing career and life, including (but not limited to): Debbie Haston, Angie Stanton, Sharla Metheny-Ybanez, Roxanne Stellmacher, Laura Cummings, Annalisa Nicole, Dawn Borbon, Suzi Parker, Jennifer Vella, Brandi Johnson, and Latisha Kahn. I know I'm forgetting people...You have all been very patient and wonderfully supportive of my eccentric ways.

A very special thank you to my editor, Chelle Olson with Literally Addicted to Detail, your skill and professionalism surpass all that I expected.

Cover art and wraparound cover design credit to Teresa Spreckelmeyer at the Midnight Muse Designs.

Finally, thank you for supporting indie authors.

PROLOGUE

London, England
March, 1816

ANDREW PENTON, THE Marquis of Drake, lifted his eyelids, heavy from the many years of undue turmoil he'd endured, to gaze into the emerald green eyes of one of his only offspring, his youngest daughter. Ellington's eyes—so much likes his own—were the only feature about the girl that resembled him. The rest was inherited from a mother she'd never known... a woman Andrew had barely known himself. Nor one he had shown any mercy to in her darkest hour.

He was resigned to an eternity in hell for his callous existence.

How he regretted so many of the decisions he'd made, the people he'd hurt, and that he hadn't honored Lorelei's memory as was proper.

She would never know how deep his love for her truly was because he'd wasted his years punishing himself and those around him. And too late, he'd realized it would not have been what she'd have wanted for him. No, if given the opportunity, Andrew would have done everything differently; he would have loved the children he'd been blessed with, not misspent years searching and longing for the child who belonged only to Lorelei, his long-lost beloved.

Lorelei's babe with no blood tie to him or the Marquisate, a boy with no knowledge of the havoc his mother had brought to the marquis' life…nor the utter destruction and agony she left in her wake.

But his Lorelei was gone…had been gone for what seemed an eternity. Yet, he was eager to be reunited with her…if there were something awaiting either of them on the other side of death.

Certainly, no place was reserved for him at Lorelei's side—heaven was too great a hope for a man as cruel as he.

For now, he was left here with his youngest child; her misery rolling off her in waves. Emotionally collapsed in upon herself, she was broken. And he was responsible. So young, only seventeen summers, yet he'd forced her to live out the emotions of someone three times her age…all because…Andrew had no excuse for what he'd put her through, at least not one that made sense in this moment.

There was not enough time for him to tell his daughter everything she needed to hear, let alone time to summon her older sister.

And he was wasting the precious time he *did* have. The words that needed to be spoken were stuck in his throat, playing through his head, yet never passing his lips.

So many years he'd searched for Peter.

So many years he'd denied the existence of Ruby.

And all the while, he'd ignored the child before him.

Ellington.

He'd so infrequently spoken—or even thought—the name that it sounded foreign even in his mind. Her heart-shaped face, red hair, and freckled nose were as distant in his recollection as so many other things he'd put from his awareness in recent years.

What he did recognize was the loathing radiating from her very person, the hatred in her stare, and the aloofness she donned to mask it all.

Because, when he'd been able to stand and look in a mirror, her character appeared the spitting image of the man who'd sired her.

The Marquis of Drake.

As steadfastly as he'd denied it to Mrs. Bee and himself over the years, his blood ran heavy in Ellington's veins.

She flaunted her superiority.

She fought with passion.

She argued relentlessly.

She made all the mistakes her father did. And she would pay for them, too—with loneliness, grief, and a life unlived.

What scared him the most was her propensity for doing exactly as she pleased. The girl did not think he noticed her comings and goings, but he was aware of everything going on in his household, even though he hadn't left his bed in days.

He knew when the day came and she gave

her heart to another, she'd love him with all her being; every ounce of her existence would be given to that person. But he feared that man would not know her worth or her loyalty. Andrew didn't trust another to mend her broken heart...return the soul he'd stolen from her. He didn't think anyone *could*.

She would cease to live if the man she finally came to trust and love were taken from her.

Much like himself...or, more accurately, the man the marquis used to be.

A memory so distant, Andrew wasn't sure he'd ever truly been that man.

The man he was now was certainly not one his ancestors would be proud to count in their lineage—one future generations would wipe from every wall in his large home.

He knew his time was near, for his breath became increasingly hard to draw in; he realized these were his last moments. He needed to tell Ellington, show her that she was his. Convince her of the mistakes he'd made and admit to her how sorry he was for...everything.

He'd found and brought Peter to her.

At first, he'd been unconvinced of the child's identity, but one look at the boy and Andrew had known his true parentage—his Lorelei...and Lord Chastain, the man Andrew had considered his friend for more years than he could count.

But he'd fought the realization for so long that there was no time left to tell the boy of his mother and the great love Andrew had shared with her, fleeting as their physical relationship had been.

It was only now, as he listened to his own death rattle in his chest, he realized that the boy's deformities were no longer of import; that the physical abilities of a man were not more significant than the willpower and fortitude one possessed.

It was his heart that mattered most.

Andrew had spent hours...days, watching the young man in his duties. For his limited years, just six months older than Ellington, the boy was good with the horses and cared much for his fellow man. The other stable hands respected him and his abilities with the livestock.

"My daughter—" His words were barely understandable as he felt his lucidity fading. He should remain quiet and take his secrets to his grave without burdening anyone further. It would be the kindest thing he could do for his child, but his history had proven that he was anything but a kind man.

Ellington's fingers tightened where she gripped his hand, warmer than the noonday sun upon his icy skin.

"Do not—" She cut off his words. "Not now, after all this time."

"I must." He pushed through the heaviness in his chest. "There is so much to say."

"It is too late."

Suddenly, Andrew was in a different time, another place...holding the dying form of the only woman he could say with certainty he'd loved. "I know what too late is, and we have not reached that point."

"What could you say to me now that you have been unable to say in the past?" Ellington whispered. Her grip on his hand faltered before tightening once more. "You have been quite clear about how you feel toward me."

"It is not your fault."

She wrenched back in shock. "You think I

ever believed that your treatment—your resentment—of me was *my* fault?" She stumbled over her words. "You are a sad, pathetic man."

"I did not mean—"

"The meaning behind your words has never been anything but perfectly clear." Ellington leaned in close to him once more, her eyes narrowing as she spoke, "You have made it well-known that I am only the daughter of a whore, not worthy of your time or your name."

His words thrown back in his face stung a thousand times worse than any bee sting could.

"I am a bastard, left upon your doorstep by a woman who'd secured her own death by spreading her legs for any man with enough shillings."

Andrew would not, could not, deny that he'd said those exact words many times over. His main goal had been to keep her at bay, suppress his own longing for love and acceptance. In truth, he didn't deserve her love nor any forgiveness found this day. If he hadn't become ill, it was likely he'd have continued to treat her harshly. Keeping her close for selfish reasons and forbidding her from finding her own way in the world. Andrew had promised Ellington no future except her measly existence under his roof.

Several times, he'd caught her sneaking into his house from God knows where at late hours of the night. He'd accused her of visiting those women of her mother's ilk, women of the night at Craven House.

And Ellington had never denied it.

He'd feared that Ellington would leave him. Abandon him to be taken in by that group of harlots. The same set who'd sent the girl's mother to seduce Drake in his time of weakness after his one true love wed another.

But Ellington had always returned to him.

Andrew had long wondered why his daughter would return to a man who gave her nothing and a home that would never be her own.

Maybe, just maybe, the one thing his daughter possessed was the only thing Andrew lacked himself.

The strength to persevere and the ability to make the best of one's situation.

Andrew had given up long ago.

But now, he had one last chance to do right by her.

"Ellie," he said, returning his look to her. He'd drifted off without knowing it, and he struggled to keep himself in the here and now and not ponder what awaited him, or dwell on what was long past. "Alex, you must trust him."

"The stable boy?" Confusion clouded her face. "Whatever does he have to do with...anything?"

"He will care for you."

"Certainly, you jest!" Her indignation at his words was exactly as he'd expected. "Have you promised me to a stable boy, Father? Is that to be my lot in life?"

She'd called him Father, something she'd only done once—and had been punished severely for, yet now, the words sounded sweet to his ears; a part of him being filled after so many years.

"Am I to live in a one-room hell with naught but what his meager salary will afford as we struggle to feed ourselves and the babies that keep coming?"

She said it as if it were far worse than death, though Andrew knew death—or the death of a loved one—was far worse. "If that were the case, would it be so terrible?"

Ellington looked around the darkened room; her eyes taking in the splendor that Andrew had always surrounded himself with. Crystal hung from the ceiling, vases adorned every table, and the best oil paintings money and influence could buy hung upon every wall.

"You never meant for me to have any of this, did you?" Ellington stood, the chair she'd sat in toppling over behind her and striking a framed landscape that leaned against the wall, nicking the wooden frame.

"No, I did not." He would not lie to her, not in his last moments. "But that is not to say I have not planned for your future."

"A stable boy...that is what you planned?" The accusation in her question cut him deeply. "You would keep my existence hidden for all eternity."

"That is untrue, I only wish for you to trust Alex." Everything was sounding so far from what he'd wanted to say to her. What he'd *planned* to say. "Ellington, my daughter, you are the only one strong enough to help him find who he truly is—it will determine not only his future but yours, as well."

Andrew hoped he hadn't made the direst mistake of his life by keeping Alex's true past hidden; he feared the boy would never discover that he was so much more than an orphan raised amongst a horde of misfortunate souls.

But with Ellington by Alex's side, he stood a greater chance than ever before.

CHAPTER 1

London, England
March, 1817

LADY ELLINGTON PEERED through the slatted railing in the loft of the stables and down on the stable hands below as they hurried to and fro; mucking out stalls, polishing horse tack, and brushing the sweat from a matching pair of greys after their daily exercise.

The activity was relatively extensive for a residence in mourning, and therefore, a household in little need of horses or carriages. Since the marquis' death, the stable had gone largely unused except for the rare occasion when Ellington's older sister, Ruby, had stayed past dark and requested a carriage ride home.

Scanning the group below, Ellie spotted the man she searched for. Up until a year ago, she'd viewed him as not much more than a boy...and a crippled boy, at that. But since the marquis had mentioned him on his deathbed, her interest in him had been renewed.

Her curiosity only escalating after their brief sojourn to Lady Haversham's Christmastide gathering.

Ember, her orange tabby, pushed into Ellie's hand, demanding attention; with a quick pat to the cat's head, Ellie went back to watching below.

Alex, two hooks in hand, swung a bale of straw out of sight below the high platform Ellie laid on, the loose straw hiding her from view. One would never know that he had one hand— and part of his arm—that were ever so slightly smaller than the other side, nor that he walked with a slight limp. In fact, all that she noticed at the moment was his bare chest and the corded muscles that ran the length of his back as he swung another heavy bale.

She must have made some audible sound, because just then, Alex looked up in her direction.

Quickly, Ellie pushed back from the railing, sliding across the dirty floor as the wooden boards below her groaned, her dress snagging on a splintered board as Ember walked the edge of the loft and mewled with vigor, exposing her presence to the men below.

Alex offered the cat a greeting from below. Ember's tail flipped back and forth as she hurried to the ladder and navigated the rungs down to the stable floor.

"Traitor," Ellie mumbled, pushing farther back into the shadows to hide from view.

It had become almost a ritual for her, lying high above the stable floor, watching and listening to the men jest about women, work, and cards, among other less thrilling topics— although Alex never said much. He kept silent when the men complained about their harping wives or the aches in their bones from their long day's work.

In the time Ellie had been watching Alex, she'd learned absolutely nothing about him besides his affection for his nursemaid, Mrs. Dutton. On his one afternoon off each week, he normally spent it reading, reciting the books aloud, even with no one about to listen. On occasion, he'd taken the brisk walk to Lord Haversham's townhouse. Ellie hadn't the faintest idea what he did inside because she hadn't wanted the task of explaining to her sister Ruby or Lady Haversham why she was there—they'd never believe she'd come on a social call without first being summoned.

No, until she found out exactly what her father had meant by his last words—that she should trust Alex—she wasn't about to let her sister and her bosom friend, Lady Haversham, in on anything. It was enough that they barged into her home every other day to 'make sure she fared well' after she'd been less than cordial at Lady Haversham's holiday gathering. They didn't understand Ellie's need to keep her distance after their return.

Ellie scooted once more toward the rail and peered down. Alex sat on a wooden bench, his shirt returned to his body—shame, that—and drank from a large jug. The container could only contain house water, for Ellie also knew that Alex did not partake in spirits as the other men did. His character was so at odds with every other man she'd known. It made no sense, but the fact drew her to him further.

Finally, a bell tolled and the men set down whatever they were working with and left the stables for noonday repast. This gave Ellie the opportunity to hurry down the ladder, out a side door used for kitchen deliveries, and make her way toward the main house.

"Miss?" Ellie paused, looking toward a man, possibly ten years her senior. "I am looking for a young woman—about your age." He shielded his eyes as he spoke, slowly walking toward her.

"Ah, well." Ellie looked about, noting she was startlingly alone in the yard between the stable and the back entrance to the manor. "I am the mistress here. Maybe I can help you find whomever you seek." She'd never seen the man before, but he appeared well-dressed and acted the gentleman.

"I would be grateful for any help." He looked about the yard as if noticing for the first time how alone and inappropriate the situation was. "My wife has been missing for several months and I have heard she may be here."

Alarm bells went off in Ellie's head—a missing wife...a few months gone...in her home.

"Oh." She took a tentative step backwards toward the closed kitchen door. "I am certain there is no one in my household that hasn't been in my employ for many years."

"Are you positive?" he continued. "She may be working as a maid, or maybe in the kitchen?"

Another few paces and she'd be within reach of the kitchen door, or at least hearing range of her servants within. "No, you have the wrong house. I hope you haven't traveled too far in your search."

Without her noticing, he'd kept pace with

her across the yard, his steps twice the length of hers. They were mere feet apart, and if he tried, he could reach out and grab her.

"You have not even heard her name." He grinned, probably thinking it would comfort her—gain her trust—but it only sent a shiver down her spine. "Daphne."

"What?" she asked.

"I am Sir Gregory, my lady. Her name," he continued. "It is Daphne."

Her back hit the doorframe, the knob digging into her back. "I think you should leave." Her voice was too shrill, terror most certainly showing on her face. "There is no one here by that name."

"In this entire grand house? Can you know all that work in your home?"

"I do," Ellie lied. However, she did know what Daphne he referred to—and he'd have to step over her cold, lifeless body to reach the girl.

"Maybe you should ask about the house," he continued. He'd stopped about three feet from her, and the distance at least gave her a measure of security. "I can come inside and we can ask—maybe your housekeeper will know her."

"I said leave. Now." Ellie stood straight from where she'd leaned against the door. Certainly, someone within could see her—and more importantly, notice that she was in need of assistance.

"I am not going anywhere until I have Daphne," he sneered. "She is my property. I am her husband."

"You will not have her." Her quickly spoken words were confirmation; there would be no denying her knowledge of Daphne any longer.

"My lady?" Ellie looked up, terror surely

etched her face from what had almost transpired. "May I assist you with something?"

Alex was at her side in an instant, a barrier between her and the man.

"Is something amiss?" The stable hand spoke to her, but glared at the intruder.

"Your mistress was about to run inside and collect—"

"I most certainly was not about to do anything of the sort." She took a confident step forward. "This man was just leaving."

Alex looked the man up and down, relaxing his menacing posture when he noticed he carried the upper hand; obviously sensing the dandy would be no match for him if anything turned physical. "Then you are both in luck. I am headed down the drive now. I can make sure you get on your way."

"Thank you," Ellie whispered close to his ear. "I am grateful."

"It is my honor, my lady. You may return to the house." Normally, she'd take offense to being ordered about, but all she could think about was getting to her room and making certain Daphne was safe. "Come, sir."

The man pulled away when Alex attempted to grab his arm.

"I suppose I may be mistaken about her whereabouts." He gave Ellie a curt bow as if mocking her. "Pardon the intrusion."

Ellie didn't pause long to watch the men make their way toward the main drive—Alex keeping pace with the man, yet behind to make sure he didn't try to turn back.

She made little sound as she raced through the kitchen and up the flight of stairs used by the household staff. Servants lowered their heads as she hurried past, none uttering even a simple greeting.

She entered her room and listened for Daphne. Thankfully, she heard the girl mussing something in Ellie's dressing closet. Ellie stripped the dusty, black fabric she was currently wearing from her body. The crushing cocoon of sorrow finally falling away with the heavy brocade mourning dress she'd donned for the last moments of sadness she'd attribute to the late Marquis of Drake.

She'd almost forgotten what day it was when she'd first woken.

It had officially been one year since the death of her *father*.

One year since she'd told her sister of their relationship, one year since Harold Jakeston, now her sister's husband, had helped to bury the awful man, and one long year where she'd lived in fear someone would come and take the only home she'd ever known.

But no one had come to claim the title or the house as his. The Marquisate had continued to lay dormant with no one stepping forward—and Ellington, the unofficial ward of the Marquis of Drake, hadn't been appointed a guardian.

Her father, Andrew Penton, was forever gone—never would she be summoned to his room to be berated over her choice of gown, or driven from her home when he over imbibed and thought it entertaining to break all the furniture in a certain room.

"Lady Ellington?" Daphne called. "I brought the gown you requested."

Looking over her shoulder, Ellie smiled at the girl, happy to see her safe and content.

When the girl returned her grin, Ellie

decided it wouldn't be wise to tell her maid of the man's visit; Daphne would likely do something ill-advised and depart Drake House, not wishing to cause her mistress any trouble.

Draped across her maid's arms was a walking dress made of the palest blue she'd ever seen, the bodice of the gown had been fitted to Ellington perfectly months before. Since then, she'd dreamed of wearing it about town, walking into Gunther's and ordering the largest ice her coin could buy.

She'd loved the color so much she'd had an evening gown commissioned in the exact color. It was unlikely she'd attend a grand ball, but the dress would have been perfectly suited to Lord and Lady Haversham's Christmastide gathering. She would save the formal dress for next holiday season.

"You are a gem, Daphne!"

With a small smile, her maid moved to Ellie's dressing room to hang the gown and Ellie followed. After her father's funeral—and when no distant relative had come to claim the estate and title—Ellington had settled into her role as lady of the manor. She'd quickly hired a proper lady's maid, took over meal planning, and made sure the house ran smoothly. It had taken a fortnight for her to realize the household hadn't continued on with her because of any loyalty to the deceased marquis *or* to Ellie, but because their salaries continued to be paid. By whom, Ellie hadn't a clue. If only she had someone she trusted who could help her. Her sister would only insist, for the thousandth time, that Ellie live with her and Harold at the Haversham townhouse.

"You will look stunning, Lady Ellington,"

Daphne gushed. "Where will you go first?"

"I haven't the first clue." Ellie trailed her fingers down the gown and over the intricate beading about the high waist. "And how many times must I ask you to call me Ellie?"

"It is not done, Lady Ellington."

She admired the girl's resolve to be the best lady's maid she could be, but most days, Ellington only wanted a friend. She'd met the girl—a few months younger than she—at Craven House, where Daphne had fled when her parents refused to take action against the maid's foul husband. Daphne had been injured physically, but harmed more internally, both emotionally and mentally, from all the man had put her through. With little recourse, Daphne had been pushed to disappear into the night.

The girl's experience only solidified in Ellie's mind that all men were the same—cruel, offensive, and uncaring; just as her father had been to her. She thought of her sister, Ruby, with her doting husband, Harold, but pushed it away. That was a rare thing, indeed. Ellie certainly could not believe that a dear husband lay in her future—which made her resolve strengthen to not even ponder the possibility.

But Ellington had felt a kindred spirit in the girl straight off, and begged Marce to allow her to live at the marquis' townhouse—Ellie's townhouse, as of now.

Daphne hadn't spoken of her past, nor whom her relations were, but Ellie sensed from her speech that she'd been raised a proper lady; and today proved it all the more. The man who'd come for her was dressed the proper gentleman, though Ellie knew his finely tailored clothes hid a rotting, black heart.

There was no question, Daphne did not need to know her husband had come looking for her — and Ellie was determined to never again allow the man control over the girl.

"Can I help you into the gown?" Daphne asked, resuming her role as the lady of the house's personal maid. "The new shifts you commissioned arrived yesterday and have been pressed and hung, as you requested."

Ellie couldn't wait to do away with the rough, coarse shifts she'd always been given and had donned until her year of mourning was up — a penance, if you will, for praying every day for the marquis' demise.

But the time had come to do away with her black garb.

Unfortunately, Ellie wouldn't slip into the fine blue material today. "No, the lavender muslin gown will suit well for the day." She watched, her gaze a bit downcast, as Daphne eyed the blue gown one last time before exiting with a sensible, sturdy violet dress with a white apron accompaniment. The dress was also a recent acquisition from the modiste on Bond Street.

Daphne lifted the gown high and slid it down Ellie's body with the nimble hands of a woman who'd dressed ladies for decades, though in truth, the maid had probably never dressed another until a few short months ago. Ellie slipped her arms into the appropriate holes and the fabric settled around her waist as Daphne began the process of buttoning the back.

"Lady Ellington?"

"Yes," she answered, shifting slightly to look over her shoulder as the maid's hands stilled.

"Is this straw in your hair?"

"Oh, poppycock!" Ellie pushed the maid's fingers away and ran her own through her long, red locks, snagging not one, not two, but four long, reedy strands of hay.

"Have you been sneaking a peek at that stable boy again?"

As if on cue, Ember pushed open the door and mewled her presence.

The conspiratorial tone in her maid's voice had Ellie on the defensive. "I was most certainly not spying on that stable *man*," Ellie said, putting emphasis on the man part. "I only passed through the stables on my way back from Craven House."

She hadn't been to Craven House in nearly a fortnight, but she hoped Daphne hadn't been keeping that close of watch on her comings and goings.

"Will you be leaving the house again today, Lady Ellington?"

Ellie turned a stern look upon the girl. "That is none of your concern, and I will have you know that..." Daphne held up two pairs of shoes, one a soft cloth unsuitable for outdoor activities and another with a hard, wooden sole. "My apologies, Daphne."

"Whatever for?" the maid inquired. "Today is a hard day for you, being the year mark of your father's passing. I will forgive you your foul mood, but only today." The girl smirked at her own cleverness.

Ellie wanted to hug the girl for giving her the perfect excuse for her unladylike behavioral outburst.

Luckily for them both, Ellie did not find delight in embracing others—ever.

Instead, she turned and Daphne continued

to button the back of her dress in silence. When she was done, Ellie thanked her, bid her to tidy Ellie's chambers then find her own noonday meal, and left the room. Taking the main stairs, Ellie made her way to the morning salon, prepared to receive any visitor who might show up to give their condolences once more on the passing of the Marquis of Drake.

The servants had seen fit to prepare the room for the day; a plate of sweetmeats and cheese sat on the sideboard next to several fine teacups.

The teacups would fetch a nice amount of coin if she sold them at the local market. She must remember to snatch a pair before her next trip to Cheapside. She'd stumbled upon the tiny shop long before the marquis had passed; the proprietor willing to given her generous coin for anything she brought round. It gave her the allowance her father denied her—and now, she'd moved to bigger, more valuable things. If she were thrown from her home, she wouldn't go penniless.

Ellie wasn't hungry, nor did she relish the idea of spending the day discussing the unexpected passing of that vile man, the marquis. She ran through responses in her head to people's kind words, '*Oh, do not fear. I have not missed that despicable man a day*' or '*Certainly, you are the only one mourning his death. I'd hoped he'd take his last breath long before he actually did, more's the pity.*'

The afternoon went on, the only company being the one-sided conversation Ellie held in her own head. Not a single visitor had shown to pay their respects on the anniversary of the marquis' death.

Not even her sister and her devoted husband, Harold, had come.

That was the only shocking part of the entire day.

Ellie looked down at her lovely gown, no longer a varying shade of black or grey.

A light tap sounded at the door.

Finally, she thought, she hadn't donned her lovely gown for naught.

"Enter," she called, standing to greet her guest. She put on a timid smile, one that said, 'thank you for coming on this final day of sorrow,' and watched as the door swung open.

Before her stood not a long-standing business associate of the marquis', or her sister with husband in tow, but rather Alex, the same man she'd spent all morning watching—not spying on, mind you—and her nights dreaming of. The servant who'd escorted her to Foldger's Hall at Christmastide—and given her Ember. She'd tried to push their time together from her mind, tell herself he didn't matter, for how could a stable hand be of significance to her. It mattered little that he'd comforted her on many occasions since his arrival at Drake House over a year before. Ellie wouldn't dwell on the fact that they'd been forced together—first by her father and then by Lady Haversham as she'd insisted he accompany her carriage to the country.

"Lady Ellington." He bowed slightly before entering the room, Ember close on his heels. "This letter arrived for you."

"To the stables?" She paused, collecting her scattered wits. "I mean to say..." Her words trailed off because she had no idea what she'd meant to say at all.

"No, I was returning from Haversham

townhouse—I took my repast there today, with Lady Haversham and baby Neill." He readily delivered his excuse, though Ellie was unconcerned with where he took his meals. Or, at least, that should be the case. "When I was walking up the drive, this note came by hired post."

"Thank you." Ellie took the proffered letter from him and turned it over in her hands. "Are you sure this is for me?"

"Whomever else could it be for?" he asked.

"Very true." Ellie had spent weeks asserting herself as the new lady of the house, much to the dismay of the servants. Though her intent had not been for their benefit, but for anyone who would eventually come to claim the house and the title, Marquis of Drake. For she knew, someone had to come.

"You may go," she said, dismissing him curtly. Her hours spent watching him, familiarizing herself with his actions and movements, likely showed on her face. When he only stared at her, she asked, "Is there something else?"

Alex stood tall in the doorway with his hands clasped behind his back, his shoulders squared, and all she could picture was him swinging a bale of straw like it was as light as a feather. "Yes, your sister requests your presence."

"Requests my presence? Did she summon you to Lord Haversham's only for you to bring the message back to me?" Ellie prodded, sudden memories of her required attendance at the holiday gathering flashing through her thoughts. "You are aware that you work for the Drake household, not my sister nor Lord Haversham? If

Ruby seeks my presence, she may call upon me herself."

Ellie sounded the petulant child, the exact impression she'd worked hard to change since Christmas. She was an adult, and as an adult she needed to command the respect of her servants, not act the spoiled youngster who threw fits to gain what she wanted.

Alex bowed. "I must return to my work, Lady Ellington. I bid you good day."

"To you, as well," she mumbled.

"And please be careful climbing up and down that rickety ladder," he cautioned before turning on his heels—like the most trained gentlemen of the *ton*—and silently closing the door. His footfalls echoed down the corridor toward the kitchen, his limp undecipherable.

The aloof attitude she donned to mask her unease at his presence fell away as his footsteps faded. Her folly at thinking she'd managed to keep her visits to the stables hidden irritated her greatly—and to think he'd known all along and got enjoyment out of her childish clambering about in the rafters.

And the only thing she'd managed to learn was how laborious it was to remove all the entangled straw from her long hair.

CHAPTER 2

"GOOD DAY," ALEX CALLED to Cook and a maid as he passed a boiling pot simmering with fresh vegetables from the townhouse gardens. The evening meal smelled heavenly after his morning in the stables.

"Good day, lad," Cook called after him.

"Fine morn," a sully maid chimed in.

"I be hav'n some supper ready for ye," another called out.

All eyes in the room followed his progress toward the back door, and he breathed a sigh of relief once he stood in the fresh air of the stable yard. The constant leering of the household servants made Alex highly uncomfortable.

Laughter floated out the open kitchen window in his wake.

"I be right happy hav'n him for me supper," one of the servants whispered, loud enough for all to hear.

Giggling, Cook said, "Only if I be done with him a'fore then."

Alex kept pace as he made his way back to the stables. He'd long ago acclimated himself to the gossip and flirtatious nature of the household staff. Whoever thought men were crude in their humor toward the fairer sex had never stumbled upon a gaggle of gossip-hungry maids.

The laughter faded, as did his thoughts on the lovelier gender—except Ellie, of course.

The woman baffled him.

Over the last year, she'd gone out of her way to avoid him, yet hid within the rafters of the stables to watch him. Even their stay with Lord and Lady Haversham over the holidays had proven that she sought to evade him, as she'd kept to her room most of their stay—no matter what Ruby and Lady Haversham did to draw her out.

At first, he'd thought she kept an eye on all the men working below in the main stable room when she snuck up to the loft, but with time, he noticed that her eyes only followed him. Several times, he'd stood a few feet outside the main stable and waited for her to safely debark from her high perch, her kitten in tow. Only the previous week, he'd been caught by the stable master, repairing the old ladder Ellie climbed daily. The scolding he'd received for taking it upon himself to mend and reinforce the rungs was well worth it, for now, he needn't worry if Ellie were to scamper down without him close.

Thankfully, the other men hadn't noticed her presence above.

"Where ye been, boy?" the stable master called. "Ye meal hour been up for some time."

The men, though never downright hostile,

had yet to fully accept him. "A post delivery stopped me on the front walk and bid I deliver a letter to Lady Ellington."

"Ah, well, get yerself ta work," the stable master said before returning to his own tasks. "Only be so much daylight left."

Soon after Alex's arrival at the Drake stables, he'd learned that the marquis himself had chosen a position for him, something he'd never done on any previous occasion. The stable master's skeptical nature was warranted, though grounded in naught. Never interfering in staff matters, the marquis had rarely spoken to Alex beyond thanking him for bringing his horse round or barking at him to make sure the bales were properly tied, lest he get hurt retrieving his mount.

Grabbing his bale hooks, Alex continued his morning chore of stacking the weekly hay delivery. The work was arduous and took much strength, but he enjoyed the physical nature of it. Every day, he felt his weaker side gaining strength; his hand rarely cramped or froze up on him any longer. He walked solidly now, his limp almost nonexistent, even to himself. It was still necessary for him to complete his nightly exercises—for hours, he'd straighten his long fingers, curl them back into a tight fist, and then extended them again. The stiffness and pain of his youth still plagued him in damp weather, but his mobility had increased since Lady Haversham had taught him the strengthening techniques she'd read about in a London medical journal of some sort.

Swinging the hooks once more, they drove deep into the dry straw and stayed firm when Alex straightened, twisting his body and using the force to lift the bale off the ground. It moved through the air and nestled atop another tightly bound block. The hooks came loose from each end when he flicked his wrists, turning to the next.

"What is this about?" The shrill voice came from the door to the stable yard. "Is this a jest?"

Alex realized the thin words were directed at him when the person kept speaking.

Eckles would be overly upset if he returned to find Alex neglecting his duties because he focused on a maid.

"Day's work will be done in a few hours' time," he called without looking over his shoulder. "I can assist you then if something needs my attention."

He assumed his answer must have been agreeable to whoever stood in the doorway blocking the afternoon sun, for the nagging voice stopped.

Ten more bales to go. He stuck his hooks into the next, lifted, and launched the bound feed across the couple of feet of space and onto the ever-growing stack.

"I am not so easily dismissed, stable hand!" The shrill voice had mellowed into a deeper, more even tone as she spoke through lips tight with anger. A voice he recognized. "I asked if you meant that letter as a jest."

Instead of hooking another bale, Alex tossed his hangers aside and faced Lady Ellington...and the indignation that blanketed her. He immediately regretted his casual demeanor. She was the mistress of Drake House—and he was, in essence, her servant to command.

He worried over his remarks about her hiding in the stables, as well. It would have behooved him to keep that tidbit to himself. He'd planned to question her on their long drive to Foldger's Hall, but the opportunity hadn't presented itself—or more possibly, Lady Ellington had made certain the chance never arose. Over the last year, he'd enjoyed playacting that he didn't notice her above, or that her fleeing the stables back to the house hadn't caught his eye. At least, if she were perched above, she wasn't spending time at Craven House amongst the women he was sure were a bad influence—or worse still, traveling the London streets unchaperoned.

"Can you speak, or do you think to stare at me for the remainder of the day?" Her clipped tone brought back the months Alex had spent listening to the marquis and Ellie hurl insults at one another, unable to stop the violent outbursts between the pair or separate their colliding natures, though he'd rushed to try. "Well?"

"My pardon, Lady Ellington, but you have caught me at a disadvantage." His best option was to play as if he hadn't any idea of what she spoke, which he didn't entirely. "May I inquiry as to your purpose?"

"Do not play coy with me, stable hand." Her hands rested on her hips and she glared, though he noticed her downward glance to his unbuttoned shirt.

Did she think him insulted that she called him stable hand? He'd grown up with words like bastard and orphan being hurled at him—or spoken when others thought him out of hearing range. Now, as an adult forging his own way in life, being called by his profession was a mark of respect and success on his part, not the slur others took it as.

One could not change their status as an illegitimate or parentless child, but one could aspire to be more than those simple words. Alex would not always live in the Drake stables, nor would he continue to accept the secondhand clothes and toiletries Lady Haversham and Mrs. Jakeston forced upon him when he was summoned to noonday meal once a week. The clothes, while not made of the finest materials, were sturdy and well suited for stable tasks.

"The letter." Ellie pulled the correspondence from her apron pocket, waving it inches from his face. "Can you say you know nothing of this?"

"I was only bid deliver it to the house." Alex hadn't even looked at the exterior of the cream note, but now he noticed no name or direction marred the envelope. He was relieved she hadn't sought him out due to his mention of her secret activities. "What has you so upset? If you do not wish a mere *stable hand* within your private sitting room, I will refrain from entering the main house."

She paused, and Alex felt remorse for throwing her words back at her, but he quickly recovered when she continued, "I hadn't thought of that in the slightest, but now that you bring it to my attention, you should stay where you belong."

"As should you. The stable is no place for a lady such as yourself, *Lady Ellington*." Alex didn't even make an attempt to hide his snide retort. "Now, if we may hurry this along, there is work to be done. What brought you to my lowly stable?" he issued a mock bow.

Irked, she looked back at the letter in her hand, as if remembering only now what she'd come for. "This." Ellie again held the letter inches from his face. "Why did you bring this to me?"

"I was told to deliver it to my master." He spoke slowly, pronouncing every word clearly. He wasn't sure what had come over him, or why he was so quick to irritation by her presence. "You are my master, correct?"

Her brow scrunched in confusion. "Well, I..."

"Do not be alarmed by my words," he prodded. "We've all answered to you since the marquis passed—and our coin continues to come as it should. Who do you suppose I should have delivered the letter to?"

Her puzzled expression vanished with his harsh words, her eyes igniting once more. "It is addressed to one Peter Davis, Duke Chastain, and the seventh Marquis of Drake.

She waited, her arms crossing.

"Do you expect the name to mean something to me?"

"Does it not?" she asked.

He racked his memory, but could not remember the name being spoken in his presence. "Of course not."

"Boy," the stable master shouted from the far doorway. "Ye about as lousy as I eva did see!"

"I must return to work, my lady," Alex said under his breath. "Go, before Eckles finds us and releases me from my post."

Alex grabbed his hooks and lowered his head, swinging into the next bale.

"If'n I find ye laz'n 'bout one more time, I be throw'n ye ta the gutter—no one 'bout ta save ye now."

"Yes, sir," Alex mumbled, using his body to block Ellie from view. The envious looks and snide comments would not end if he were linked to Lady Ellington, as well as the late marquis. "Please, go!"

"Who ye be talk'n ta, boy?" As Alex feared, Eckles entered the stables. "M'...m'...m'lady. I be right sorry for interrupt'n ye."

ELLIE PINNED THE stable master with her iciest stare, daring him to continue—one of the only useful talents she'd learned from the marquis. The truth was, she was beyond angry, and anyone who stepped in her path was likely to feel her burn. Answers, she needed answers, though she suspected Alex, a mere stable hand, could offer her nothing.

"This does not concern you."

With a curt bow, Eckles said, "Aye, m'lady."

Eckles fled the room, sure to spread word of his mistress's presence in the stables, alone with a servant, but that did not concern her as much as the prospect of losing the only thing she considered her own—her home, Drake House.

Her only recourse was the small amount of coin she'd gathered over the last year in case it was needed; though she'd hoped it never would be.

The marquis was dead...and after all the years spent locked in his townhouse with no one for company, she *deserved* her home. If some gentleman of the *ton* thought to come in and take what was hers, he had another thing coming.

Peter Davis, the seventh Marquis of Drake. She'd never heard of him.

A duke in his own right. What did the man need with another title and her home?

If she had her way, never would a man hold the title of Marquis of Drake again—or at least not in her lifetime. It could continue on in its dormant status for as long as she took breath. However, the possibility of someone stepping forward to claim the estate still hung over her head.

"Do you realize what you've done?" Alex stood before her, his irate expression mirroring hers from moments before. "I've worked myself to the bone every day since I arrived here to gain my place in this stable. And you decided to ruin everything…in mere moments."

"Why are *you* cross?" She'd been the one wronged. "He had no right to speak in that manner."

"He had every right—this is his stable!"

"If what you said before is true, these are my stables." How she wanted that to be true, to proclaim her right to ownership before all and sundry, especially the seventh Marquis of Drake, should he be man enough to present himself. "Besides, no one should speak to another in the manner he does you."

He shook his head as if to tell her she knew nothing of the servant class. "He can do as he pleases, just as you address me as you see fit. Though, I am touched that you worry yourself over how your servants are treated."

"Have I been so cruel?" The words slipped out before she could stop them. "Not that I care about the mere opinions of servants."

Alex laughed—a cold, distant sound.

She was making everything worse—her pride taking blow after blow. Ellie should quickly retreat and behave as if the man, tempting as he was, didn't exist. Act as if she could truly care less about servants or their opinions and silly notions. That her mother wasn't the ultimate servant, for she not only provided a service to her masters, but also her body—willingly.

Or that most days, Ellie felt like little more than an idle servant herself since the marquis' passing. She was reminded daily of her true place in life; one she refused to accept and would never willingly submit to.

With the arrival of the missive naming the man who'd take everything from her, her future was highly uncertain. Part of her needed him, Alex, on her side...and maybe that'd been the marquis' plan all along. Perhaps he knew the day would come when Ellie was cast from her home, and he'd hoped Alex would take care of her, making it unnecessary for his charge to earn her way in the same manner her mother had.

But why a stable hand? Her father had had enough influence before his death to secure a match for her—even the lowliest baron would have taken favor with wedding the ward of a marquis. Though, Ellie had given her father no indication that she'd be keen to accept any plan he had to safeguard her future. Did he assume she deserved a match no nobler than her mother would have achieved? In Drake's eyes, she would never be more than a fallen woman's bastard child. It was only right and fair that Ellie be as downtrodden as her mother before her.

"Please," she sighed. "I will speak with him. I shall tell him it was I who distracted you from your duties with my senseless feminine questions."

If it were possible for Alex's stare to freeze her where she stood, it was likely she'd be as solid as the blocks of ice in Craven House's cold box.

"I think it would be best if you leave. I can care for myself, my lady," he snarled. "I am at least capable of that."

She'd done many things that made no sense, uttered many degrading comments to those who surrounded her, but this...this anger at her, was something she'd thought him incapable of. He'd dealt well with her sullen demeanor on their journey to Lady Haversham's holiday celebration, had stuck up for her on numerous occasions—why would he not allow her to do the same for him?

He was the one person not allowed to be angry with her or cast blame for her actions.

"That you are capable of." She peered down her nose at him—as best she could with him standing a head taller than she—and reverted to her cold ways. "I will be going out, then. *Please*," she said, emphasizing her manners during her request, "fetch my horse."

"I will call for your maid."

"I am in no need of a maid, only my horse."

"Then I will accompany you," he retorted before turning to the row of stalls behind him.

"I am not a child in need of a nursemaid," she called, her indignation increasing. "I have traveled the London streets for years on my own, today is no different."

But her protest didn't stall him, as she watched him prepare two horses. Her normal, mild mare, and another sturdier horse for himself. There was no point in arguing over his insistence on accompanying her out; for in truth, the day grew late and she wouldn't mind the company. Once she was safely at Craven House, she would bid him depart for home and leave her to her own devices. "If you insist, you may accompany me—discreetly, of course."

Their short jaunt passed much as their carriage ride to Foldger's Hall had at Christmastide—she rode in silence while he kept a close eye on their surroundings, even guiding her horse to a lightly traveled area away from the vendor carts and merchant stalls lining the worn district. The journey between Drake House and Marce's home was as familiar to her as her own room. She knew which alleys to avoid, who was out of place, and what vendors to never buy fruit from.

Stopping at the walk not far from the door to Craven House, Ellie dismounted her side saddle, startled that Alex was a mere foot away, ready to accept the reins.

"I will await you in Craven House's stables, my lady." His heated breath cascaded over her, warming her exposed neck.

When he pulled away, a chill raced down her spine and she realized she'd been in such a huff, she'd fled the townhouse without so much as a shawl or wrap. Unfortunately, the afternoon air was likely to turn even more frigid as the sun descended on the horizon.

Ellie fought the urge to lean into him, allow him to wrap her in his warm embrace, even if only for a moment. She'd wanted to do it for so long, especially since he'd stepped in and rid her of Daphne's angry husband. It frightened her to think what might have happened if he hadn't stumbled upon her in the stable yard. He was there, even when she was certain she didn't need him.

"My lady?" Confusion laced his tone as he

took hold of the reins. "Do have a pleasant visit. I will await your call to depart."

She was only inches from him before she caught herself and took a step back to put distance between them, the bustle of the late-day traffic filling her ears. She'd lost her good sense for a moment, actually believing she could embrace the man before her with no lasting consequences—with all of London mere feet away, and Marce Davenport, with her sisters close by, likely peering from the large windows facing the street.

"Very well." Ellie smoothed her dress and with the time it took to do so, dispelled the urge to step close to Alex once more, consequences be damned. Before her body saw fit to betray her, she started for the door, belatedly forgetting to instruct the stable hand to return to the townhouse.

When she turned, Marce's lone manservant had arrived to assist Alex with bringing the horses round to the stables.

The elderly man, Mr. Curtis, nodded to her when he noticed she watched the pair. He'd been with Madame Marce since long before she was called Madame, which meant he would certainly have been acquainted with Ellie's own mother—though she'd never brought herself to broach the topic with him. He was always kind to her, especially during her many late-night visits after Ellie and the marquis had had one of their many arguments.

Avoiding the man was necessary to escape his pitying gaze, though she was unsure if the look were meant for her or for all of the unfortunate women who called Craven House their home. She preferred to believe Curtis only felt sorrow for the paths each woman had chosen, even if that choice hadn't been made willingly.

The building before her, well-maintained and towering three stories, was a refuge for many luckless souls, her mother finding solace within its walls during her final days. Ellie continued to come because she felt a closeness to the mother she'd never known when surrounded by Marce and her sisters—Ellie wasn't permitted to associate with the many working girls who came and went almost daily, but she spent many long days—and nights—ensconced in Marce's private parlor.

Before she knew it, Ellie stood poised to knock on the double front doors—with no idea why she'd chosen Craven House as her destination this eve.

Something about the place, the people— beyond her mother's soul—drew her, much like the invisible cords that linked her and Alex, the stable hand. It was unexplainable, but very much present.

CHAPTER 3

"MY DEAREST," MADAME Marce called when the door swung open. Ellie was immediately enveloped in the petite woman's embrace and then thrust away at arm's length. Marce had long given up on Ellie returning her hugs. "I was wondering when you would come. Today is *the day*, is it not?" Marce paused, looking Ellie up and down. "From the dress, I would say today is, in fact, the day."

Ellie was shocked someone remembered the significance of the day.

"Yes, it has been one year." The words should fill Ellie with relief. The cold truth was that today was only a postponement of the eventuality of her losing her home.

"Do come in." Marce released her and gestured for her to enter. "We have a few hours before my evening clients begin to arrive. Are you hungry?"

The woman had always looked after Ellie, much as a mother would—though Marce was only ten years her senior. "No, thank you." She followed her down the dim hall into the interior of the house. Her blonde curls bouncing around her shoulders and down her back as she walked, her hips swaying. Ellie could see why the men of London chose Craven House for their nightly entertainments, besides Marce's discreet manner.

"Tea, then?" Marce said with a glance over her shoulder, a smile on her face.

Ellie had a difficult time turning down the woman's offerings, knowing Marce still carried the regret of her mother, Sasha, who'd failed to save Ellie's mother after Ellie's birth. "That would be nice."

They turned down a second hallway and entered Marce's private salon—a gaudy gold and red monstrosity that should cause Ellie's head to hurt at the many candles reflecting off the brass adornments on the walls.

Marce pulled the bell cord, signaling her housekeeper to bring refreshments, and perched on her favorite chair. Ellie moved to gaze into the crackling fire, giving Marce no chance to assess her emotional status. At this, the woman held a true talent. Her success, and her mother's before her, was due to her uncanny ability to read people, their intentions, and use that to her advantage—or, more commonly, to help a person who didn't realize they were in need of assistance.

"What ails you, Ellington?" Marce called from across the room. "Your shoulders are tense and your back ramrod straight. Despite all my efforts, you have never taken to the importance of posture. Maybe you are finally feeling the loss of your father?"

"Certainly not." Ellie put all her remaining strength into those two words.

"It is completely normal, my dear, everyone handles their grief and healing differently. Do not be ashamed to admit your father meant something to you."

"Truly, it is not that." Ellie wanted to crumble and confess all her troubles—beg Marce to fix everything, but the Madame did not hold an all-powerful magic wand. It was possible she could advise Ellie on what to do next—for if she were thrown from Drake House, Ellie had nowhere else to go but Craven House. "I received a letter this morn."

"Oh," Marce sighed, allowing Ellie to speak at her own pace.

"Yes, it was addressed to a Peter Davis, Lord Chastain and seventh Marquis of Drake."

"My goodness." Marce kept quiet when the housekeeper arrived, wheeling a tea cart into the room. It didn't pass Ellie's notice that five delicate cups adorned the tray. "Thank you, Darla. Please tell the girls—"

Whatever Marce had meant to say would not be known for Marce's three younger siblings bounced into the room, the twins' arms clasped as they giggled while their school-aged youngest sister followed—a dour look upon her delicate, fair-skinned face.

"I most certainly do not turn red as a rose petal at the sight of him!" Payton, a medium-height brunette whined as she crossed her arms and glared at her older sisters. "I don't even know his name—plus, he's nothing more than a stable boy!"

Ellie was instantly alert to their thread of

conversation—for she and Payton were mere months apart in age, which meant...

"No man, whether he be servant or proper lord, will take a whining ninny to wife," Marce scolded. "Now, the pair of you need stop teasing your sister."

Sam and Jude managed a contrite look for Marce's benefit. The pair, along with Payton, couldn't look less like siblings. Payton, her dark hair and light complexion, was the polar opposite of Marce's blonde locks and olive-toned skin. And in the middle, Sam and Jude had hair of the deepest auburn—Ellie was regularly envious of the shade, for her own was as bright as a flame. Marce's sisters were a sheltered lot of misses, kept far from the many sorted things that transpired at Craven House.

"Hello, E," Payton greeted. "Lovely dress."

Ellie looked down at her frock, hints of dirt clinging to the delicate fabric. She really must remember to don her riding cloak before leaving the house in a huff. "Thank you, it is the first sent from the modiste."

"It suits your coloring," Marce chimed in as Payton moved to a seat close to the fire, dropping into it, her sulking continuing.

Ellie had tried to like the girl, but despite their close ages, they were very different. Payton had been coddled by her mother—and then her sisters—her entire life, while Ellie had been thrown to the wolves—or wolf, singular—not long after her birth.

"You agree with us, don't you, Ellie?" Sam called as she took over her sister's hosting duties and poured four cups of tea, with nary a drop on the intricately embroidered cloth below. "Payton has an eye for your stable boy."

Ellie gave herself away when she looked between Payton and her sisters, astounded by Sam's revelation—wondering if it were possible that Alex felt the same for Payton. A spike of jealously lanced through her. The brunette wasn't a striking beauty like her eldest sister, but she would be considered stately and demure—except for her incessant whining.

"Now, stop that at once," Marce cut in before Ellie questioned the girl further. "Ellie was just telling me about a missive she received today."

Ellie really didn't want to speak about the letter before everyone, but with four pairs of eyes trained on her, she saw little option, for Marce would likely cancel her evening until Ellie spilled all the news.

Suddenly, the room was overly crowded and too warm for her liking. "I was telling Marce that a letter arrived today, addressed to a Peter Davis, the Marquis of Drake." She wrung her hands before her, taking a step away from the burning hearth behind her and slipping her fingers inside her apron to retrieve the missive. "So, I guess it is official and the newest marquis should be arriving in short order to throw me out with the rubbish."

"What did the letter say?" Jude called in her singsong voice, the only thing that helped tell the twins apart.

"Do not keep us in suspense," Sam said, her voice deep, earthy. "We must know all the sordid details at once." Both girls leaned forward on the lounge with their chins perched on their palms, tea forgotten.

"I haven't read it." Though the missive had been burning a hole in her apron pocket since it arrived. She hadn't planned to tell anyone of its arrival, but it was too late for that now—she now held the letter tightly in her hand.

All three women gasped as if they were viewing a drama upon a stage and the playwright had destined the lead to perish in a vile, painful, drawn-out death.

"Do not act so," Ellie demanded. "It is only a silly letter. For all it is worth, I could burn the thing now...as if it were never delivered." She turned back to the blazing fire in the hearth, ready to toss the letter into its burning embrace.

How easy would it be to be rid of the unread letter, and go on as she'd been for the last year?

"Ellington, do not be so hasty." Marce reached around and tugged the envelope from her fingers. Her position at Ellie's side caught her off guard, as she hadn't noticed the woman leave her seat. "There is much for you to consider."

"Like where I shall lay my head—in your stables, or beg for lodging from Ruby? Or maybe I can solicit one of the many workhouses in Cheapside. But most of all, who *is* this man?" Her hands were still outstretched before her, her fingers poised as if she clutched the envelope, now safely in Marce's possession. "It is very likely I will be relegated to the poorhouse in a fortnight's time."

"Do calm down with the dramatics," Marce said, regaining her seat. "Nothing is ever so dire. Besides, I am certain our stables are well equipped for a new tenant."

Ellie whipped around to face the woman she'd always viewed above all others. "You would..." She let her words trail off at the smile beaming back at her.

"Do not be silly, my girl," Marce confided. "You are much too disagreeable to burden my livestock with. You will drive them mad within a day, I suspect."

The room filled with Sam, Jude, and Payton's laughter, their voices blending into a melody of sorts. Again, Ellie's envious nature threatened to take over. These four women—sharing a mother, but different fathers—knew the bonds of blood were strong. They lived together, laughed together…and loved one another. It had her pondering the notion of throwing herself at Ruby's mercy and requesting a place to live—maybe, just maybe, they could forge a similar bond.

Unfortunately, that would give her elder sister an increased amount of control over Ellie—and certainly her comings and goings. It was something she'd given no one; the marquis had thought he controlled her, kept her securely under his thumb, but he'd been mistaken in the extreme.

Her sister would certainly revel in the fact that she'd been raised as the daughter of a baron, given the love and attention Ellie had had withheld from her by their father. A constant reminder of what Ellie would never have—a happy home.

"Of course, we shall burn the evidence, but we'll know what it says before we do." Ellie was helpless to do anything, as Marce slipped her finger between the folds of paper and opened the envelope, crushing Ellie's hopes of burning the letter and being able to pretend nothing had changed.

"Please tell us we finally learn who this mystery man is," Ellie mumbled.

Clearing her throat and shaking the creases from the parchment, Marce started to read.

Peter Davis, Duke Chastain, and the seventh Marquis of Drake,

I apologize for my absence this past year. My father, the fifth Marquis of Drake's solicitor, fell ill some time ago, which required my full attention. My assistant was instructed to handle your finances while I was away and await your call. I am inquiring now as to a convenient time for my lord and I to meet with you to review the estate ledgers and make a plan for your future investments.

James Adams

No one said a word as Marce inspected the letter a final time, re-folded it, and slipped it back into its creamy white envelope.

"Ah, this is not as dire as I feared," Marce sighed in relief.

"How can you say that?" Ellie asked. Her heart beat rapidly at the thought of a solicitor showing up on her—no, correction, the seventh Marquis of Drake's—doorstep and demanding an audience. He obviously thought the newest marquis had been notified of his inheritance and had taken his rightful place at Drake House. "I am possibly days away from being without a home."

Marce's siblings only looked to her, each trusting their sister's ability to handle any situation.

"It is simple," the blonde said matter-of-factly, "We will find someone to pose as the new Marquis of Drake, set up a meeting, and then allow the newest lord to retire to the country for an extended stay." She sat a bit taller as her sisters looked on in wonder.

But it was only Ellie who voiced her doubt—or possibly, she was the only one sane enough to have doubts. "That will never work. How do we not know that the solicitor is not previously acquainted with Peter Davis?"

"How do you know that he is?" Marce questioned. And she was correct, Ellie didn't know for certain if the solicitor and Davis had met previously. Nor was the solicitor's name familiar to her. Her father hadn't conducted business at his London townhouse, and truly, Ellie had never wondered overmuch about his finances or business dealings. "We do not know anything about this solicitor, the newest marquis, or their past meetings or correspondence. If any."

Sam and Jude shook their heads in unison.

Payton stared into the hearth, having lost interest in Ellie's dilemma at some point.

"What is our plan?" Jude asked.

"Yes, how can we help?" Sam echoed. From what Ellie had noticed, the twins had taken to switching places lately—and did a fine job of mimicking one another.

"You will do nothing," Marce stated. Both the girls whined in protest at being left out of what they deemed as fun. "I will not involve the three of you in this matter. Now, go prepare for supper while Ellie and I chat."

The twins huffed but obeyed their sister, standing and making their way to the door, their long, auburn hair trailing down their backs unrestrained.

"Payton?" Marce snapped her fingers to gain the girl's attention. "Heavens, I do not know what has gotten into you lately. If you keep daydreaming away the hours, I'll start to think you do have a tender for this boy."

Payton pushed to her feet and sulked from the room, much as she'd entered it.

Ellie sat on the lounge the twins had vacated and waited for Marce to speak—hoping she did indeed have a plan...and one that would not see her sleeping in the Craven House stables.

"All we need find is a man willing to pose as the new marquis." She smiled, as if a wolf in sheep's clothing were all they needed to pull the wool over society's eyes. "Garrett would do it with no questions asked," she mused, "...but he is off gallivanting about the country or some such—and we cannot wait for him to return." She tapped her finger against her lips as she thought.

"How about that stable hand, Ellie?" Marce offered.

It was likely that he'd question her request, but she trusted him above any other man in her acquaintance—besides her sister's husband, Harold, of course, but asking for his help was certainly out of the question.

"The boy Payton is infatuated with..." Marce continued when Ellie didn't immediately praise her idea. Ellie kept her pose relaxed, as if a twinge of possessiveness hadn't sparked within her. "Oh, do not fret, she's long had her sights set on a certain baron's wayward son."

"Why would I fret?" Marce's perceptiveness rivaled that of an inquisitor. "He is only a stable hand."

"That is good to hear." The blonde eyed her closely.

To avoid her stare, Ellie paced before the fire once more. "You suggest I ask him for assistance?"

"I do not see the harm in it. You are his

employer, and he will likely do anything you ask to keep his position."

Ellie didn't doubt her thinking. "And I believe I can trust he will not share the news about an heir with the other household servants as he's not one for gossip and such—which makes him quite the bore."

Marce looked at her, brow raised in question.

"Oh, not that I notice him overmuch, it is only I have heard he journeys to Lord Haversham's townhouse on his afternoons off—and chooses not to visit the local inn for ale with the other servants." Ellie couldn't tell if she was making the older woman's suspicions worse.

The tall clock against the wall chimed the top of the hour, and both women jumped as the sound echoed through the room, slipped around the door that stood ajar, and continued down the corridor beyond. The chimes had barely faded when a knock could be heard from the front of the house.

"Oh, my," Marce said, standing quickly and handing the missive to Ellie. "Time has gotten away from me. You must be on your way. I am not expecting anyone, but mayhap I forgot another meeting."

"One other thing before I go." Ellie stopped, remembering her other unwanted visitor of the day. "Daphne's husband came round, looking for her."

"And what did you tell him?"

"That I did not have anyone in my household by that name, but he knew I lied. I could tell." Ellie despised the feelings of terror the man had instilled in her in those brief moments. It had been a rare pleasure—an entire year free of her father's abuse. But Ellie should have known it couldn't last indefinitely. However, she wouldn't allow it to have her flinching again at every raised voice or slammed door; she would be strong, for herself and Daphne. "But it is unlikely he will return. One of my servants intervened and took care of the matter. My butler was instructed to not allow him entry, and to alert me if he comes round once more."

"I will do what I can to dissuade him from pestering you again," Marce said with a smile, and Ellie sensed she didn't want to know exactly how Marce would dissuade Daphne's husband from his search.

Slipping the note into her apron pocket, Ellie departed the room—no more confident in her future than when she'd arrived, but if all else failed and she was thrown from her home, there would forever be a place at Craven House for her.

She only feared her life would mirror that of her deceased mother.

CHAPTER 4

THE HOUSE APPEARED the height of respectability, if not ringing with wealth, with a neatly trimmed landscape, cleanly swept walk, and windows polished until they sparkled. Even the sign out front proclaiming the manor's name as Craven House was freshly painted.

Alex paced in the darkening evening outside the stable door, awaiting Lady Ellington's summons to depart. He'd begun to wonder an hour earlier if the woman meant to have him wait all night for her orders, only to slip past him—and disappear into the twilight unchaperoned—to punish him for insisting on accompanying her.

He would never understand her. She fought to be in control of Drake House, but sulked like a child when they'd been at Foldger's Hall at Christmastide. She'd been serious in observing society's strict rules during the mourning period for the marquis, but spoke harshly of the man.

She was the most beautiful lady he'd ever seen, and yet, wanted nothing to do with balls or other matters within society.

It was past time Lady Ellington realized she could not live her entire life hidden away in that dusty, old townhouse, only leaving under guise of the setting sun or a fool's noonday errand. It was no way for a woman to live—or any person, for that matter.

Though Mrs. Dutton—and Lady Haversham—said his choices in life were suspect, as well. They'd both urged him relentlessly in the past year to retire to Foldger's Hall, or take a position at one of Lord Haversham's estates. He'd have the opportunity to train horses, while caring for a stable much grander than that which could be housed in London proper. No matter the promises made, Alex couldn't leave his post. Something kept him securely tethered to the marquis...and Ellington.

He had the sense that if he left, she'd see it as him abandoning her—leaving her without someone to watch over her. And it was no secret that he did not trust the women of this house— Alex didn't understand their interest in Ellie, nor why the girl continued to come to this house of ill repute. Though, at Lady Haversham's insistence, he'd kept a close eye on Ellie and her time spent at Craven House. She always arrived during the late morning hours and left long before the Madame's clients began arriving. This was the first time she'd stayed later than he felt was safe.

He peered into the dim interior of the stables where Mr. Curtis sat, shining a bridle with a sturdy cloth. Alex weighed his options for removing Ellie before the eve deepened further.

He could send the old man to the main house to check on his mistress, at least then he would know she was safe and still inside, but he'd likely receive a tongue-lashing from her—pushing him to depart.

But the night was settling, and with it came the unpredictable evening travel through the dark London streets. Alex pushed his hands deep into his trouser pockets to warm his chilled, aching hand. His thigh pulsed slightly with discomfort from the long day's work stacking bales. It was times such as these that Alex truly pondered his future if he were to take a more prominent position at another stable; maybe he would not be charged with such backbreaking labors, giving his body time to heal further.

But no, he knew as well as Lady Haversham that the hard work was exactly what had mended him thus far. The honest labor was good, not only for his injured body, but also kept his mind from churning. When his thoughts weren't continually focused on his future, Lady Ellington dominated his consciousness—her sadness that went far deeper than Alex's physical pain, her preference for solitude similar to what had led to Drake's downfall.

She needed someone by her side.

He'd promised himself to be that man. Not Lady Ellington's man per se—but someone who'd remain close and keep watch over her. Pull her from her continued melancholy.

After their time in the country, Ellie had returned to ignoring his presence, but he noticed her body's reactions to his closeness—a slight stiffening, her shoulder's straightening, or a sharp inhale of breath.

He could not be imagining such things.

Those reactions were the reason he'd agreed to Lady Haversham and Mrs. Jakeston's request to watch out for her. Both ladies felt responsible for Ellington, but the girl would let neither of the older women in. Though Alex had briefly seen the woman's defenses crumble, and she'd allowed him in—not on one occasion, but two. And so, when Mrs. Ruby had again asked for his continued watch over Ellie, he'd readily agreed. He watched every day as Ellie became more and more withdrawn, preferring to journey out alone, even though it put her safety in jeopardy.

Despite Harold and Ruby keeping their distance, as Ellie requested, they remained close to London, their newly acquired townhouse undergoing major renovations at present. But Alex saw Ellie's resistance to Ruby.

Alex swung around when he heard the clop of hooves behind him, coming from the stable. Mr. Curtis led Lady Ellington's and his horse, saddled and ready, in his direction.

"Me mistress sent word, ye be summoned to depart," the old man said, handing off the reins to Alex. "But ye looked ta be deep in ye mind, so I retrieved ye horses." The man clapped Alex on the shoulder before he turned and returned to his task of endlessly polishing the Craven House tack. It likely soothed his aching hands and fingers, much like the more arduous labors in Drake's stables that kept Alex's crippling pain from taking over.

With one final look at the man, Alex led the horses around to the front drive of the manor house. It was located in a respectable part of town—and for that, Alex was grateful, for Ellie would travel to Cheapside if that were where Craven House was located. The women kept to themselves, operating a quiet business under the guise of a family home, but no one sought to publicize what happened within Craven House's walls. If Alex hadn't heard through the servant's gossip about what the manor truly housed, he would be hard-pressed to believe it.

Another man on horseback entered the drive behind Alex as the front door opened and Ellie walked out, slipping something into the front of her apron. She moved quickly to his side without a word.

"Shall we depart, my lady?" When she only nodded in agreement, he assisted her onto her horse, mounting his own as she fussed to rearrange her skirts. "I hope your visit went well."

"Let us be off." Ellie eyed the man dismounting his own steed as Mr. Curtis rushed to take his reins then led the horse around to the stables.

"Of course, my lady." He spurred the horse into action with Ellie at his side and they started home. He watched her from the corner of his eye, her face clouded with concern. She kept her gaze trained on the path before them, her eyes never scanning the area around them—which was peculiar. The girl often journeyed through the dangerous London streets, keeping aware of her surroundings, but this night something burdened her.

Alex had no doubt Ellie had fled here due to her unease over the letter. If he'd known it would cause her such dismay and unease, he would have gotten rid of the offending missive. Maybe Lady Haversham was ill-advised in thinking Alex was the one to best take care of Ellie—there must be someone better suited to care for her well-being. Certainly someone she'd take into her confidence and actually speak to.

The ride passed without incident, and Alex sighed with relief as the townhouse came into view down the block. Once she entered, he was certain she would not journey out again until the morrow.

Instead of stopping out front, Ellie continued down the small lane between her townhouse and the next, toward the stables, and pulled her horse to a stop in the shadows, still three hundred paces from the open stable doors.

"My lady, is all as it should be?" he asked, taking in her lowered head. "Please, tell me what worries you."

It was a long time before she lifted her head and spoke. "Can I trust you?"

She spoke so quietly he wondered if he'd heard her correctly.

"My lady?"

"I asked if I could trust you, stable hand," she spoke firmly as if she'd made up her mind on some matter of import and needed to have it out before she doubted her decision. "We do not know one another that well, but obviously, the marquis trusted you—as do Lord and Lady Haversham." His mind stuck on the mention of the late marquis as she continued to speak, "But I need to know if you are loyal to me—will you hold my confidence in all matters?"

He sensed this as a turning point of sorts, but where it would lead he couldn't guess. In the darkened evening, stopped upon horseback and secluded from the prying eyes of London, this woman asked for his allegiance.

Something dug deep to his core—a call to duty ran through his whole body. It was an uncomfortable sensation, one he'd never felt but, to some degree, knew he'd been waiting for—as if the blood of a protector ran red through him.

"Always, my lady," he pledged, knowing he'd risk all for her, though, he could not imagine any real threat facing her. "You can trust me."

He dismounted and stood before her, reaching forward to assist her down.

"Please, ask of me what you need. I will do all in my power to help."

Sliding from her saddle, her green eyes glowed in the darkness—and stared directly at him. He was unsure why, but he felt as if this were the first time she truly looked at him and not through him, as if they were equals.

She squared her shoulders, preparing to make her request. "The letter you delivered to me this morning was from the late marquis' solicitor." She paused, as if he should know what that meant or what cast a shadow over her now. "It was addressed to the marquis' heir."

"So, the new Marquis of Drake is expected at any time?" He wasn't foolish enough to see Lady Ellington as the rightful heir. "Has the man made contact with you? Has he done anything improper?"

"No," she sighed. "I've never heard the man's name before, not from the marquis anyways. Nor has he called upon me since my father's death. But it is only a matter of time before he does, I am certain."

"How can I be of assistance, my lady?"

Her hesitation sparked a warning in him. "The solicitor requested a meeting with the new marquis, he seemed unaware that the man hasn't taken over the title as of yet."

"How can Drake's solicitor not know this?"

"He wrote that his father had fallen ill and he'd been away caring for his family, leaving many duties to his assistant." She crossed her arms and paced as she continued, "But he has returned and is eager for a meeting to discuss several business ventures and estate matters. Apparently, the marquis' various stewards at his estates have not seen fit to send word to Adams, the solicitor. Maybe they are like us, we keep doing as we always have—as long as their salaries continue to be paid and funds for repairs are approved, no one is eager to meet our new lord."

She'd lumped herself in with the other servants, like himself, as if she, too, were property of the Marquisate, belonging to the estate like chattel. He'd never witnessed her uneasy and insecure in regards to her place, yet, she laid her vulnerability out before him like an evening meal, terrified he would pounce on her timidities.

He'd heard no question in her response, yet he was hesitant to interrupt her. It was a rare occasion when she said more than five words to him—and he found he was enjoying their moment alone, though the topic was bleak.

"I knew this day was coming," she said, continuing to pace. Three steps and turn, three steps and turn. "I truly should have had the foresight to—"

"Ellie." He spoke her given name as if he used it every day—which, in his mind, he did. "You cannot take all the burden on yourself. Please, ask of me anything."

She stopped before him, looking deep into his eyes. "But I have no right to ask this of you."

Just as he had no right to call her by her Christian name. "I am your servant to command."

Ellie took hold of his hands and squeezed.

"Your hands are like ice, my lady." He held her fingers firmly to keep them in his warm palms. "I think we should continue in the stables, where it is warmer, before you become ill. You haven't even a coat to ward away the coming night."

"No." She shook her head. "We mustn't speak of this where anyone else can overhear, I fear. If you agree to what I ask of you, we could both find ourselves in much trouble if we are discovered."

His mind raced, searching for what she could ask of him. "Much trouble if discovered?" he repeated. If he remained to hear what favor she asked of him, there would be no changing his mind. The urge to flee before she said another word hit him.

But his body didn't heed his mind, and he stayed rooted to his spot in the alley, continuing to hold her hands to warm them and awaiting his call to action.

She kept her head lowered as if she went through her request once more in her mind, before lifting her eyes to meet his gaze. "I need you to pose as the new marquis—meet with the solicitor and see if we have anything to fear."

There it was again—if we have anything to fear—as if the pair were in equal jeopardy. So many questions and concerns clouded his thoughts, each pushing to the forefront and demanding an answer before agreeing to anything, yet again, his brain and body did not align. "Of course, my lady."

Not a question passed his lips as her mouth turned upward with a smile and the tension drained from her.

"Truly? You'll help me?" She squeezed his hands once more in her excitement. "I see no other way to untangle myself from this mess."

Finally, some sense came back to him. "Maybe we should ask Lord and Lady Haversham if they have any association with this man before we get too deep into this charade." It was a rational idea, and Alex prided himself on thinking of it while Ellie was smiling at him, her face so close to his that he could feel her breath against his cheek.

But her smile disappeared as quickly as it had arrived once the words left his lips.

"No," she protested, releasing his hands and stepping back. "I cannot allow anyone to know of this."

"Maybe the new marquis is not a horrible man." He tried to get her to understand. "What if Lord Haversham is acquainted with him? Would it not be in all of our favor to make a fair impression on the man instead of being caught tangled in a web of lies and deception?"

"And what if the man is not honorable? If he is a relation to Drake, then it is quite possible they share that similarity. We could very well all be left without a home within a fortnight."

He halted before mentioning that Drake's blood ran through her, as well, but he could never see her as anything but perfect.

She began pacing once more, her footfalls sure upon the ground as she started on the same path as before.

He knew she feared for nothing. "How are we to know Adams has not met this man yet?

What if I walk into his office and am pointed out as a fraud?"

"I have never heard the marquis speak of Peter Davis, nor has this solicitor ever visited the townhouse. But if you are uncomfortable with this, I am sure I can ask someone else for help."

He shuddered at the notion of what another servant might request in exchange for participating in her harebrained scheme. "I did not say I would not help you," he conceded. "What is the rest of your plan?"

Ellie took the few steps to him, taking his hands once more. "Oh, thank you! I haven't all the details thought out yet, but it should be very simple to have the marquis' trousers and coat altered to fit. Then we send word with an agreed upon meeting place and time. From there, all you need do is meet the man, see how much he knows of Davis, and set the man's concerns at ease over your ability to take over the Marquisate."

It sounded anything but simple to him. "But I am not a lord, nor do I believe I can fool a man whose entire livelihood is based on his interactions with men in possession of wealth and title."

"Come now," she sighed. "Did you not tell me once that you might have been a lord if the accident hadn't occurred and your family hadn't abandoned you?"

He had during a weak moment on their sojourn to Foldger's Hall. They'd spoken of many private things, and that she would remember that one utterance took him aback.

The words stung—he knew enough to know that *if* he were born into the noble class then his title still awaited him—unless his *family* had been able to prove his demise. But he pushed the thought from his mind as he did on the many previous occasions he'd been lonely enough to ponder the *what-ifs* of his life. Donning a fancy suit and meeting briefly with a solicitor was the least he could do to keep Lady Ellie from worrying herself to death—and if she chose not to include Ruby or Harold in her guise, then he felt some measure of ease knowing if anything went wrong, Alex could send for Lord Haversham or Harold.

However, the risks were very much on his shoulders. It was he who'd be impersonating a lord, a marquis, nonetheless. If her ruse were found out by anyone, the penalty would fall on him—not Lady Ellie.

Alex should deny her request and walk away, tell her the risk was too great for them both to undertake, plea with her to rethink her future. There were so many things he should say and do, but he only wanted to please her—give her hope that things to come would be more stable and secure, not only for the household but also for her.

The only way to accomplish that was to find out exactly what the solicitor knew—and how Lady Ellie could use it in her favor.

If that put him in jeopardy, he'd worry about that when the time came.

"How quickly can you have the marquis' coat altered to fit?" he asked, hoping he didn't come to regret his decision.

CHAPTER 5

ELLIE LET HER heart settle. Once it had, the hum of blood rushing through her veins faded. The feel of her soft blanket, hand quilted by Mrs. Bee when Ellie was still toddling about on unsteady feet, always comforted her. Whether it had been after an angered fight with the marquis or her own inner battles.

This night, her unsettled nature had nothing to do with either of those things.

But rather him, Alex.

He'd agreed to assist her in her outlandish scheme to retain her position as mistress of Drake House. It both shocked and unnerved her. She'd never given him reason to believe in her.

It was as if fate had tossed them together—or more likely, the marquis in his last twisted design to dictate her life and increase her distrust further. If his plan had been to solidify that stable hand into her mind, then he'd succeeded beyond his wildest dreams.

When faced with the choice of whom she trusted amongst her known male acquaintances, her list had only included Alex.

A night did not pass without her thinking of him as she fell into slumber—his kind heart at giving her Ember at Christmastide, or his gentle yet firm clasp on her hands in the alley. Her overwhelming feelings toward him scared her, yet at the same time also excited her.

After agreeing to see the solicitor, and being fitted to one of the marquis' older but pristine coats, they'd parted ways until the time came to meet with Adams. Ellie longed to speak with him—ask if she were sending him on a foolhardy mission, one that could land him in Newgate, but that seemed the exact wrong thing to say. And Ellie desperately wanted to say the *right* thing.

So, she'd recently relegated herself to hours hidden in the rafters of the stables, where she could feel close to him without putting herself out there for his judgment. Many hours lying prone on her stomach, made the softness of her bed seem all the more inviting. Tonight had been more fruitful than most, for Alex had appeared, his shirtsleeves discarded at some earlier point. He'd worked arduously to complete the evening feeding.

Ellie yearned to help him half as much as he'd helped her.

His single-minded dedication to his chores reminded her of that late evening, well over a year ago now, when she'd first laid eyes on him. He'd been focused and determined, so much so that he hadn't heard her sneak into the house and walk down the corridor, nor enter the room he sat in. She'd stood mere feet from him for several minutes as he recited from the open book in his lap. She noticed that he read faster than he turned the pages, as if he'd memorized the passage long ago. The book, like an old friend, only there to guide him if he were to go astray.

Ellie closed her eyes where she reclined atop her bed, remembering that night. A time when she'd never felt closer to anyone.

She was cold after being out long after dark, when a sudden storm unleashed wind and rain far exceeding the normal London drizzle. The damp chill settled into her bones, having passed through her riding coat within moments. Her hair, always wild and untamable, fanned about her face in disarray from her mad dash through the downpour back to the Drake townhouse. Her only concern upon returning home was that the marquis did not catch her. She'd been forbidden long ago to leave the house unattended, and that she'd been with Marce Davenport at Craven House would be inexcusable.

With that in mind, she'd left a window unlatched in the downstairs parlor—a room seldom used because, well, the marquis did not entertain.

That was exactly why she risked dripping water down the hall and allowing it to pool about her feet as she listened to the voice drifting from the marquis' study. It did not belong to the marquis, nor to anyone belonging in her home. She could not place the cultured, smooth tone wandering its way through the slightly ajar entry.

Ellie stepped into the warm room after pushing the door open. The urge to reprimand the room's occupant was strong. She wondered who dared enter her home, for she knew the marquis was still out for his coach and horses hadn't been in the stables when she'd slunk down the alley moments before.

No, sitting before her wasn't a vagrant nor someone meaning to do her harm.

He wasn't more than a young man, no older than she.

And he sat in the marquis' favorite seat, a book open across his lap with a raging fire in the hearth, illuminating his contoured face. It was only upon further inspection that she noticed his feet planted solidly before him and his hands were those of one used to manual labor.

His words flowed evenly, though slowly. His head lowered and his knuckles white where they clutched the book. Concentration radiated from him, yet his eyes barely looked to the pages.

Ellie wondered what held his attention so, if it weren't the words before him.

Startled, she was unconcerned about whom he was.

His voice blanketed her with a deep sense of security.

"What are you reading?" The words came in her voice, yet she was unaware of speaking them.

His head lifted slowly and his eyes met hers. Brown—his eyes were brown, that was the only thing she was sure of in that moment.

And that, despite his cultured tone, he was not of the noble class.

"I beg your pardon," he said. Closing the book, he stood. Taller than she'd expected, he loomed before her, his back to the fire. "I should return to the stables."

He moved toward the shelf he'd retrieved the book from, his free hand rubbing against one thigh.

"Are you hurt?" Again, she asked the most irrelevant question. "I mean, you are…"

"It is the weather," he said as he slipped the book back into its place and turned back toward her and the exit. "I fear the cold, damp weather here in London does not agree with me."

Ellie wanted to laugh at his words. It was the excuse she'd expect from a man three times his age. Yet, she sensed the subject was nothing to scoff at.

He moved quicker than before as he crossed the room. No doubt headed for the door behind her. It was then that she noticed one foot did not lift as high as the other, and he tilted ever so slightly to the left to compensate for it.

"Do have a good evening, Lady Ellington."

"You know my name?"

"Of course." A sheepish grin lit his face.

"Then it is only proper you introduce yourself, as well."

"I am nobody, my lady. Only a lowly stable hand sent to fetch the week-old pickings from the garden."

Ellie looked about her. "This is not the garden."

"That it is not."

"But here you be."

"I confess, Cook was not about the kitchen, and so I thought to spend a bit of time until her return in the warmth of the house. The stables are awfully wet and dank during storms."

"And you thought to spend your time in the marquis' chair—reading his most favored book?" she questioned.

"I thought you knew naught what book I read."

Hesitantly, she smiled, for, in fact, she knew the book well, though not the words it contained. She'd spied the marquis with it across his lap many a night in this very room.

When his head dipped in embarrassment, she continued, "I promise, I will not let on to your secret."

"That is overly kind of you." His fingers again massaged his upper leg. "I must see if Cook has returned. Undoubtedly, the stable master will not agree with your generous words or my tardiness."

"What ails your leg?"

"I am told I was in a carriage accident before I could walk. While my nursemaid took care of me after my parents had decided I was beyond repair, I fear my leg and hand still suffer damage."

"And the marquis was agreeable to hiring you?"

"I can handle a horse better than men twice my age and with four healthy limbs." His affronted words had her regretting her question.

"I did not mean to imply—"

"You would not be the first, nor the last, to think a cripple cannot handle the tasks in a stable," he cut her off. "Besides, the marquis and the stable master know of my shortcomings. I truly must return before he questions my whereabouts. Good eve, my lady."

"Wait," she said. He stopped a few feet from the door when she laid her hand on his arm to halt him. "Can I not have your name? If I see you about—which I likely will—I would have a name to address you by."

"Alex."

"Only Alex?"

"Alex is all I have to give."

Ellie was at a loss for words...

It was much the same with her. She was 'Lady Ellie' or 'Lady Ellington', no surname, for no person had claimed her as their own.

"Well, Alex, you may call me Ellie."

"That is not proper, my lady."

"I assure you, it is quite proper, for you see, much like yourself, it is all I have to give." It was all she had to give, the amount of her worth in a single leather-bound tome, the writings of a man who'd be forgotten in time, much like herself.

He nodded. "Very well. If we ever find ourselves alone, it will be Ellie."

That was the most she could ask for. Any servant, no matter the favor bestowed by their master, would be punished for daring to call a lady by her given name—even if said lady was not actually a lady.

"Before you go..." Ellie turned and rushed farther into the study, she looked over a few titles before selecting the book she sought. "Take this."

Ellie held the book out to him.

"The Task," he read, but didn't take the tome from her outstretched hand. "What is this for?"

"It seems you have memorized that last book." Ellie looked to the ornately engraved book in her hands. "And this book was given to me years ago. I have heard that Cowper has a beautiful way with words. Please, take it. I am not much for reading."

Reluctantly, he took the book, tucked it under his arm, and issued a curt but formal bow. "My deepest thanks, Lady—"

"Ellie," she said. "We are alone, after all."

"Your kindness will not soon be

forgotten…" He paused. "Ellie."

Her name sounded divine from his lips. Few addressed her in the household, many preferring to act as if she didn't exist rather than associate with the rumored bastard child of the Marquis of Drake—little more than a ward of the Marquisate and someone to take pity on.

"Lady Ellie." A hand grasped her shoulder, shaking gently. Why was he back to calling her Lady Ellie? They were still alone. She hadn't heard the marquis return from his evening out. "Lady Ellie, you have a visitor."

With a start, Ellie sat up, the bright, noonday sun streamed through her windows, blinding her for a moment. She must have fallen asleep, and slept through the night—for the first time in over a year she hadn't awakened, a nightmare fresh in her mind.

"Daphne, heavens, stop jostling me so." Ellie pushed her maid's hand away. "I am awake. It certainly must be too early for visitors."

"You slept through your morning repast, my lady." Her maid rushed across the room and picked up a cream dress draped over a chair, presenting it to her with a flourish. "Miss Ruby…I mean, Mrs. Jakeston awaits you below."

"Has it been a week already?" Ellie mused. "How many times must I tell her I am a grown woman and do not need her checking on my welfare?"

"At least one more time, my lady."

"Stop it with the *my lady*, Daphne."

"Why are you ever so riled up?"

Thoughts of Alex, that's what, but there was little chance she'd share the object of her frustration with her maid. The girl already went on and on about 'how handsome he is' and 'do you think he fancies anyone?'. It made her sick to think of Daphne or Payton enjoying Alex's longing looks.

If Ellie hinted at her dream or that it had wandered far past where their actual encounter had ended, she'd never hear the end of it. How had her dream progressed so that she now, in the light of day, found it hard to draw breath? In her dream, he'd thanked Ellie for her kindness with a kiss—and she'd allowed him to wrap her in his solid embrace.

Strong, capable, uninjured arms.

"Come now, my lady." Daphne shook her once more. "That stable hand cannot keep her occupied all day."

"Stable hand?"

"Yes. Mrs. Jakeston requested to see him when I told her you weren't seeing callers at the moment." Her maid returned from Ellie's dressing room with a pair of cream slippers to match her gown. "Said she would stay occupied until you were ready to see her."

During her and Alex's brief talk in the alley—and his subsequent agreement to help her—he'd given his vow of assistance more willingly than she'd imagined possible. She was aware that her luck would not last forever, but she needed more time to figure out what her future would hold before she was thrust from her home and forced to make any decisions.

Ellie pushed from the warmth of her bed, slipped from her night shift, and donned her fresh undergarments and gown with Daphne's help and sure hands. Next, she sat at her dressing table, allowing the girl to brush through her mess of red hair, gently working her way through the many knots from falling asleep without plaiting it first.

"Oh my, my lady," Daphne sighed, pulling the brush through a particularly difficult tangle. "You must have had a fretful sleep for it looks like you fought a war during your rest."

"Ouch." The brush twisted in another knot. "Can you not just sweep it back and pin it as best you can for now?" Ellie didn't want to admit it but she hoped to catch Alex before he departed for the stables.

"Why the hurry now?"

"It is rude to keep Ruby waiting."

Her maid smiled into the mirror before them. There was little doubt the girl thought her mistress finally saw the rudeness of her ways. In truth, Ellie only wanted to complete her mandatory weekly visit with her sister—and if she gained a glimpse of Alex in the process, that would be most fortunate.

Ellie entered the drawing room, a serene smile on her face; but she was only greeted by her sister—Alex already having taken his leave.

"Ellie," her sister greeted her with a quick hug, releasing her and regaining her seat before Ellie's displeasure showed itself. "I am sorry for missing our visit a few days ago. The work required to make a dilapidated old house livable is quite cumbersome, to say the least."

"I had not noticed you'd missed a visit, though I take such joy in seeing you." Of course, she'd noticed her sister had failed to show on the anniversary of the marquis' death, but she'd rather be entombed along with the man than admit it to Ruby. "But you are here now and I will tamp down my elation at that."

Ruby tried to maintain eye contact with her

younger sister, but Ellie noticed the woman's hands clutching and unclutching. She needed to give Ruby credit for her persistence in persuading Ellie to accept her into her life, though she was met with snide retorts and avoidance.

"Baby Neill is doing well," Ruby said, changing the subject. "I have so much enjoyed helping Vi with his care. Having a child about—his laughter and precociousness—is something I never thought to experience."

"I am sure at your age, you had given up hope of a family." Ellie knew she was being cruel, but she would not get into another endless discussion about children and marriage—and family. "But you've been blessed with Mr. Jakeston and a new home. Things will work out as you've always dreamed."

Ruby stared at her in silence, the quiet becoming almost deafening between them before she continued, "That is exactly it. I never thought of a family of my own—neither wished for one nor expected it. However, once Vi wed Lord Haversham—and then Harold captured my notice—I found it was something I truly longed for."

"I commend you on your life's discovery."

"Ellie—"

"Can we please not have this pointless argument again?"

"You are the only one who turns our discussions into arguments—though I blame your quarrelsome nature on our father."

Ellie sighed and held her hands wide, signaling her to speak.

"What I was trying to impress upon you is that marriage—and a family—wasn't something

I realized I desired because I felt it was out of my reach."

"And you think a family and marriage is within my reach?" Ellie held her sister's stare, refusing to look away. "Or that it is something I have ever wanted?"

"Everyone wishes for family."

"Well," Ellie said. "I have never been impressed with the family I was given—nor would I wish my life circumstances on another. Who is to say my child would fare any better than I did?"

"You are not our father." Ellie saw the fight draining from Ruby, knowing their conversation would end shortly. It always went in much the same direction each time Ruby set about pushing this topic. "I only think you should think about your future a bit more."

"I assure you, I think about my future often." Ellie slipped her fingers into her apron pocket and touched the letter from their father's solicitor. "It has never included a family or children because one must think to keep their home before anything else."

"You will always have a home with Harold and me." She'd said the same sentiment over a hundred times since Drake passed, yet Ellie was no closer to accepting the offer than she was a year ago.

"Again, that is a most generous offer, but I must politely decline." Ellie stood, hoping to get her point across that their *visit* had come to an end. "Please give my best regards to your husband."

Ellie pasted a bright smile on her face, one that anyone who looked closely enough would notice didn't reach her eyes.

Ruby remained seated for a few moments before shaking her head, standing, and taking her leave.

Ellie crumpled in the seat Ruby had vacated, allowing the many thoughts she wished she could say to her sister to bounce around in her mind.

There were so many things Ellie was sorry about, and hundreds of others that she owed apologies for. She wanted to accept her sister and everything she had to offer. The idea of another caring for her—truly taking care of her—seemed like a dream outside Ellie's grasp.

To embrace all Ruby offered, Ellie would need to open herself up and let everything in, but that would also allow many terrible things to escape her. Making herself vulnerable before her sister, letting Ruby envelope her in a net of safety, would only bring out all the harsh memories Ellie had worked to suppress, things she'd sworn never to trouble her sister with.

They ate Ellie from the inside out—and she'd die before allowing them to do the same to Ruby.

CHAPTER 6

ALEX PACED BEFORE the dressing mirror in one of the upstairs guest chambers, turning to and fro, assessing the skill with which the maid had altered the coat to fit him. The cut and fabric were long out of fashion, but with Drake's shrinking size as he aged, Lady Ellington had been forced to locate a trunk in the attic that housed clothes from the marquis' younger years.

The coat draped as it should—pulled tight across his shoulders, its tails falling precisely as he'd noted of Lord Haversham's coat. Lifting the hem of his pressed pantaloons, he took special notice of the Hessians securely on his feet. They were unlike any boots he'd ever worn before, and shockingly, they fit as if they'd been crafted for his feet only, not those of a man over a year in his grave.

Alex felt a twinge of unease and remorse over donning the clothes of the late Marquis of Drake. But he reminded himself, as he had numerous times each day since he'd agreed to orchestrate Ellie's plan, that this was for a good cause—he was only doing this to prepare Ellie for the eventual transfer of the Drake townhouse...buying her time to figure out her own future, whether that was with her sister or forging her own path.

"Do you think I shall pass?" he asked. "The clothes fit well, but I worry I do not know the mannerisms of a true lord."

When no response came from behind him, he looked over his shoulder to where Ellie sat by the closed door, lost in her thoughts, though she stared directly at him. He took the opportunity to watch her. When her face wasn't pinched in displeasure and she wasn't working overly hard to make her discontentment apparent, she looked almost angelic in nature; part of her hair had come loose from her pins and created a halo of light around her head. Her expression, neither pensive nor perplexed, lent a childish air to her visage. She'd tucked her legs up under her, her skirt falling over them and stopping a few inches short of the floor. Today, she wore a dress of the most delicate peach, with a white apron tied about her waist. Since she'd come out of mourning, he'd looked forward to seeing what colors and styles she chose to wear—not that he knew a thing of ladies' fashions, but no matter her choice, it far outshined the dull black, sturdy gowns she'd worn.

He was leery to bring up the task before him, knowing it would disturb her peaceful air, vanquishing her calm gaze.

Smiling, he realized he could dress every morn with her sitting thus, lost in her own thoughts or watching him—it didn't matter—as long as she was close. He'd always thought his connection to the marquis was the elusive man himself, but now, he wasn't so sure. Maybe, the possibility existed that his destiny was tied to the woman before him...not the marquis.

"You look dashing." Her words were no more than a whisper, and likely not meant to be spoken aloud.

He raised his brow, catching her eye in the mirror. "Dashing, yes." He twisted this way and that, puffing his chest and dancing a little jig. A small smile pulled at her lips at his antics. "But will I pass for a marquis?"

She unfolded from her chair, stood, and walked around him, her fingers pinching her chin with concentration as she inspected him. Finally, she stopped, her hands falling to her sides. "I confess, I am not the appropriate person to judge. You look to be any gent conducting business on Bond Street or promenading through Hyde Park."

"And my hair is not too long?" he asked, smoothing his palm along the part at his crown. Lady Ellington's lady's maid had trimmed his hair to where it tucked neatly behind his ears and barely brushed his collar in back. "It still feels a bit disorderly."

"I think it perfect, my lord." He turned from the mirror as she covered her smirk with her hands. "I could not help it," she giggled.

"This is for one meeting, correct?" It was all he'd be able to handle—though he should not have agreed to the farce at all. "After this, we will accept the cards as they fall. If this new marquis appears, we will accept him with open arms." *We?* He hadn't any idea when he'd started thinking of her and him as a 'we,' but it had happened sometime since she'd asked for his help. He wondered if after this were done, she'd go back to ignoring his existence. "At that time, you must tell the other servants—and your sister, too."

"It has not come to that yet. It is time you are off, or you will be late." She hurried about the room, gathering his discarded clothes—ignoring his earlier statement. "You have the horses waiting in the drive?"

"Of course," Alex confirmed. He'd wrestled with the best way to arrive at the solicitor's office. If he took the Drake carriage, then a driver would be necessary, which would cause word to spread through the household about him leaving in fine garb by the master's coach. But, he'd needed a horse—for no London nobleman would walk to his solicitor's office. And riding out of the stables would certainly have drawn the eye of Eckles, the stable master. "Are you certain you can ride astride?"

Ellie only laughed, not bothering to look up at him. "I have done it more often than you'd suspect. Besides, it is not far. Daphne and I shall meet you around the block. No one will question your attire or why you are slipping from the house and neglecting your duties."

He nodded as she slipped out of the room and closed the door behind her, leaving him alone in the outdated, shabby guest chamber. Though the furniture and décor were reminiscent of times past, Alex could settle himself in such a room—it was more than he'd ever had at the orphanage in London, and far more than the stables provided him currently.

With one last look in the mirror, Alex became rooted to where he stood. He hardly recognized the man before him: freshly bathed and dressed in such finery, his hair parted and combed to the side, with the marquis' signet ring upon his finger. When he'd arrived to bathe and dress, he'd noticed the small box that held the ring perched on his clean trousers. He'd set it aside at first, not wanting to mar the cream fabric that covered the box, especially if it wasn't meant for him.

Ellie had assured him that if they were to have any chance of fooling Adams, the ring would certainly help.

Though he was a fraud and a phony, everything about this situation felt right. Both his attire and his determination to put Lady Ellington's mind at ease.

He could do this.

He would do this.

It was one short meeting between him and a solicitor. If the man prodded him overly much or asked too many questions, Alex would excuse himself and depart.

That was exactly as he and Ellie had agreed.

Though he did not relish the idea of failing her. They'd known one another for over a year, yet she was still hesitant around him, never sharing much about herself. Nor did she ask many questions about him and his past. Many times when he looked at Ellie, her red hair flowing down her back unrestrained, or her green eyes alight with fury or mischief, Alex wondered if he truly knew anything of value about her—or if she'd only ever let him know what she wanted him to know, keeping all else to herself.

After this task was complete, he expected her to finally realize he could be trusted; that he was beneficial to her for more than what any common stable hand could offer. Ellie could call on him if she found she was in trouble or needed anything.

He eyed the mirror once more, astonished by the fit of his jacket and the way his boots shone. Maybe one day he would not only be playacting at being a gentleman, but would have more to offer those in his life in truth.

He only prayed that when the day came, Ellie was still in his life.

Glancing at the clock positioned on the dressing table, Alex noticed sufficient time had passed. He could depart the room without fear of anyone noticing Ellie had recently been present.

ELLIE KEPT TO her saddle as she walked her horse up and down the narrow alley two blocks from her townhouse. Her maid's mare, saddle empty, followed, the horses' hoofbeats echoing off the tall structures on each side of her.

She'd called Alex dashing in his fine clothes. A thought she shouldn't have spoken aloud, but it was better that utterance than her other thoughts—she'd never seen him more confident—and somehow, in his element—than in that very moment. It was as if the only thing that fit him better than the clothes on his back was the sense of rightness that surrounded him, enveloping her, as well. Wave after wave of pure self-possession and composure had filled the room. It was as if he donned the clothes—or ones just as fine—every day and spent his time attending his responsibilities in Parliament or hosting gatherings to discuss current world events.

Not a single person would think him anything other than a marquis—she was having a hard time reconciling the man she'd seen with the stable hand of hours before.

As soon as they'd entered the alley, Daphne had departed back home—without any questions. She valued the maid's ability to hold her tongue when her mistress sought out inappropriate escapades.

Now, she need only await Alex's arrival.

It had taken everything she possessed to leave him in the first place; he'd looked finer than any man she'd had chance to witness dressing—not that she'd ever watched a man dress. It was as if he were stepping into a role that should have belonged to him his entire life— and she'd thought back to when he'd teased if he hadn't been injured as a babe, and his parents hadn't abandoned him, he might very well be a grand lord.

And as most noblemen had a tendency to do, he was taking much longer than she'd expected—keeping her waiting. A part of her feared he'd thought better of their foolish errand and had decided to not play the lord after all.

Looking up between the buildings to the sun above, Ellie noted the time. Close to noonday, the time James Adams expected the Marquis of Drake to meet with him at his office—still a ten-minute ride from where she sat; though a lord was easily forgiven for his tardiness, especially a marquis.

Alex only need meet with the man, reassure him that he was in control—and most importantly, keep Adams and the rest of society from gaining any further interest in the Drake estate and Marquisate; and in turn, buy Ellie time to remedy her situation. Namely, being the bastard child of a deceased marquis with no money to her name nor any prospects for her future, besides her continued ruse.

Many days she wished she were strong enough to walk away from it all—seek refuge with her sister or at Craven House—but after her many years of abuse, Ellie *deserved* the marquis' townhouse and everything that came with it. No one, certainly not some long, distant relation of her father's, was going to usurp what was rightfully hers. She'd paid with her pain, her many years of tears—as her mother had paid with her life.

A chill ran through her at the thought, even though the day was unseasonably warm for this soon into spring.

The icy feel within threatened to have her buckling. She pulled her riding jacket tighter with her free hand, hoping to ward off the coldness that she knew came from within.

They could not fail—it was not an option.

She pushed her remorse and second thoughts about putting Alex in danger from her mind, for the punishment for impersonating a lord would be severe. He knew to depart the solicitor's office if anything went wrong with the meeting, or if his line of questioning became too deep and unsettling—for all they knew, her greatest fear would be realized, and Alex would be called a farce to his face, the magistrate summoned, and Ellie would be able to do nothing about it.

Thankfully, she'd thought through this outcome. She knew she'd have little choice but to beg Lord Haversham for assistance if Alex were taken by the authorities.

Ellie held her horse still when Alex finally arrived in the alley.

The sight of him fairly had her gaping—he looked every inch the refined, educated marquis. His walk even held an air of aloofness that the previous marquis had developed over years of practice; this man had mastered it in far less. His chin tilted up slightly as he stopped before her with the hint of a smirk upon his face.

His light brown hair had come free from behind his ear and flopped slightly over his forehead, lending him a devil-may-care look. Her maid had fit the coat perfectly across his broad shoulders, though the arms seemed a bit too tight, as if his muscles within begged for room.

Whatever had she been thinking that he could fool anyone with his attire?

It was likely he'd do far more than that.

"My lady?" he asked, plucking her from her wayward thoughts.

"Oh, yes." She shifted, preparing to dismount, and he was before her, his arms outstretched to lower her to the ground. "Thank you." His assistance was something—as much as she hated to admit—she'd grown accustomed to.

His hands settled about her waist and didn't release her until her feet were firmly planted on the packed dirt of the alley, and even then, she sensed that he hesitated, holding her a moment longer than was necessary. She closed her eyes, imagining she could feel his warmth through her corset and gown, though all she detected was the light pressure of his firm hands.

It unnerved Ellie how many times over the last several months she'd envisioned herself in his arms—a place she had no right to claim.

"You should be on your way." She took a

large step back, knowing he needed the distance as much as she. "Are you certain I cannot accompany you?"

He shook his head at her offer. "No, it would certainly complicate matters—and distract me."

"Distract you?" she asked, puzzled. "How so?"

"I would not be able to focus on the man's questions because I'd be worried some harm had come to you waiting outside."

Ellie had done all in her power to discourage his concern and thought for her—back when her father had passed and then on their journey to Foldger's Hall—yet, their last few days together had rekindled his watchful, protective nature.

"Then it is best I await you here." The deserted alley was also secluded from the eyes of passing persons, the deep lane swallowing the light and hiding her from view.

Once again, Alex shook his head in discord. "No, it is far too unsafe for you to loiter here without a chaperone. I think it best you return home and await me there."

"Someone is taking a little too quickly to his newfound power," she huffed, her hands landing on her hips. "I requested your help, I did not ask for a guardian, nor do I need a mere stable hand to keep watch over me." She was unsure why she took such great exception to his request—likely because it wasn't a request at all, but more of a command.

He glanced over his shoulder to the busy street and then up at the cresting sun. "We do not have time to bicker if I am to arrive on schedule." With the reins clutched in his left hand, he took hold of her hand with his right, looking her square in the eye. "Please, if something untoward were to happen to you while I was off playing the lord, I would never forgive myself—and this whole farce would be for nothing."

His eyes searched hers—digging deeper than she wanted and past the wall she'd constructed around herself—gently urging her to let her guard down and believe in him. But how could she ever have confidence in the fact that he'd take care of her and not simply seek what would benefit him?

The marquis' words floated through her mind. With his last breath, he'd bid her to trust Alex—but why? And more importantly, how? It was a security she'd never been afforded—even the marquis was not worthy of her trust, nor had she granted Ruby any measure of confidence.

Squeezing their clasped hands, Ellie nodded. "I will await you in the front drawing room." Then she released his hand and moved to her maid's horse, readying to depart. "Do stay safe— and thank you."

"Anything for you." He paused for only a second before continuing, "Ellie."

She could picture him saying her name thus—on the whisper of his breath and only for her hearing as he proclaimed his willingness to go to the ends of the earth to please her.

He assisted her onto the horse and swung up onto the other; his solid grip on her waist could be felt through her layers of clothes long after he'd let go. "I will depart the alley a few minutes after you, so as not to catch the eye of anyone."

Ellie wondered if it would be that horrid to have their names linked, to be seen in his company in public—but then no one knew the pair. One could not create a scandal if no one were the wiser of his or her identity.

CHAPTER 7

ALEX'S CONFIDENCE WANED the closer he rode to the solicitor's office, his brow broke out in sweat and his neckcloth seem tighter than a noose, restricting his airway. The only comfort he took was in the sway of his horse as he navigated the crowded lane, searching for the building he sought. Adding to his unease was the fact that he was unfamiliar with the area—it neither being in the shopping district nor on the route to the more influential townhouses of London.

The street narrowed and he made the last turn, recognizing the name on the shingle hanging outside a small office in need of fresh paint and window scrubbing.

Pulling his horse to a stop before the building, Alex glanced about. Normally, he or a footman would keep watch over the marquis' carriage or horse while the lord was occupied—not that the Marquis of Drake left his townhouse often but to attend his gentleman's club.

He was baffled—did he leave his horse tied to the post in front of the building? Eckles would surely whip him if he lost one of Drake's prized horses, even if he were on an errand for Lady Ellington.

"M'lord?" a boy, no more than twelve, called as he rushed around the building. "Ye be the marquis?"

"Undoubtedly, lad," Alex answered after suppressing the surprise of being called 'm'lord.'

"Then I be take'n ye horse round back while ye be meet'n." The boy grinned, his teeth stained from lack of hygiene, yet they were straight as an arrow. "He be wait'n for ye inside, m'lord."

Alex slid to the ground as the boy took his reins. "What is your name, boy?"

"Daniel, m'lord." Bowing quickly, the boy started back the way he'd come, horse in tow.

There was nothing further to delay things. Brushing his stray hair behind his ears once more, Alex started for the door, which opened before he reached it.

"Good day, your lordship," a spectacled man greeted, stepping back to allow him entry. "Thank you for coming. May I offer you a refreshment?"

"No, thank you, Mr. Adams." Walking past the man, Alex noticed the disarray of the small, two-room office. "It is Mr. Adams, correct?"

"You are correct, your lordship. Please, come this way." The man, at least thirty years Alex's senior, shuffled toward an open doorway leading to another cluttered office beyond—with no hint that he suspected Alex of being anything other than whom he claimed to be. "I have your papers right here." He moved behind the desk, motioning to a fairly large stack of files with a capped tube of sorts leaning against them. Noticing Alex's bewildered expression at the sheer size of the tower of parchment, the man continued, "Do not feel overtaxed, my lord. When I journeyed to the country, I took all the marquis' particulars with me, in case an emergency arose."

Alex nodded, taking a seat.

The man cleared his throat and shuffled through the closest stack of papers. "Well, I am, once again, sorry for my tardiness in contacting you."

"All is well," Alex answered. "The marquis' year of mourning only recently passed."

"Ah, yes," he said, clearing his throat once more. "I am sorry for your loss."

It was on the tip of his tongue to tell the man his kind words were unnecessary since he barely knew the previous marquis beyond that of a servant, only seeing him in passing.

But a serious expression settled on the man's face, his brow pinched in thought. Nerves flooded Alex, awaiting the solicitor's accusations as to Alex's true identity.

"May I speak frankly, your lordship?" When Alex nodded, Adams sat forward, settling his clasped hands upon his desk. "I must admit that I was taken aback when the previous Marquis of Drake requested the papers to name you as his heir, but now the resemblance to your mother—and father—is clear."

"Mother?" The word squeaked past his lips before he could stop it. He wanted to demand what this man could possibly know of his mother—or father. Instead, he kept silent, hoping he'd share what he knew without Alex demanding it from him. Besides, the solicitor was certainly mistaken in seeing any resemblance between him and an associate of the marquis'.

"Oh, yes." The man was as uncomfortable at the turn of the conversation as Alex was. "You have your father's hair and eye color—but certainly your mother's French complexion."

Alex held his breath, hanging on the man's every word—even though, certainly, it was all a mistake.

He reminded himself that he was posing as another. This man did not know him, or his family. That was impossible.

"I was uncertain whether you had received the decree I sent to your townhouse, as you sent no reply," the man continued. "But it seems all is well with both the Drake estate and your Dukedom. I was certain you'd continue to occupy your father's estate, and instructed my assistant to continue with the salaries of all Drake servants."

While the solicitor's words brought answers to many questions, new ones arose. Alex's head ached with the thought of explaining even their conversation thus far to Lady Ellington.

"Am I correct in assuming you prefer to use the title, Lord Chastain, as your father before you?"

Chastain? Alex ran the name through his mind once more, wondering if he'd heard it before or only *hoped* he had. Ellie had told him of both names listed on the correspondence but neither meant anything to him.

"My apologies, your lordship." The man stood. "I am overwhelming you with matters that must still be raw for you."

"No need—"

"Please, I will not keep you further," he

continued. "I can have the papers sent round to you to review. I admit, I've been curious to have a look at you for many years now."

"Me?" Alex stuttered, certain he was nothing as the solicitor had expected. "Whatever for?"

The solicitor lowered his head before speaking, "Ah, well, the marquis was very adamant that the papers go before the appropriate counsel and gain the proper seal not long after your parents perished. I assumed he would seek legal guardianship of you—being as Lord Chastain and he were close friends—but he never requested the papers drawn up. I suppose he was in agreement that your upbringing at your father's country estate was acceptable." When he only stared, the man finally stopped talking, his mouth gaping open before snapping shut.

Alex was tentative about responding; the chance he could convince the solicitor he knew an ounce of what he was talking about was highly questionable.

"Again, my apologies." Adams pulled a kerchief from his pocket and blotted his forehead. "I do not mean to bring up all sorts of unpleasantness."

The man stood awkwardly before him, only the desk and mounds of papers separating them; yet Alex felt as if the distance between their statuses were of oceanic proportions. "It is all in the past." Alex waved his hand as he stood to depart. "Please, send any correspondence to the Drake townhouse."

"Very well, my lord. But before you go," Adams paused as if uncomfortable with the direction the conversation was about to go. "Your mother was so very young—but she was always kind the few times I had the honor to be in her company."

"I appreciate your kind words, sir."

"They are as much for you as for your mother's memory. She deserved better than what happened to her."

"I will see myself out." Alex had no idea if it were done or if the proper thing to do was to allow the solicitor to escort him from the office. Either way, Alex needed a few moments alone to think through all he'd learned—and how much to share with Lady Ellington.

He breathed deeply, reminding himself once more that this wasn't his past or his mother the man spoke of—though, he desperately wished it were.

Alex hurried from the solicitor's office with an agreement to meet again after he reviewed all the papers. He couldn't help but worry he'd taken a solid step into taking over another man's life, which did not sit well with him.

With a cautious look about, sure that no one watched, Alex mounted and rode back to the Drake townhouse.

ELLINGTON THREW HER needlepoint aside and launched to her feet in boredom...and unrest.

How she wished she'd been born a man— something she knew the late marquis had wished, as well. If she had been, she would not be relegated to this dreadful room to await the edicts of men.

She'd be in control: of her life, her home, and her future.

Not be put in a position where she was a passive participant in her own life—her every prospect and aspiration to be granted at the whim of men; whether he be the late marquis, his solicitor, some man named Peter Davis—or even Alex, a bloody servant.

Ellie could not sit, she was not kept occupied by pacing, nor had the tea and bread with marmalade soothed her. It was as if she were a caged animal, awaiting her fate.

Hearing footfalls, she rushed to the door and swung it wide.

"What kept you so long?" she called. "You better have a compelling excuse for keeping me waiting!"

"Pardon, Lady Ellington?" The butler paused. "Can I have Daphne bring you more tea?"

She'd give the man applause—if it didn't make her look less than stable—for he neither jumped at her suddenness nor looked the least bit surprised to have a door flung open before him.

"Are you awaiting someone?" he asked, looking over his shoulder and then farther down the hall in the direction he'd been headed.

"No." She closed the door in the man's face. "Drat!" Pulling it open again, she saw he hadn't moved. "Good day, Alfred," she said before slamming the door once more. She was on edge, preparing for the worst—hoping her plan wouldn't explode in her face. It would only see Alex in harm's way. She'd forced him to do her bidding, and now it would be all her fault if he were caught. Ellie's breath hitched at the consequences he'd face—certainly time in a goal, but impersonating a lord might see him in far worse danger.

Wringing her hands, she walked across the room to the bookshelf she'd taken to keeping her favorite books arranged on. Maybe a good tale would distract her thoughts from Alex—and what could possibly be keeping him so long. She took a seat next to her discarded crossstitch after selecting a book and glanced at the clock.

It had been over three hours since they'd parted ways in the alley.

It would have taken him another ten minutes to get to the solicitor's office after he left her, which meant even with the journey home, he'd had ample time to return. She didn't want to ponder the notion that the solicitor had called Alex out as a sham and sent for the magistrate.

She stood once more, the book clutched to her chest.

"I do not want to call on Lord Haversham. I do not want to call on Lord Haversham." Her steps matched her chant. "I do not want to call on Lord Haversham." But time was running out, and soon she'd have no other choice; she could not allow Alex to sit at Newgate for her doing.

Ellie was a fool for asking so much of him.

A soft meow drew her attention to the door as it was nudged open, wide enough for her kitten to squeeze through. Ember hurried to her side, rubbing against Ellie's leg, begging to be picked up. But she kept pacing—and soon, the animal followed, two steps behind.

Ember had been a gift from Alex at Christmastide.

As if she needed the reminder of the man's kindness—and her own selfishness.

She set her book down and scooped the cat—no longer the tiny kitten she'd been—into her arms, snuggling her close. She'd hated that he'd been right about her needing the animal as much as Ember needed her. She'd looked for every excuse to leave Ember behind at Foldger's Hall to stay with the other stable cats, but the adorable little beast hadn't allowed it. As her time at Lady Haversham's holiday gathering came to a close, the kitten had become increasingly dependent on Ellie, following her all about the house, even taking to her lap during meal times.

And bloody curses, if Ellie hadn't enjoyed it.

"Whatever shall we do?" she asked. The cat's resounding purr in reply didn't give her answers, but it did comfort her. "We cannot allow him to be punished for doing my bidding. It would ruin his entire life...and he would likely protect me. How could I ever forgive myself if he is suffering in a goal while I live as I always have? I certainly could never live with that outcome." The cat brushed her head against Ellie's cheek.

The clock chimed the top of another hour and Ellie began rehearsing in her head the least painful way to request Lord Haversham's assistance without involving her sister or Lady Haversham.

"My lady?" The butler's voice startled Ellie. "You have a few visitors."

"Tell them I am not receiving." She had to find out what had kept Alex—and if he needed her help. "I am not feeling my best," she continued when the man remained inside the door. She hadn't any idea who'd be calling on her today...let alone a *few* visitors.

"Do not think you can send us away that easily," Ruby said, pushing past Alfred with

Lady Haversham on her heels.

Can my day get any worse, she wondered. Of course, it could, and it was. Normally, her sister was polite enough to badger her only once a week with her requests that Ellie move to Haversham House, or agree to meet this gentleman or that gentleman, or accompany her and Lady Haversham to the opera.

With Alex still not having returned, her mind was elsewhere—her patience short.

Both women invaded the room—and Ellie had the sinking feeling they were on a mission, their visit not purely social. Lady Haversham went immediately to the teapot, felt the outside—and tsked in disapproval.

"Please, have a fresh pot sent in directly," she spoke over her shoulder to Alfred. "Thank you."

"Certainly, my lady." He issued a curt bow and fled the room.

Ellie wished she could follow him, but no such luck would be hers.

Both women settled on the lounge, moving her book and needlepoint to the table.

The final blow came when Ember jumped from her arms and settled between the pair of ladies, demanding their attention.

"Are you not going to ask why we are here—unexpectedly?" Ruby asked with a suspicious smirk.

"To further ruin my life?" Ellie retorted.

Her sister's smirk was replaced by a frown. "No?"

"Possibly," Lady Haversham laughed. "It depends on how you feel about meddling."

Ellie didn't like the sound of that—at all.

"Oh, meddling is not the right term at all,

Vi," Ruby said, turning a stern look on her friend. "Maybe it is best to think of it as...being helpful."

"Meddlesome," Ellie sighed. "I'm certain meddlesome will be the correct term."

Daphne pushed a cart loaded with tea and pastries into the room, and for once, Ellie was happy to see her trusted maid in lieu of another servant. "Your tea, Lady Ellington."

"Thank you, dear," Lady Haversham said, ever the perfect hostess. "We can serve ourselves."

Daphne turned a worried look to her mistress, but Ellie nodded, motioning her to leave.

Ellie took the cup Lady Haversham offered her and sank into the chair across from the pair—to await whatever fate was her due. The quicker they all had their tea and were settled, the faster the women would share their reasoning for their visit...and the closer Ellie would be to finding Alex.

"We are throwing a grand ball to introduce you to society," Ruby blurted.

"No." Ellie shook her head. "That is an absolute, irrefutable no."

How many times—how much energy—did she need to spend dissuading her sister's never-ending schemes? Ellie was worried sick over Alex; she needed to be free to search for him. But instead, she was trapped here, talking of extravagant gowns, a room full of strangers, and fancy food—all in one large, stuffy room.

The room they currently occupied was rather stuffy at the moment, as well. Suffocating even.

"You see, it is not only for you—it is for Harold and me, too. An introduction for our whole family, if you will."

The explanation didn't make the idea any more appealing.

"Absolutely not." Ellie had spent the last year avoiding society—keeping the news of the marquis' death as quiet as possible. "You both know I've waited this last year for someone to appear on my doorstep and throw me out. I cannot see any advantage to being known by society. Besides, how would I be introduced? As the bastard daughter of Drake and his strumpet?"

Both woman recoiled at her wording—her sister appearing more injured than shocked at her tone.

"That can be said for the pair of us," Ruby whispered.

"But at least your mother is a member of the *ton*—not a woman who sold her body to anyone with enough coin."

"Does that make me any less a bastard?" her sister asked. "Should I stand a bit taller because my mother chose to be his mistress as opposed to being hired? Does society recognize and acknowledge that difference?"

The questions kept coming—Ruby's voice breaking more with each one.

Ellie had never believed Ruby was as damaged from their parental circumstances as Ellie was. Somehow, she rationalized that since Ruby had been brought up with a last name—and a proud father—she was not bothered by the bastardly conditions the *ton* had no knowledge of.

"Why do you care what society thinks?" Ellie asked, avoiding her sister's many other—more pertinent—questions. "They do not matter in the least to me."

Ruby handed her tea to Vi, her hands trembling. "I care because these are the people my husband does business with. These are the people whom we seek to make long-term relationships with. They are good people—at least most of them."

"But they are nothing to me," Ellie said before sipping her own drink, hoping to convince Ruby and Lady Haversham that this topic of conversation was of little interest to her. "I do well here. I do not need to make friends, I have a small group who care for me." Truly, she could count them on one hand, but she'd rather have a handful she trusted than a dozen who were no more than acquaintances. "I have no plans to be part of society, to follow their foolish rules, to keep my mouth shut lest I speak of something only fit for gentlemen's ears. It seems a fate worse than death."

"What about marriage?" Lady Haversham asked. "Do you not plan to one day find a good, honorable man to love—possibly start your own family?"

"My days are never guaranteed, and tomorrow I could find my home taken," Ellie retorted, knowing the topic would eventually be discussed. "Especially if I were to be introduced into society—surely that would have people talking." She paused. "And it would certainly increase the chances that a legitimate heir will come forward."

"You are always welcome at the Haversham townhouse or any one of my husband's, or father's, estates," Lady Haversham offered. The woman meant well, but it still felt like the charity it ultimately was. Never did she want to become one of Foldger's Hall's orphans.

"I can take care of myself if I am thrown from this house, but," Ellie breathed deeply, calming herself. "I will not actively go about society flaunting myself and my past, inciting gossip of the worst kind. That would reflect poorly on you and Harold." Relying on Ruby's nonexistent vanity was a poor choice of paths—and they both knew it.

"Do you think having a sister—no matter the circumstances around the relation—would ever be viewed as an embarrassing thing to Harold or me." Ruby shook her head in obvious disgust. "You are the only sibling I have—and I would shout my joy about it from the rooftops if that would convince you I love you and cannot see my life without you in it."

"Ellington," Lady Haversham broke in. "I think Ruby is trying to say she wants you to be happy, though she is unsure how to go about giving you all that you deserve in life."

"I have all I *deserve*." She'd prayed, begged every day for the powers above to take the marquis, make sure he never hurt another person again. When Ruby came into her life, her prayers changed slightly, she hoped upon hope—wished on every falling star—that the marquis would perish before he was able to destroy Ruby as he had her. In turn, she'd taken from her sister the chance to obtain her own closure of sorts. She hadn't been able to face the man who'd used and discarded her mother, never claiming Ruby, instead allowing another man to raise her as his own. Then, after that man had died, the marquis hadn't stepped forward to support Ruby in any way, making it necessary for her to gain employment as Lady Haversham's companion.

"I am alone and refuse to continue the pattern of manipulation our father left as his legacy."

"You truly think you are capable of causing harm to others—treating them as the marquis treated you?" Ruby asked, her brow knit in confusion. "After all you lived through, it is unlikely you would ever do the same unto another."

Ellie lowered her head, the tears pooling in her eyes. She'd never been so weak as to cry before the marquis—she would not sink to that level now because the truth was, she didn't know what she was capable of. She wanted to believe she could overcome her tendency for harsh words and never resort to violent outbursts, but there were many positions she'd yet to encounter; such as someone trying to force her from her home.

There was likely to be a violent outburst if someone tried to take what she saw as hers.

She looked up, directly into her sister's eyes, and for once, spoke the truth. "I have done nothing but treat you poorly since we met. I am harsh with the servants. I do as I please, no matter the worry it causes others—and I am unlikely to change." Ellie sighed from the effort. "I do not deserve to stand next to you—or you, Lady Haversham—in polite society. And not only because my mother was a courtesan. I do not know if I am capable of change, or that I want it."

Ellie stared at her sister—and Ruby stared back, something new and different in her eyes. Defeat? Sorrow? Regret?

A terrible pain in Ellie's chest threatened to send her running from the room, but the stark realization that she never wanted Ruby to give up on her had the pain subsiding. Her sister always thought the best of her, gave her chance after chance, took Ellie's harsh words—but never gave up.

But now, Ellie recognized the defeat in her sister's eyes—for it was the same look their father had given her moments before he passed. She wanted to scream, *Do not give up on me! Never give up on me! Please, keep trying!*

Instead, she said nothing, giving her sister a confident stare in return.

"It is only one ball," Lady Haversham bargained. "After that, neither your sister, nor myself will pressure you. I know it means a lot to Ruby."

Ellie was unsure what to do—she cared nothing for society and their frivolous and wasteful parties, but as much as she tried to convince herself and others to the contrary, she cared deeply for Ruby—and her husband, Harold.

"Will you allow me to think on the matter?" she asked.

"Yes," Ruby gushed. "Please, think about it. We are planning the ball for two nights from now. Harold and I would like you at our side to greet the guests."

"Would I be able to invite a few of my own friends?"

Ruby and Lady Haversham exchanged a puzzled look, but quickly nodded in agreement.

"The thought of spending an entire evening amongst people I do not know is daunting."

"Whoever you'd like to come—"

"I am only thinking of Marce and her sisters," Ellie rushed to explain. "Ruby, you remember Marce, do you not?" Before Ruby had taken Harold as her husband, Craven House's Madame had assisted Ruby. "They are very nice women—and have been my friends for my entire—"

Lady Haversham held up her hand, silencing her. "You need not explain. If you count them as friends, they are welcome and shall receive an invitation." She stood, Ruby following her. "Can we assume you will attend?"

She didn't want to commit to anything, for she truly had no idea where she'd be in two days' time. For all she knew, things had gone dreadfully wrong with Alex and she'd land herself in the Tower—that was if she were able to prove she was a lady and not a common criminal. Or worse yet, she'd be forced to ask Lord Haversham for help and she'd no longer be welcome at the ball.

"If I attend," she paused, "I'd ask that you allow me to forgo any formal introductions."

CHAPTER 8

ALEX DISMOUNTED, CAUTIOUSLY peering about the deserted stables before leading the horse inside, quickly slipping the saddle from its back and brushing the sweat and dirt from her coat. The hour was close to meal time, all the servants and stable hands likely with their families or collecting their bread and stew from the back kitchens.

His stomach let out a loud protest at the thought; a warm piece of bread dripping with honey and a hearty pheasant stew would settle his frayed nerves and allow him to think clearly—before meeting with Ellie. He'd stalled returning to the townhouse, wandering about town until the sun began to set and the temperatures dropped.

"Where have you been?"

The sudden question startled Alex and he dropped the brush he'd used on the horse moments before.

"Why are you lurking out here in the dark?" he asked, searching the shadowy reaches of the stable to find where Lady Ellington waited.

"Lurking?" she asked. "I was examining the many ways I could ask for Lord Haversham's help without him taking my troubles to Ruby and Lady Haversham."

"What troubles?"

"You!" she exploded. "I have been pacing the halls and now the stables, awaiting your return for hours. I was so worried."

"I am here." He meant to soothe her irrational anger.

She quickly stepped from the shadows and hugged him quickly, before pushing him away and stepping back. "I was preparing to garner the earl's assistance in collecting you from the magistrate."

"The magistrate?" Alex asked. "Why would that be necessary?"

"You fool." She picked up an old woolen cloth and threw it at him, missing his shoulder by inches. "I thought you'd been found out—and detained!"

"So, you were worried about me?" He was caught between chuckling at her ire and listening with bated breath for her response. When she only huffed her displeasure with him, he continued, "No, the man did not know I was not whom I claimed—and even went so far as to boast about my resemblance to my sires." Alex had thought about the man's insistence on the similarities, and decided the solicitor saw what he expected to see—and that was all. Adams had set up a meeting with a man of French heritage, and so to him, Alex had indeed looked French. "He didn't suspect a thing to be amiss."

Ellie's shoulders sagged, and he regretted worrying her needlessly.

"I did find out a few things about the new Marquis of Drake," he continued, hoping his words would ease her apprehension. "It seems he goes by another title, Lord Chastain—a duke. Have you perhaps heard of him?"

She slumped to the bench near the door leading back to the main house. "I do not know. Sometimes I feel as if I did not know the man I lived with my entire life—he's as much a stranger to me as any person walking down Bond Street."

"Do not look so downcast." He'd thought giving her the news would relieve her concern, but it seemed to worsen her mood. "If it makes you feel any better, it is unlikely the new marquis will make an appearance anytime soon."

"How can you be so certain?" she asked, pulling her legs up under her skirts. It was a pose he'd come to know meant she was thinking overly much and her mind was occupied elsewhere.

"Mr. Adams sent word to the Chastain townhouse when the marquis passed away."

"Why does that mean anything?"

"Lord Chastain has not shown up to claim his title or the townhouse. Who's to say the man even wants it?" Alex snagged the brush he'd dropped earlier and returned it to its proper place. "Adams said he'd be sending all pertinent paperwork here for me—I mean you—to look through. Maybe we can learn more of the man from it. Though, I was able to learn that Drake's heir is not from his blood, but a special allowance by King George III."

Her gaze snapped to his. "No relation, you

say?"

Alex only shook head.

"Then maybe I still have cause to fight this." She sat up a bit straighter, a small amount of confidence returning. "It is highly unlikely, but not unheard of, for a female to inherit a title when no other male relations exist—but a bastard female will certainly be difficult, especially since the marquis never publicly acknowledged my existence. I can at least have his claim to the title contested."

"There may be more we can learn in the papers—something of your connection to the late marquis?" Alex had little hope any proof existed to substantiate Lady Ellington's claim to the Drake bloodline.

She laughed, a rough, dry noise that sounded painful, as if it clawed its way up her throat to escape. "The man was a spiteful, vindictive, shell of a man—not even worth the title of a gentleman. His dying wish was that I be thrown from my home, left with nothing. Do you think he'd risk committing my name or our relationship to parchment?"

Alex wanted to think the man was better than Lady Ellington declared; he'd given him a chance in his stables, after all. That spoke to some compassionate spark in him, or that the marquis was not concerned with such things. He'd never been outright cruel to Alex or any of the other servants—yet the other staff spoke of his cruelty toward Ellington. Alex had witnessed his wrath only once, hearing the marquis berating the woman; though Ellington was quite capable of standing up for herself. He'd been too new to his employ to say anything of the situation when Lady Ellington had found him lurking in the library that long ago night.

But Alex could not believe the marquis was such a horrible man as to leave his ward without a penny to her name or a roof over her head. It was inconceivable that a person could do that to another. Mrs. Dutton had left her sister's home—overcrowded as it was—and journeyed to London with a toddler in tow. She'd given up having her own life to make sure he was properly cared for; she'd taken it further when she'd begun taking in other young who needed a home. It was possible Mrs. Dutton had successfully hidden society's true nature from Alex all these years, for he'd never met another who'd watch a child starve to death without offering what little they could manage.

"He was not always the man he presented to you and the other servants," she sighed. "He—"

"You need not explain yourself to me, no need to convince anyone of his mistreatment of you," Alex confided, sitting next to her on the bench. "My worry and loyalty belong to you alone. I have no need to pledge my allegiance to another. If you are banished from your home, I will go with you."

"And what have I done to deserve such an action?" He continued to stare straight ahead as she continued to fuss with her skirts. "I have not treated you kindly."

"Maybe it is that you are unaware how to treat another with kindness." He felt her stiffen beside him. "You were not given the proper upbringing, and, therefore, are not trained in the art of cordiality." He paused to allow her to process his words—and add impact and meaning to his next. "And for that, I blame the marquis."

She finally brought her eyes to his—a deep sorrow filled not only their depths but her entire body, as well. "Am I not as much to blame for my inability—or unwillingness—to change?"

He wanted to tell her he could never blame her for anything. Even if he'd been caught as a fraud by the solicitor and the magistrate sent for—leading to his eventual stay at Newgate— Alex would never fault her for it. She was as much the product of her life as any other person. Some, as Lady Haversham, lived charmed lives and things were changed by their own actions. But people such as Lady Ellington—and to a certain extent, himself—were not dealt a childhood without disappointments, complications, and undue sorrows.

It would be preposterous for Alex to blame himself for his injuries suffered during infancy, as it would be outlandish for Ellington to believe she was at fault for the Marquis of Drake's hurtful demeanor and treatment of her.

For not the first time, Alex pondered the similarities between them.

The only difference being, Alex had decided long ago not to fall prey to the harsh realities of life, but to rise above it—and accept the love given to him by Mrs. Dutton and Lady Haversham. Though he may be an orphan without the comfort of a surname, he would not allow that to define who he was and what he accomplished. For all her strength and cunning, Lady Ellington seemed unable to do the same, or was at a loss for where to begin. She rebuked every advance Ruby made to show her love.

Booted steps and the throaty chuckles of grown men drifted into the stables—dispelling their moment of calm, their time of plainly existing—side by side—despite all that stood in their way. And with the spell lifted, Alex discarded his own rush to compare their circumstances.

"It is time you return to the main house, my lady." Alex stood, moving deeper into the stables so as not to be caught again with the mistress of the house. "The solicitor promised the appropriate filings would be delivered before sundown tomorrow.

She didn't say a word in response.

His only guarantee that she'd actually been there was the sound of her retreating footsteps as she left the stables; the servants returning from their meal greeting her with hushed, 'good day, m'ladys.'

With her departure came the sense that things would revert to how they once were; she'd recede to her place of lone existence, ignoring those around her whenever possible.

A part of him wondered how he could live his life every day knowing he'd been abandoned and left for dead by his parents, but the thought of this woman acting as if *he* didn't exist crushed him so.

CHAPTER 9

"I AM NOT to be interrupted," Ellie whispered to Alfred, the butler. "No one spoke to him, is that correct?"

He nodded, taking in her odd clothing. His dismissive nod indicated he didn't approve of whatever she was up to. "No, my lady. Your guest insisted on carrying everything, unassisted. May I inquire as to what is going on?"

Ellie paused in the hall outside her father's study, patting her unruly hair and running her clammy palms down her freshly ironed apron, the butler pausing at her side.

"No, you may not. I have everything under control. You may go, Alfred, but remember, no interruptions—by anyone."

He gave a curt bow and returned to his post by the front door.

Ellie knew she couldn't keep the servant's questions at bay endlessly, but she hadn't the time to deal with him now.

It was imperative she calm herself before entering the room, or she'd never pass as the housekeeper. If her tender age didn't already give her away as a fraud. Her nerves were enough to have her perspiring profusely, she only hoped the man within didn't notice.

With a deep breath and a serene smile, Ellie pushed open the solid door and looked at the stranger standing before the desk, a large pile of crates and a few trunks littering the room. Her deep breath left her on a sigh. She'd frequently wandered the townhouse in her youth, paying little mind to the comings and goings of Drake's business associates. Their visits were few and far between.

Ellie had never seen this man before.

"Good day," she greeted, donning her cheeriest voice. Although it sounded a bit high-pitched and strained, even to her ears. "My lord is not at home this morning."

He glanced nervously at the piles around him and then back to Ellie. "Ah, well..." The man was as apprehensive as she. "He was expecting all the papers, but I did not confirm that I would be coming personally to deliver them. It is my fault."

"He did tell Alfred and me to expect the papers."

"I was hoping to give my sincere apologies once again for the unorthodox handling of the estate." Adams' tall, slender form seemed to give way, and his shoulders hunched over as if he were a man used to leaning over a desk for days at a time. "I understand if he is to seek out another solicitor. You see, my father—"

"Mr. Adams," Ellie said, and the man's eyes met hers. "There is no need to explain anything to me. I will inform my lord that you delivered the papers personally with your apologies."

"Oh, that is very kind of you, miss."

Ellie found the man's scattered wits endearing. If a man became this flustered over his duties—or when he thought he'd failed at them—he was certainly a man to be trusted.

"If my father caught word of how I handled everything—I rightly bobbled everything up—he would be ashamed to call me son."

"I am certain it is not such a dire situation," Ellie reassured him.

The sentiment seemed to ease Adams' fears and his shoulders straightened once more. "What is your name again?" he asked as if noticing her for the first time. He looked her up and down, his gaze stalling on her red hair a moment longer than was proper.

"I did not say, Mr. Adams." Ellie mentally visualized her sack of coins hidden in a shoe box in her dressing closet. If he were to sound the alarm on her, she only hoped he'd allow her to return to her room before the magistrate was called. She didn't think there any harm at posing as a servant, thankfully, but the ruse she'd concocted for Alex would certainly garner consequences for them both. "I am only the housekeeper here, no one important, I assure you."

Adams held eye contact for a moment longer, as if searching for an answer to a question he hadn't asked. Reluctantly, he looked away and continued, "Thank you for meeting with me. Give the duke my regards—and let him know he can call on me if he has any questions."

"Certainly." Ellie turned. "I will show you out."

The man hastily departed the room, his feet shuffling as he made his way back to the foyer where Alfred held Adams' hat, the door wide for him to depart.

"Good day to you both," Adams said before hurrying down the steps and climbing into the waiting hired coach.

Alfred inspected her from head to toe once again. His look of disdain even sterner than before, signaling he found her appearance dreadful, but Ellie hadn't any better way to convince the solicitor that she was a servant than to wear Daphne's plain dress and frayed apron. Keeping his distaste for her attire to himself, the butler asked, "Why did that man say the trunks and crates were for 'my lord?'"

It was an obstacle neither she nor Alex had considered when she'd learned Adams was having everything sent to Drake House. Of course, everything would be delivered to the current Marquis of Drake—which was still, as of yet, unfulfilled in the servants' eyes.

Ellie optioned to don her usual mask of aloofness and returned to the study, closing the door behind her and cutting off any further discussion on the matter. Avoidance of situations and discussions had worked best for her since her father's death; she circumvented Ruby's continuous need to discuss her future, she averted the servants' questions about their future, and she evaded Alex's need to watch over her. And she'd thought she was doing a marvelous job at it all until she realized that Alex knew exactly what she'd been doing, and the servants' questions would not go away until answers were given.

Unfortunately, she had no answers to give at

the moment, but with any luck, she'd know much more after she searched the crates surrounding her—if those answers would be helpful to her or the servants, was still to be seen.

The amount that must be stored in all the crates and trunks in the room far exceeded what Ellie thought the man had accomplished in his life—certainly more than was ever done since her birth. Her father had rarely left his home during those final years—and then, only to visit his club for a hand of cards or the occasional *ton* entertainment.

"I cannot imagine you did anything worthy of all this," Ellie spoke aloud, hoping her father, rotting in hell, was privy to her musings. "Though, to have me rifle through all your most personal things will be my greatest joy. And to think, you cannot do a thing about it. Where to begin?"

Ellie felt silly speaking to an empty room. The man wasn't here, nor would he be anywhere that allowed him to keep an eye on her—but still, it brought her satisfaction, knowing the man who'd spent her entire life keeping her at arm's length was now to have his life bared before her.

She tapped her forefinger against her lips as she looked about the room, determining where to start. There were crates of every size, and trunks that must have needed two men to carry. Poor Mr. Adams must be sore from loading and unloading everything. Walking between the stacks, Ellie removed the lids from several crates and lifted the top of the largest trunk. Neatly arranged folders filled each one.

With no particular box catching her attention, Ellie decided to start with the one closest to the lounge, making it easier to pull out papers and stack them on the table before her. It had crossed her mind to request Alex's assistance with sorting through everything, but she'd quickly changed her mind in favor of respecting his wishes for her to keep her distance while he worked.

The aloneness suited her, she found, as she removed stack after stack, finding nothing of import in the first box but old estate ledgers and detailed lists of the property's assets. It was interesting to know that twenty years ago, there had been a count of seventy-eight chairs in the Drake townhouse. Maybe one day—when boredom overtook her—she'd walk the entire house and count.

She stood, venturing to one of the farthest crates and lifting the lid. Inside, another box was nestled. Lifting it, Ellie noticed it was the size of a hatbox, but didn't weigh enough to have one inside. And, if she discovered her father had an obsession with ladies' hats, she would be shocked beyond imagining. Balancing the box on one hand, she tried to lift the lid, but it wouldn't budge.

Retaking her seat on the lounge, she set the white and blue box atop her lap. It appeared far too personal an object to be housed at a solicitor's office, and it likely held nothing of value or meaning; but if that were true, then there was no reason for it to be kept.

Ellie slipped her finger under the brim of the box to find what held it shut, but nothing impeded her as she slid her hand all around it. Pushing the box between her legs to hold it steady, she grasped the lid and pulled. With a small amount of reluctance, whatever held the box closed gave way and the lid came off, revealing a haphazard stack of envelopes and simply folded notes.

Tentatively, she reached in and took the top few letters from the box; they were all sealed, some addressed to a Lady Lorelei and others to a Lady Chastain. She recognized the name from Alex's meeting with Adams, but why would her father be writing Lady Chastain and not her husband, the duke? More puzzling was why he'd kept those letters mixed with the ones addressed to Lady Lorelei. Who were the women to Drake?

She set the closed letters aside. Opening the sealed correspondence seemed like an invasion even she wasn't comfortable with. There were plenty more crates, plus the large trunk, to go through before she relegated to breaking the Drake wax seals on the letters addressed with the marquis' own hand.

Ellie separated the closed envelopes from the loose pages and folded letters, most many years old as evidenced by their yellowing paper.

The last was a scrap of paper, torn from a newspaper with a scribbled note written in the margin. It was a marriage announcement from one of London's many gossip columns. It was dated 1800 and announced the marriage of Lady Lorelei de La Valette to Benjamin Davis, Lord Chastain. A duke wedding the daughter of French nobility—a comte. At the edge of the fraying paper it read, 'Traitorous! Why Chastain?' It was barely legible, and if Drake had written anything else, it was long lost.

Lady Lorelei and Lady Chastain were one and the same.

Next, she opened a folded piece of paper to find a list of sorts, some of the items written in a bold print while others looked rushed without care.

She quickly scanned the list for anything that would help her ascertain the connection between Lady Chastain and her father, but nothing made sense. Extinct title…no comte or comtesse…searches leading to nothing…disappeared without a trace…injured babe…still no explanation for plans…no hope left.

Nothing made sense—it was a jumble of words that Ellie couldn't seem to connect.

Turning the paper over, she saw two lines:

Search for Alexandria Dutton has turned up nothing. All familial connections have been investigated. The child not found.

It was the only writing so far not belonging to the marquis—and surprisingly, the only string of words put together to make a legible sentence. But still, it meant nothing to her.

Ellie traced the words with her finger, concentrating on each letter, hoping something would come into focus or that the meaning behind the note would spark some kind of memory long forgotten. Though something about it nagged at the back of her mind, it remained hidden, just out of her mental reach.

Several other lists noted various places around England and France, each crossed off; the marks becoming increasingly erratic and almost violent in nature—if mere ink on a page could be violent.

With no loose papers left, Ellie realized she had no other choice but to open the letters addressed to Lady Chastain. It was likely the other boxes in the room held nothing but more accounting ledgers and business correspondence, which gave her no information about how this woman's son, Chastain, had come to inherit her home.

Privacy was something her father had never allowed Ellie, and her hesitancy to break the seal on the first letter confused her. The man was gone—over a year in his grave—he'd never know she invaded his private correspondence. He was no longer here to berate her for her many insolent actions. In fact, there was no one who knew the letters existed but her...and Adams. And he'd left everything in the hands of the new marquis—or so he thought.

But it was something else, something deeper than her fear of her father, which kept her from opening the letter. Once she read the correspondence—possibly even this very first one—she'd be privy to her father's most personal thoughts, for they were letters written to this woman and she'd clearly never received them. Which told Ellie they contained such delicate writings that Drake feared sending them.

She'd never known the 'intimate' or 'private' marquis. For her, he'd always been cold and distant—a recluse in his own home—never one with enough internal emotion to write—and then retain—such keepsakes. She'd drawn the marquis a picture once, of a dog she longed to have, and he'd crumpled the paper right before her eyes and tossed it into the hearth. She couldn't reconcile the memory of the man who could disregard such a gift from a mere child with one capable of all this.

It was time she knew exactly who the marquis was—for while she doubted he was anything but the cruel man who'd raised her, she suspected there was more to him. A time when his entire life wasn't driven by his suppressed rage and fury. The way each letter in her hand was written—changing as she flipped through the dozen or so next to her. Almost as if the message inside became more erratic and unpredictable. On one, her father hadn't allowed the ink to dry before running something over the top of the letter, smearing the ink. Or maybe it wasn't that the ink hadn't time to dry, but liquid of some sort had dripped on the page—possibly from an unsteady hand holding a tumbler of bourbon. But something told her it wasn't the amber liquid marring the pristine surface. But the only way to know for sure was to read them—all of them.

Once Ellie broke the first seal, the Drake insignia cracked in half easily and the aged wax crumbled to her lap, she knew she wouldn't stop until every letter had been removed from its sealed envelope and read.

The note slid from the envelope with ease, its color not as yellow as the envelope.

Ellie looked to the closed study door, a sudden sensation of being watched overtaking her.

She was being silly. The room was empty but for her—and no footsteps had sounded in the hall.

Taking a deep breath, she unfolded the letter.

This one was apparently written before Lady Chastain married, as it was addressed to Lady Lorelei. Inside, Drake had written her name in flowing letters, the 'L' making a dashing loop. His bold script was undeniable, yet the ink caressed the paper as if luring the woman with his words. It hinted at something deeper within the marquis—the loving way his words moved across the page brought light to the room, not the gloom of the dark and brooding person Ellie had known.

And so, Ellie read…

My Dearest Love, Lorelei,
I count the days until you return to London—and me. My days drag on and on, my nights are filled with the sweetest dreams. The day will come when you and I are once again together. I have journeyed to my country home to pass the time—and all I see are the many things that must be tended to in hopes of preparing my simple home for its new mistress, my marchioness. Our time apart has only shown my heart that it cannot beat without you.
Until we are one,
Andrew

Andrew.

Ellie had rarely heard her father's given name, and never had she seen it written.

The man had preferred his title—a way of showing his superiority to others instead of creating more intimate connections. The last person to call the marquis by Andrew was Mrs. Bee, his old housekeeper, but she was long deceased now.

Next, Ellie opened a letter addressed to Lady Chastain, obviously written after she'd forsaken the marquis for another. It was more formal, as if written to an acquaintance as opposed to a woman he'd loved with his whole heart and soul only months before.

Lady Chastain,
Congratulations on your recent nuptials to Lord

Chastain. It is with great pleasure that I send this letter wishing you and my good friend a life full of happiness. I sincerely hope you receive everything you are deserving of.
Cordially,
The Marquis of Drake

Ellie filled with an unexpected sensation—pity, sorrow, sympathy? Certainly not, possibly empathy. She could understand the sense of betrayal he felt at Lady Lorelei wedding another. It was similar to the emptiness that filled her after Alex left her side—not that her dependency on the man could be comparable to losing a love that must have run very deep.

The next letter instantly brought Ellie to tears.

My Shining Light in this Dark World,
I fear I have a confession to make, though it is made all the easier knowing you will never read this. All these years, and I have never told you of my daughter. Ellington. She is the exact image of me in both appearance and manner, though I am uncertain that this is for the best as she has taken on my worst traits, as well. I am a man you will not recognize—a man who cannot put forth enough effort to love his own child. Most days, I cannot stand the idea of laying eyes upon her. She should have been given my name and my protection, raised as the daughter of a marquis should, but instead, I hide her within my home. I do not want her close, yet cannot stand to let her go. I should blame this all on you—my inability to show my love to and trust another, but it would be one more sin that will undoubtedly send me straight to the fires of hell—and so, I will not even think the ill thought again.

Faithfully yours,
Andrew

He—her father—had spoken of her. The letter had never been sent, and in turn, never received or read by another…but he'd written of her.

He would confess his blood connection to this woman, but not Ellie herself? All those lost years, and he'd never brought himself to speak to her in anything but anger. She could have had— *they* could have had—a life and relationship unlike the one they'd shared. Maybe not love, because Ellie was still uncertain if either father or daughter were capable of that, but one of contentment and ease, if only he'd spoken to her like he'd written to this woman, a complete stranger to Ellie.

Would he have taken her upon his knee and read her a story?

Taken her for rides in Hyde Park in his fancy carriage?

Ices at Gunther's?

Most certainly not—but they could have sat at the same supper table without insults hurled in each direction, or weeks without speaking a single word to one another.

She was unsure what hurt worse; the way he'd treated her all those years, or the fact that everything could have been different but *Ellie* wasn't worth it to him.

Lifting the hatbox to her lap once more, Ellie removed all the letters and loose papers remaining, feeling for the bottom of the box— and the last sealed letter.

It wasn't as handled as the others. This one must have been written, folded, sealed and placed directly in the box.

> *My One Love,*
> *This is the final letter I will write. You are gone from me and I must accept that, but know I am drowning without you. Years of searching for Peter and his nursemaid have given me nothing but false hopes and a continually damaged heart. This day I am accepting nothing is left of it. Which means I have failed you—your memory and your son. There is one last thing I can do for him...I will not give up on finding him. He cannot stay hidden forever. For now, I will use my time to make sure London is safe for his return.*
> *Yours in this world and in the next, Andrew*

Her father had referred to the child as 'your son.' A product of Lord and Lady Chastain's union? One he cared for far more than he'd ever cared for either of his own flesh and blood offspring.

She'd only known the marquis as a man proud of his status, flaunting his place as lord of the manor. It lacked any support for why he'd given everything to a boy that wasn't his—and left Ellie with nothing.

His letters were not worth the paper they were scribbled on. He wrote of his regret at this treatment of Ellie, but that was for another's benefit, not hers. The marquis had never intended for Ellie—or anyone else—to read these letters. His only regret was that this woman—Lady Chastain—would look unkindly on him for these behaviors. He wasn't asking for Ellie's forgiveness or giving her any apology to warrant it. He was confessing all to a woman who'd loved another and forsaken Ellie's father.

She was as faithless as Drake.

Pity, they would have made the perfect pair; each only thinking of themselves while those around them were left to suffer.

It was as if he loved this one woman so entirely that he had nothing left to give her—or Ruby.

Drake had clearly been lacking sense when he'd instructed his solicitor to draw up and file the paperwork.

Ellie collected everything and returned it to the box, securing the lid.

There were many more crates to consider before the day ended.

Finding that her father had lost his lover was not what she'd expected to discover, and it did not answer any of her questions.

Namely, how he could knowingly leave his child with nothing—and give everything to a man that might still be missing—if he were even alive.

She lifted a crate and placed it on the floor, allowing her to open the box beneath it. It was a newer box, the corners sharp and undamaged, the cardboard not discolored from age. It must hold the marquis' most recent business dealings and files.

Lowering to the rug, Ellie sat next to the box, fearing it too heavy for her to lift. The box did hold papers more current, the top dated 1816, January 9. It was a few months before he'd taken ill and finally succumbed.

There were many letters of correspondence between Drake and Adams, a few notices of issues needing attention at his country manor, and even a letter from Lady Haversham about Alex's suitability as a stable hand. It indeed appeared her father had taken an interest in hiring the man for his London home—even handling the correspondence and salary negotiations personally. Ellie wasn't versed in such matters as household and stable staff, but Drake's interest in Alex seemed out of place. It was no wonder he'd taken such a hard stance on her visiting him in the stables.

At the very bottom of the boxes several loose papers were gathered and clipped together. The scribbled words across the top were not those of the earlier papers, these appearing rushed as the quill barely pressed hard enough to leave a trail of ink behind it. It was less decipherable than the note left on the newspaper clipping.

She focused on reading every word, though she started crying before she'd finished even the first line. By the fourth line, Ellie's hands were shaking uncontrollably and she needed to wipe away the tears in order to see.

Control—the one thing Ellie had lacked her entire life. The thing she'd finally gained with the marquis' passing, and now, he was giving power over Ellie to another.

A complete and utter stranger was to determine her fate. Flashbacks of Daphne's massive bruising and nights spent quietly crying herself to sleep, thinking Ellie couldn't hear her, flooded Ellie. It had taken weeks for the outer damage to disappear, but the inner harm still plagued her maid.

And her *father* had given another the power to do the same to her.

If she hated the marquis before—Ellie had every right to *despise* the man now.

CHAPTER 10

"WHY ARE YOU so upset by this new information?" Marce asked.

Ellie continued to pace the confines of the glassed-in room at the back of Craven House, not answering the woman's question. The humid air made her arms sticky to the touch; however, it encouraged growth from the many plants housed here.

"While surprising, you cannot think this is something Drake would not resort to in his final hours."

She hadn't time to dwell on the immense heat and sticky air, nor the overwhelming floral scent permeating the room, making it hard to draw a deep breath—which Ellie was in great need of following her mad dash to Craven House.

"Do stop pacing, Ellington," Marce scolded. "I have told you numerous times that my plants can feel the emotions we expel. And you, my girl, are a ball of nerves—and rage. Very unhealthy for both you and the greenery."

Ellie stomped down the long row of tables, heavily organized with potted plants, some with blossoms, others without so much as a single leaf; the hard-packed earth below her feet as solid as her resolve to fight the marquis' intentions. The nerve of the man, to think even after his death he could still order her about and dictate her life—and to this extreme? It was certainly unacceptable.

The Madame clutched the small clippers in her right hand, holding a thin branch steadily between the two blades with her left; a quick movement sheared the stem from the plant she'd been trimming since Ellie's arrival.

"How can you be so calm?" Ellie threw her arms wide. Her exasperation quickly turned to fury at the situation she'd been forced into. Her anger hadn't reached such a level since the marquis had *dared* call *her* his child on his deathbed. "I have gone through all the files sent from the solicitor's office and—"

"Ellington," Marce snapped, setting her clippers down on the solid wooden table with more force than Ellie thought her capable of, then petting her plant as if asking its forgiveness for her cross words. "Do stop your pacing and fretting." She took a deep breath as if it were she who needed the calming effects, not Ellie. "Now, what do we know of this man?"

"Only that the marquis hadn't been able to find him in many years and he is not from Drake lineage...and that I'm betrothed to him." She couldn't believe she uttered the word aloud—*betrothed*. "I am unsure what is worse—being betrothed, or the fact that I've never met my intended…" Ellie paused, sucking in a deep breath. "Or that I am betrothed to a stranger who has been conveniently missing since infancy."

"Intended is a bit severe," Marce replied. "You are a woman capable of saying no. It is highly unlikely the man will insist you wed him if you are not in agreement."

"Allow the marquis to think of every possible way to betray me." Ellie's irritation increased. "If I do not wed this stranger, then my father dictated I am to be thrown from Drake House, never to be allowed in again. And what if the man is dead—I cannot wed a deceased person."

"Many do not have the luxury of meeting their betrothed until shortly before the actual ceremony." Marce didn't comment further, ignoring Ellie's lapse into self-pity, which was certainly for the best because Ellie could not think of an answer that would soothe the fire burning within her.

Instead of holding her breath and awaiting some man to come take her home, Ellie was now waiting for a stranger to take possession of her home and her *body*. Her first instinct was to flee the Drake townhouse—pack all her worldly possessions—and seek refuge with her sister. Tell Lord and Lady Haversham of all the injustices forced upon her by the late marquis, and hope they would champion her cause—or at the very least, take pity on her. Ellie could not fathom Ruby—or the Havershams—forcing her to wed a man she did not know.

"Have you asked about town if he is an honorable man?" Marce walked down the long table of plants, seeking out another in need of trimming. Ellie kept silent, for admitting she didn't have anyone in *town* she could ask, seemed pitiful; even more wretched was that she'd no one in all of England to ask. "It is quite possible he has no intention of marrying a stranger either—he may be as oblivious to the marquis' dastardly plans as you were mere hours ago."

"No," Ellie answered. "I suspected he would only be concerned with taking my home—not the woman he was forced to wed."

A light drizzle assaulted the paned windows surrounding them as it turned into a heavy downpour—the afternoon sky dark with warning. Funny, but Ellie had been in such a mood as she'd quickly saddled a horse in her stables and then rode as if the devil himself were on her heels that she'd completely neglected to notice the storm rolling in. Thankfully, she'd had the foresight to take an overcoat this time.

She watched the drops pool on the windowpanes and slide down the glass, some making a straight, quick path while others slowly zigzagged their way to the earth below. She wondered if her fate would come swiftly, or if it would be drawn out with many twists and turns still to come.

"Marriage is not always the worst thing to happen to a woman," Marce commented with a shrug.

Ellie laughed. "Coming from a woman who's been free to choose her fate her entire life."

"You think I would choose the life I have?" Marce's hard stare belied her gentle, reserved exterior. Many thought the dainty, blonde woman younger than her true years—and many would mistake her for an idle society miss, but Ellie had never underestimated Marce

Davenport. She'd spent her life caring for her siblings—and others in need. "But my choices—or those not so much within my control—are not the important matter at hand."

"Tell me how to fix this," Ellie sighed. She'd known the woman for many years, and she'd never failed to find a solution to all of the challenges Ellie had faced. "There must be a way out without marrying this man."

"And what if you are rather taken with him?" Marce asked with a raised brow.

"I cannot envision being smitten with this man—or even granting him the opportunity to meet me." The idea was preposterous. Though Ellie had endured much in her life so far, the fact remained that she was barely out of the schoolroom age-wise. Far too young to be expected to take a husband.

"Maybe you will yet be spared," Marce mused, retrieving a potted plant from the ground at her feet. "This contract may have been signed a decade ago and the man never located. If he were still missing, or presumed deceased, surely Drake changed his mind since then."

"It was signed a fortnight before my father's death."

"Oh."

"Yes, this is dreadful," Ellie moaned.

"And was it signed by your intended or, mayhap, his father?"

"No." Ellie retrieved the folded paper from her coat pocket. "It seems to be a letter outlining the match, the specifics of my dowry, and what is to happen if the marriage does not come to be."

"Ah. You see, it is not as you think." Her plant forgotten, Marce walked to Ellie's side and snatched the letter. Her mouth moved slightly as she read the words, her face clouding with concern the further she read. Marce was optimistic, thinking the marquis had left a way for Ellie to walk away from the marriage, to let her feelings be known, and not be made to continue with the sham; but as everything was with her late father, it was not a simple thing. "It says here that only Peter Davis, the seventh Marquis of Drake, can nullify this contract. If you do not marry him, you are to immediately be forced from all entailed properties without a farthing to your name."

"The nerve of that man." Ellie paced up and down the long row, away from Marce and then back toward her. As if on cue, lightning lit the sky beyond the windows, illuminating the room—followed by the rumbling of thunder in the distance. "Am I to give in? Maybe call on the new marquis...give my kind regards on his fortune and introduce him to his future wife."

"Your sarcastic tone and negative thoughts will not help the situation." Marce crossed her arms, the letter wrinkling in her hand. "There must be a way to meet the man—or find out if he is still missing—without him suspecting who you are and what your intentions be."

"I have no intentions."

"I did not mean it to sound like you do." Marce turned, her long hair falling behind her shoulders as she returned to her task. "I only mean it would be advantageous for you to learn something of the man before you give up everything that should be yours. He may be kind."

"Or maybe he's a lying, cheating, stealing rogue." Ellie thought through all the information Alex had imparted to her upon his return from the solicitor's office. Adams hadn't implied the new marquis had been found—or even that he had been missing—in fact, he'd let it slip that he'd known Peter's parents, Lord and Lady Chastain, before they passed away. "He is possibly already married—or betrothed. A year is certainly long enough to meet an eligible debutante and come to an agreement of her dowry."

"That it is," Marce mused, inspecting yet another plant. "But there must be a way to learn something of this man."

It dawned on Ellie then, she'd had the perfect opportunity waiting all along, all she'd need do is send word that she would attend the ball Ruby had invited her to.

She paused before telling Marce of her idea.

"Go on, out with it."

"How do you know I have something to say?" Ellie asked. "You are not even looking at me."

"Simple—the negative energy fled the room and all my plants sighed in relief."

"You jest."

"Maybe," Marce laughed. "You stopped pacing. Now, please share what you've thought of. I have much to do."

Ellie looked out the glass windows in alarm at the darkened sky beyond. "Your clients will be arriving before long," she said with a rush. "I will not keep you any longer. I can come round tomorrow."

Marce set her hands upon her hips, a stern look on her face. "You will do no such thing—leave me to worry all evening at how to solve your dilemma if you already have an answer. Besides, my clients—as you call them—will likely wait until the rain subsides, if they come at all. Now, please share."

"Lady Haversham is hosting a ball—to introduce Ruby and Mr. Jakeston to society." Ellie couldn't believe she hadn't thought of the idea sooner. "Ruby requested my presence by her side—to properly introduce me, as well."

Marce laughed.

She couldn't help but feel a twinge of hurt at the sound. "Not that I have agreed to attend, mind you."

"And it will allow you the perfect opportunity to ask about the man. " The woman sobered, the sound of her laugh fading so quickly it was as if it had never happened. "Of course you will attend."

"Why?" Ellie questioned.

"Someone in attendance is likely to know if the new marquis is still missing, and besides, being sponsored by a countess and presented to society..." Marce huffed with exasperation, as if Ellington were daft. "With Lord and Lady Haversham vouching for you, there is not a door that would remain closed to you. *If* you chose not to marry the new marquis, you'd likely have your choice of any man within the *ton*."

"I do not want to marry." It wasn't that she'd never expected to be wed and have her own family, it was only that she could not envision it for herself at this moment. She'd spent her life under her father's unbending rule—and now, with a spot of independence at her disposal, Ellie only wanted to experience freedom for a while. "But I confess, it would be nice to attend a ball or possibly a recital or tea."

Marce smiled. "You are not the cold, selfish child you once were. It is not wrong to order a pretty gown—and live a bit before making any lasting decisions."

"You think so?"

"Certainly," she said, turning away from Ellie as she fussed over plucking a flower. "If the marquis meant for you to wed immediately, then he would have handled all the particulars before his passing."

It was more likely his illness had taken a horrible turn before he'd had the chance.

"When is this ball?" Marce asked. "You will need a gown, shoes...and oh, so many things."

"Tomorrow."

Marce gasped. "Why ever did you not tell me sooner, child?"

"I hadn't planned to attend," Ellie confessed. "But I did garner an invitation for you and your sisters."

"I certainly have not received any invitation."

"Lady Haversham is awaiting my answer before sending your invitation, I suppose."

"Then you should hurry home and send word that you'll be attending the ball." Marce rubbed her hands together, dispelling any dirt that still clung from her work. "Now, I will set about preparing a dress for you. I am certain Payton has something that will suit your color—"

"That will not be needed."

"Do not be foolish," Marce scolded. "You are going—"

"I did not say I was not attending, only that I will not need a dress." Ellie thought of the stunning dress she'd had commissioned a few weeks past, made of the softest blue cotton with an overlay of eyelet mesh.

"Do you plan to attend in those rags that the marquis insisted on having made for you, or possibly," she paused in horror, "arriving in your mourning garb."

"Heavens, Marce," Ellie sighed. "Never. I had a dress made, a silly overture really, during my mourning period. I dreamed of wearing the dress—to where, I did not know, but I finally had the gown made. It awaits me in my dressing closet."

"That is wonderful." A bell chimed deep within the house, and Marce looked to the doorway, a signal from the parlor maid that someone had arrived for the evening. "My dear, sweet, Ellington. I have much to do and you have word to send to Lady Haversham."

Ellie looked to the windows beyond to see that the rain had indeed subsided—and it was long past time for her to depart. Surprisingly, she felt lighter than she had in months. "Yes, I should be going. I will have an invite sent by morning."

"Then all is settled for now." Marce smiled. "I really must be going. I will have your horse brought round and have Mr. Curtis accompany you home."

Ellie shook her head. "You know that is not needed. I've made the trip so many times I could likely sleepwalk my way home."

"It is not you that I worry about, Ellington," she said, sorrow filling her voice. "It is the actions of others that give me such reservations about sending you without an escort."

"I will arrive home safety," Ellie soothed. "As I do every other time I visit. Goodbye, until tomorrow."

Ellie gave her a quick wave before ducking

out of the room. She hoped the next time she came to Craven House it wasn't seeking a sanctuary and new home.

The back halls of the house were eerily quiet, as if this part of the manor were unaware of what was only just beginning in the rooms closest to the front entrance. Light shone from under several doors as she journeyed through the house; Payton, Sam, and Jude likely tucked within for the evening.

The sisters were very blessed to have Marce as their flagship—like her, their eldest sister would never allow anything untoward to befall them.

Keeping her footfalls light, Ellie entered the library before reaching the heavily used portions of the house where sounds of revelry were already drifting to deeper sections of the cavernous building. The room housed an impressive collection of old, dusty tomes; Alex would enjoy this room with its deep chairs and large hearth. Perfect for an evening of reading ancient texts and discussing the great poets of the time.

She used the double doors in the room as a means of unnoticed escape whenever she'd stayed longer than intended and wanted to depart without alerting any of Marce Davenport's *guests*. Many times, she'd felt the urge to stay, take a room next to Payton's and have the comfort of knowing Marce and her sisters were always close—but that would mean living under Marce's rules and dictates, which were not horrible, but more than Ellie was comfortable with after Drake's harsh treatment.

The last year, while lonely, was freeing in so many ways. She'd done what she wanted, when she wanted, and hadn't perished because of it.

The time was coming when she'd need to accept Ruby's interference in her life, but, for now, Ellie was...

A tap on the glass drew her attention.

Her horse—or whichever horse she'd hastily saddled in the Drake stables—was ready.

Ellie slipped out the double door that looked out on the short lane that would take one to the stables to the right or the front entrance to the left. Sure enough, the elderly man held the reins of her horse, a black steed much taller than she remembered from her ride to Craven House.

"Good eve, m'lady" he said, assisting her up. "Thank ye, again. Me mistress be too proud ta ask for ye help. God speed."

"Did Daphne come round this morning?" She glanced over her shoulder to make sure no one was close enough to hear their conversation. To anyone passing, it would appear Ellie thanked the old man. When Mr. Curtis nodded, Ellie continued, "Do let me know if you require anything else. My stables—and my home—are at your disposal."

"Ye dinna have ta be so kind, m'lady." A single tear slipped down the man's face, and he brushed it away quickly.

The Marquis of Drake owed Craven House more than Ellie could every repay them. Madame Sasha had cared for Ellie's mother during her final days, and then Marce had kept watch over Ellie—both things the late marquis should have seen to.

It was Ellie's responsibility to pay back the debt she felt was owed to the women.

"My stable never misses the grain, I assure you. And do have a fair eve as well, sir." She'd never had the heart to treat the man with anything other than kindness. He'd been with Marce and her sisters since long before Madame Sasha had fallen ill and left her four daughters and one son to care for themselves, which meant he'd also known Ellie's mother. She nodded, pushing his thanks from her mind. What little she could do to help Marce keep at least a couple of horses in her stables was far overshadowed by the care she'd shown Ellie all these years. Besides, no one at Drake House was the wiser. "Keep warm, the night is fabled to be a blustery one."

With a light kick, Ellie sent her horse into the dark evening at a gallop.

The wind and deserted streets greeted her, and she spurred the horse ever on—how she dreamed of riding for much longer. Away from London, away from all the questions and concerns. To another place, one where she had a surname and family who'd known her for as long as she'd been on this earth—and no one would ever come to take what little she possessed.

She'd fancied a large country manor with doting parents, siblings who argued, and loyal servants who slipped her treats of baked sugar and plum dressings.

The Christmastide country celebration had brought back many dreams from her childhood, ones where her mother was still alive and healthy and her father—certainly not the marquis—took joy in his family. She hadn't wanted to consider why she'd been so unhappy to journey to Foldger's Hall at the time, but here—riding through the darkened London streets toward an empty, quiet home—she let herself dream of what could have been...had her mother not sold her body for coin and her father been anyone other than the Marquis of Drake.

Spurring her horse fast, Ellie visualized many of the papers she'd read. Each showing her father's quick decline into the abyss—one he'd willingly gone into filled with anguish, isolation, and rage. He must have been a very different man before he'd had his heart broken, if that were indeed what happened. All the papers only showed her one side—Drake's—and if there were one thing she'd learned over the years, it was that her father could not be trusted.

The many kind letters addressed to Lady Chastain, even after her betrayal and marriage to Lord Chastain, pointed to a completely unknown man.

Certainly, Lady Chastain had made the right choice in her son's nursemaid, for it was more convincing that the woman had instructed the maid to take the child far away and keep him from the marquis' clutches.

Ellie wished she'd been blessed with such a caretaker—what had her name been?

Dutton, Alexandria Dutton.

She pulled back on the horse's reins, stopping the beast.

"Watch ye self," a man shouted.

Ellie looked up to see a carriage, its flatbed loaded with supplies of some sort.

The answer to everything had been right in front of her the entire time—from her father bringing an injured man to work in his stables, to Drake pleading with her on his deathbed to trust Alex, to the letter detailing the carriage accident that had killed Lord and Lady Chastain...

"Move ye blasted horse, ye senseless twit!"

A horse galloped quickly by her, Ellie not seeing its rider before they disappeared down the darkened street.

But she couldn't bring herself to speak—or even use her heel to spur her horse back to action.

She'd met Mrs. Dutton, spent Christmas with the woman—and she'd also met her ward, injured in infancy.

It was him. Alex.

All along, he had been within the marquis' house, with no one the wiser.

Ellie had feared a stranger—someone she didn't know—coming and taking everything from her. She'd waited with bated breath for over a year, each day filled with unrest and fright, dreading the day, the hour, she'd be thrown from the only home she'd known, to be left with nothing.

Instead, the man who'd destroy her sense of stability and belonging was someone she'd thought of as a friend. A man Ellie had spent many long, lonely nights dreaming of. She'd trusted him far more than she'd trusted anyone.

Her greatest ally and her greatest enemy were one and the same. Alex was the one person who could take everything away from her.

CHAPTER 11

"NOW GO!" ALEX commanded, knowing Ellie would likely do the complete opposite of what he—or anyone—desired. "Leave before Eckles returns."

When she'd entered the stables, atop the horse, he'd been shocked to see her. Not that she'd managed to leave the house and the stables—with a horse no less—without anyone the wiser, but that she'd returned in such a state. Her hair hung tangled down her back as if she'd been in a windstorm, though judging from the labored breathing of the horse, she'd rode the beast hard—and recklessly.

His back was to her as he led the steed back to his stall, the very first on the left, denoting the significance of the beast. It took no urging for the animal to seek out his area, exhausted from the hard ride through London's residential area, lather still dripping from his sleek, auburn coat.

Alex turned after securing the gate to see Ellie standing where he'd left her.

A maddened look crossed her wind-kissed face, confounding him. He was the one likely to be punished for her escapades on that damned horse, should Eckles discover the beast had been ridden.

"Do not stand there...go."

"I most certainly will not take orders from the likes of you." Her words, as always, cut him deeply. Her aversion to him—yet her continued interest in his activities and her pleas for him to take part in her charade—confused him ever more. "Maybe I want the stable master to know it was I who dared ride Drake's prized horse."

"Then you are a bigger fool than I'd thought."

"How dare—"

"Yes, I know...how dare I speak to Lady Ellington in such a manner." He stalked toward her. "I will tell you *why* I dare. You, *my lady*," he annunciated each syllable, "are incapable of exercising common sense. You think yourself above reproach and untouchable by all."

"I...do not...well..." she stammered.

"From now on, I will do exactly as you do," Alex seethed. He was being overbearing and unfair, yet could not help his words—or his feelings. "This—" He gestured at the stable around them "—is mine. I live here. I toil for eighteen hours a day here. That— " He pointed out the open stable doors "—is your home. I do not command you within those walls. And you shall not command me within these."

"Everything on this property, and entailed to the Drake estate, is mine." Though her words were spoken firmly, there was doubt in her eyes.

An uncertainty he'd never seen in her before.

Whether Ellie was the bastard child of Drake or no more than a ward to the marquis, it made no difference to Alex. He knew the feeling of growing up parentless, without the benefit of a surname or family. Their circumstances—though she was loath to admit it—were almost identical.

"I will not argue against your claim, but you must leave before Eckles returns."

The fight drained from her and her defensive stance crumbled.

Something in his words soothed her, though he hadn't any clue what. There was no time to discuss it.

Grasping her shoulders, he turned her about and gently pushed her toward the door and the safety of the main house.

"I do not need you looking after me," she called over her shoulder as she marched toward the door.

Alex hadn't the time to address her less than aware notion of the situation.

Quickly, he retrieved a brush and moved to the horse's stall. He worked rapidly, brushing sweat and filth from the animal's coat, and with it all traces of Ellington's wild flight. He'd been positive that she'd meant to harm herself, what other purpose did one have for riding in such a careless manner down unknown, dark alleys and crowded streets?

And so, he'd waited for her return, noting the horse missing.

She'd still not imparted the reasoning behind her actions. Not that Alex expected any answers from her; the girl was as close-lipped as anyone he'd ever met. Many times, she had him questioning his own reserved nature. When one was alone—truly, unequivocally, without the benefit of another human soul, alone—it took a little time to remember that others existed. Outside his own insignificant sphere, others were living their lives, completely separate and unaware of his hardships. Not that he believed others should concern themselves with the lives of people who did not impact their own way of living, but to be so ignorant of other's suffering…Alex had fallen into that same trap.

Folly. Foolishness.

Madness.

He'd lost his capability to see others for whom they were and, most disconcerting, to recognize their circumstances.

That had happened with Ellington.

And he had no idea how to go back, start over, show her he cared—and discover what torment she hid.

And then there were the added pressures of all he'd learned from the solicitor—which hadn't been overly significant. He'd heard a large amount of crates had arrived at the townhouse—as the solicitor had promised—and Ellie had spent the greater part of the day locked in the study reading every page.

Alex was only beginning to understand her demons were nothing new, but rather something born from years of misgivings, unfounded lies, and deplorable actions.

He wanted to know what haunted her. Needed to understand how he could help her—take away the hurt and replace it with…something else. He had nothing to offer her but his loyalty. He couldn't help but think that would never be enough to banish all the hurt within her.

His world was developing, expanding past what had fulfilled him before.

It was no longer enough to work diligently, earn his place, and keep his head down, focusing on one day being more than a mere stable hand.

No, he needed someone else in his life. Suddenly, the solitary nature of his past was unappealing to him.

Alex took the comb that hung on the hook outside the stall door and applied his steady hand to combing out the knots from the beast's long mane.

Ellie's actions tonight had spoken volumes.

But, at the moment, he only had time for calming the horse before him, readying him for the long night and praying that Eckles did not suspect a thing.

"Boy!" Eckles' shout called from the main room of the stable. "Where ye be?"

"I am here." Alex looked about the small stall for anything out of place. Thankfully, all appeared as it should be, nothing leading one to think the steed had been from the stable. The horse's breathing had calmed sufficiently and he'd relaxed, his eyes closing in exhaustion. "I will be out in a moment."

He hung the comb back in its place, double-checking that the stall was secured for the night, and entered the main stable room. Part of him longed to search above, to the rafters, for confirmation that Ellie had indeed returned to the house as he'd commanded, but the look of displeasure on Eckles' face held Alex's full attention.

"Sir?" Alex said. "I was about to retire for the eve. Is there anything further you require?"

Eckles only eyed him.

It had taken several months for Alex to acclimate to his role with Drake's staff. He'd been too quick to assimilate himself with Lady Vi, now Lady Haversham, at Foldger's Foals. Everyone had been close as family, not that Alex knew what that truly meant, but if he ever had a family, he suspected it would be much like his time spent there. But here, in London, the servants had families and lives outside the marquis' household. They came and earned a wage—that was all. They did not hang about on their one afternoon off each week. They did not stay on after the evening meal unless their position demanded it. They had family, friends, and homes away from this townhouse. And those who didn't, sought out the servants' quarters as soon as their responsibilities were complete.

He had nothing.

No family, no friends, no ties to anyone or anything.

He'd always thought this gave a person a certain freedom—the ability to go where the wind took you—but all Alex felt was a crushing loneliness that had grown unavoidable over the last year.

Yes, he spent his free hours at the Haversham townhouse—at Lady and Lord Haversham's request—but never did he feel like he was amongst family. The Havershams had the newest little lord to care for. That world—proper society—was not something Alex desired. He did not understand their customs nor their stringent rules. Being served by another was something he'd never longed for. And not because he saw it as out of reach, but because he saw others as his equals, no one above another.

It was inconceivable for Alex to believe that a person was superior to another simply because of their sires, because he was born to a fancy house, vast estates, and immense wealth that made him any more important than a stable hand—without benefit of his nature. That a cruel man, such as Drake, was any better than the stable master at Craven House—a kind, noble man who looked after the occupants within the large manor, no matter what entertainments happened within.

Mrs. Dutton, the woman who'd been the closest thing to kin as he'd ever known, had run the orphanage with a light, but firm hand. She did not run her home like a workhouse, as many orphanages were—the children were never required to work to earn their keep.

It was only in recent years that he'd found out why. They had a benefactor. Their necessities were provided for, allowing Mrs. Dutton to use her extra coin for tutors and books for learning.

As the eldest in the home, he'd taken on more of a leadership role with the other children. He'd led by example, dedicating himself to improving his speech and putting behind him his accent. He had been assured by Mrs. Dutton that if he wanted to work in the finest of London's stables, he'd need to act the lord, though he wasn't.

And so, he'd learned to read and recite, he'd studied geography, and even tried his hand at the piano—which he'd found helped with his injured hand, strengthening his fingers and adding to his range of movement, so much so, that many did not notice his shortcomings unless they witnessed the slight limp that came after a long day's work.

He'd been unable to bring much when he'd left Lady Haversham's country estate to work for the marquis. He had brought several books with him, though the musty air and moisture in the stables had rotted the pages quickly. It had warmed his heart when Ellie had given him the book by Cowper. He'd managed to keep it in a dry spot, treasuring the time he was able to read in the evenings when the light allowed.

A creak above brought him back to the present where he noticed Eckles was staring at him, waiting for a response to a question Alex hadn't heard.

"Well, boy?" Eckles slurred. "Ye da not deny it?"

Alex remained silent; the man was drunk.

"The miss'n grain—ye been skim'n off the top," Eckles continued.

"No, sir." He had no idea where the accusation had come from, though it was clear the other servants and stable hands watched him closely, looking for any infraction to hold against him. "I know naught of a grain shortage."

"Ye com'n in here with ye superior talk an' sparkle'n manners, think'n ye so much betta 'an the rest o' us. An' all the time ye be a thief."

"I never—"

"Ye doona have ta say it, boy." Logic and reason were beyond the man.

"I do not know anything about the missing grain." Alex had been pulled in so many directions of late, keeping up with Lady Ellington and her antics was more work than his responsibilities in the stable—he'd been away nearly an entire afternoon with the solicitor alone. But assuredly, if he weren't keeping up with his chores about the stables it was likely the grain had disappeared on his watch. "How long has this been going on?"

"That not be concern'n ye," Eckles said, his distrust clear. "But I like ta put an end ta it here an' now."

Alex watched in stunned disbelief as the stable master grabbed the dressage whip from the wall and snapped the tip at the ground with one lightning-fast flick of his wrist.

"Sir." Alex's voice rose as he tried unsuccessfully to keep his panic at bay when he heard the creak of floorboards above his head. He'd heard several times how the stable master dealt with disobedience, unruliness, and deception within his stable. "I have said it was not I, nor do I know who is responsible. But, if you give me time, I can help you locate the wrongdoer."

"Oh, now ye fancy yerself one a those Bow Street gents, do ye?" Alex took a step back toward the long hall of stalls when Eckles stumbled toward him, arcing to the left. "Come out here, lad."

Alex kept his eyes trained straight ahead to avoid looking up to where he suspected Ellie hid. Of all the times for her to flout his command, this night was the worst. Alex would see the whip along his backside many times before dawn, but to have her witness his degradation? It would sting worse than the lashes.

But he would take the lashings. While he did not deserve them for the grain theft, his negligence made him responsible for Ellie taking the marquis' prized horse. And for that, he should be punished.

The rain outside assaulted the roof and side of the stables relentlessly as the storm grew in force. He only hoped the pounding would also drown out his cries of pain, for it was unlikely he'd be able to keep them at bay.

There was naught else to do but accept it, let the lashing begin, for it would end all the sooner. With confident steps—Alex worked hard to make his leg cooperate for the few paces needed to reach the center of the main stable room—and his head held high, he walked as Eckles made a circle around him and continued his haphazardly arcing steps.

There had been no whippings since his arrival at the marquis' townhouse.

Eckles likely looked forward to this very moment as he continued to stalk his prey in his drunken haze.

The whip lashed out at the ground every five or six paces, in every direction.

The man had no control over where the tip landed, which didn't bode well for Alex.

This beating would come from a fit of drunken rage, and therefore, end quickly once the stable master had expelled his last burst of energy, his stupor taking over.

Eckles, normally superbly skilled with a whip, was surprisingly lacking precision as he continued to lash out at the bare ground, dirt jumping in the air each time it was struck.

"Turn about, lad," Eckles commanded, a bit of his self-assurance returning. "Face the grain bin."

The silo was situated next to the ladder that Ellie used to reach the rafters.

He would not look up, he would not look up, he would not look up. The words repeated themselves over and over in his head as he took the final step toward the bin and placed his hands on the rough lid, leaning slightly forward as splinters of wood punctured his palms. It didn't hit him until now how quiet the stable had been since he and Ellie had returned. He'd expected to be caught long before he was able to brush the sweat from the steed's coat.

It only left one reason; Eckles, and the other servants, had known this was coming—and the stable master had lain in wait for him…and from the smell of him, finishing a full bottle of liquor in the process.

Alex relaxed his back and neck, planting his feet firmly into the ground. He knew if his skin was taut in anticipation, then the tip would split his back clean open, and the healing would take all the longer.

Cowering was not an option, nor was debating his punishment or supposed crimes.

His back would see the whip regardless.

The first strike came out of nowhere—and hurt far beyond anything he could imagine. He'd always assumed his pain tolerance was high due to the daily agony and discomfort that persisted from his childhood injuries.

But this…the lick the dressage tip made was much more than any pain he'd endured. With the second strike, his shirt fell to his waist, having been sliced in half.

He concentrated on the feel of the warm blood oozing down his back and settling into the waist of his pants, soaking in and creating a layer of warmth below the chill of his exposed upper body.

Each strike was more precise than the last—something Alex had hoped the man incapable of in his disheveled state, but not a single lash missed Alex.

Alex did exactly what he'd said he wouldn't do. He braced himself for the third strike, flexing his back and readying it to take the next blow — and allowed the sound of the rain above to fill his mind and transport him anywhere but here. He thought of the many hours he'd spent reading, first at Foldger's Foals, then by candlelight at Drake House. He focused on the remembered touch of Ellie's smooth skin when she'd grasped his hand in the alley. He concentrated on the feel of Ellie's waist as he'd lifted her from her horse all those times. Ember, sitting upon the woman's lap as Ellie stroked her fur; Ellie unaware of how calm she appeared without her shoulders tense.

"Stop!"

The single word, though spoken softly, thundered through the room, pushing the lull of the rain from his mind and bringing him back to the stables and his pain.

Words continued to fly into the room, yet he could not make any out for the blood pumping through his veins and thudding deafeningly in his ears.

New marquis...your master...drawn and quartered.

Ellie's feet came into view as she clumsily rushed down the narrow rungs of the ladder. One foot, covered in a mud-stained kid boot, missed its purchase and she stumbled down three steps.

Instantly, he was no longer leaning against the grain bin but reaching to stop her fall, his throbbing cuts forgotten.

As he did, the next strike from the whip traveled past him, only slightly nipping his ear as it did.

Too late, Alex realized its course.

THE SEARING PAIN didn't confine itself to Ellie's upper arm where the whip had struck her, but traveled through her body. Even her legs shook as wave after wave of fire rocketed through her, reaching every nerve ending.

She wanted to scream, to curse Eckles' cruelty, to take responsibility for everything.

But first, she had to get her footing back—and suppress the fear that'd kept her frozen above, watching helplessly as the man took his drunken aggression out on Alex.

It was much like her father had done, but he'd used words instead of a whip—though that didn't mean it injured her any less.

Ellie stifled her cry at the fiery hot current traveling through her—it was only one whip on her arm, and not the back-splitting lashes Alex had received. And endured.

She'd heard rumors of Eckles' brutality within the stables, his need to keep all in their place—which was below him.

The marquis had lavished praise upon the man for his forthright nature and efficiency, never questioning the flow of help in and out of his townhouse. Little had she known both the marquis and the stable master suffered from a tendency to find comfort in a bottle.

No more, this would *never* happen again within her home!

His home.

The truth should have been more apparent, especially after the marquis had insisted on his deathbed that Ellie trust Alex.

He was not the stable hand he appeared—and was far more than he knew.

His injuries during childhood, his many moves during his youth—but it had been his caretaker's name that had sparked the true recognition.

Alexandria Dutton.

Mrs. Dutton—the woman who'd raised Alex and even now resided at Foldger's Hall with the rest of the children.

The woman that Drake had blamed for absconding with the baby of his one true love.

Lord Chastain, Peter Davis—a duke.

Born of Lord and Lady Chastain.

And Andrew Penton, the Marquis of Drake—her father—had given him everything that should be hers and Ruby's.

She'd had Alex pretend to be exactly who he truly was.

Pushing the jumble of conflicting thoughts from her mind, Ellie refocused on her physical pain. Her feet were on the ground, and two hands held her waist securely, keeping her upright.

Her body had wanted to collapse when the fire had shot through her moments before.

"Alex?" It had to be his arms holding her steady.

His eyes were filled with such devastation she almost cried for him.

"Are you hurt?" The words were ripped right from his soul. "Your arm."

She held back, her injuries nothing compared to the lashings he'd taken. His tattered shirt hung loosely about his waist and blood trailed down his torso—the red, drying now to a muddied brown, appeared as cracks in a desiccated riverbed.

"Lady Ellington," Eckles squawked, his hand making an attempt to tuck in his loose shirttails. "I bid ye return to the main house while I be handle'n servant matters."

She pushed Alex's hands from her waist, stepping around him to face the stable master. The movement pulled at the gash on her arm, but she pushed the pain from her thoughts.

"I will do no such thing. You, you miserable excuse for a man, will gather your belongings and depart this stable." When he only stared at her, the whip hanging at this side, she continued, "Now!"

"With respect, ye canna be tell'n me what ta do." She shrank back at the foul odor on his breath. This man had no sense of what he was doing, too far gone in his cups. It would be similar to arguing with her drunken father—nothing penetrated the fog that enveloped his brain. "Run along, a'fore ye find yerself on the end a another lash, lass."

Alex was around her before the stable master had finished his thinly veiled threat—a brief pause—and Eckles' sneer dropped from his face, his eyes filling with alarm, some sense pushing past the haze.

The man focused on Alex as his body teetered back and forth.

"You will never speak to her in such a manner." Alex's face was a mere inch from Eckles'. "And you shall apologize for your actions and leave here as she requested."

Ellie saw his back—a sight she'd come to know well from her many hours spent watching...and judging him as he worked endless hours. It appeared nothing as it had only hours before. His corded muscles were now splayed open with cross cuts in every direction, blood dripping in paths down into his waistband. The muscles flexed along his shoulders, re-opening the thin trails the whip had inflicted. She reached for him...to stop him...to protect him...to shelter him from more harm, knowing he could take more lashes from the whip.

For her, it was the harsh words that burrowed deeper than any physical whipping could. His movements were too quick, his determination taking over, moving him from Ellie's reach.

Eckles hadn't a moment to say anything before Alex had him pinned against the wall, his fingers—from his weaker, injured hand—trapping the man's throat to the wall. His other arm held the stable master solidly at his chest. Alex's back rippled with the strength it took to hold the man in place.

The man's face turned a deep scarlet and his mouth opened and shut as if he wanted to issue a retort, but couldn't find the words or the breath. His nostrils flared in anger. To be ordered about by a stable hand, and one as damaged as Alex, must be the ultimate insult to one of Eckles' position.

Alex lessened his hold, allowing the man to speak. "I will not—"

"That is an incorrect response." Alex increased his hold once more. "I would've accepted your beating, but I could never accept this. You will apologize to the lady, or I can keep at this all night if you wish to be difficult."

Eckles looked at Ellie. As if he were seeing her—and the injury he'd caused—for the first time, he winced as his eyes drifted over the torn arm of her coat.

"Alex," Ellie breathed. "He is not worth your temper. Let him be gone and out of our lives." Not once did she look away from Eckles as she spoke, favoring to turn a scolding stare on him. "If he ever seeks refuge here or speaks ill of you or I, you are allowed to do away with his miserable hide."

She hoped her words were enough to help Alex calm himself and allow Eckles the chance to flee, yet his shoulders remained taut and his arm continued to press the man into the wall.

"Go," Alex finally said. He dropped his arms, but his back never lost its stiffness. "And do as my lady says, never return."

"O'course." Eckles issued a lopsided bow and almost stumbled to the ground. Recovering, he turned on the heels of his worn boots and zigzagged down the long hall of stalls toward his boarding room beyond.

"Let me tend your back—"

Alex brushed away Ellie's hands as they reached for him. "I will be fine."

"It must hurt dreadfully, please." She tried again, but her outstretched arms caused her own pain to flare and she winced.

"It is you who is hurt."

"I—" The sentiment eluded her. Ellie needed to explain all, tell him what little she knew before he recognized the significance of his position— and possibly used it against her. He had every right to throw her from Drake townhouse, as had happened to Eckles. If anything, he had more cause to expel her if what she'd read in her father's papers were true. "Alex, please listen…" she started up, catching the many thoughts going through her mind and mentally arranging them into some semblance of explanation. Something to encompass all she needed to say.

But no arrangement of words or phrases said exactly what needed to be said.

Please, do not leave me. You are the only constant I've had in a long while.

Please, do not throw me from my home. I've never felt welcome anywhere else.

Please, forgive me.

All things she longed to tell him, yet were inadequate in so many ways.

Her fright had nearly kept her hidden, never coming to Alex's aid. She cringed at the thought of how badly Eckles would have beaten Alex had she not pushed past her own fear and stopped him.

"Your arm." The softness in his voice had her looking back at him. "Are you hurt?"

They were the same words she'd asked him moments before. Blood, drying now, carved trails down his back, yet his only worry was for her and her minor, insignificant injury. She'd thought before, because of her birth—dubious as it was—that she was far above this man, destined to be more than anything he could give her. The truth was, it was she who did not deserve him.

"It is my fault."

"It most certainly is not. You—nor I—can control the madness of a man in his cups." He shook his head to dissuade her accusations. "Do not speak that way. If it hadn't been me, it would have been another, less tolerate servant."

"If I'd left the stable like you said—listened to you this one time—I never would have been here." She couldn't bring herself to tell him the truth, it had been she who'd pilfered from the grain box to help feed the two horses at Craven House. "Besides, it only stings a bit. Your pain must be close to unbearable."

"You quite possibly saved me from months of agony," Alex said as he inspected her arm pensively. "These will take weeks to heal, but imagine the scarring if he'd kept at it for another ten lashes. Does this hurt?" He pressed lightly on the area.

It did hurt...but she'd be damned if she'd admit it. Thankfully, the physical hurt was far less damaging than her father's cruel words had been.

"Remove your coat." He turned her as if she were a child and began to unfasten the long row of buttons. His fingers faltered. Ellie wondered if his childhood injury ailed him, or the pain from his back. "We cannot know the damage until we can see it. I will have Cook put together a salve for you."

Ellie brushed away his hands. "It is you that is hurt and in need of care."

His fingers returned to their task. "It would be wise to heed your earlier advice and listen to me. Infection can lead to greater discomfort."

Many things ran through her mind; if something weren't applied quickly, Alex's back would scar and possibly fester, as well. If she could only send word to Madame Marce for a salve to ward off any infection. Her concoctions were far superior to any Cook would mix for Alex.

More importantly, how long until her angry shouts as she climbed down the ladder, sank in— and he began asking questions Ellie wasn't prepared to answer—even if she possessed the information to give them to him.

Could the duke and Alex truly be one and the same?

Peter.

The name did not suit him as Alex did. It would take time for her to think of him thusly, if that were his true birth name…and if he decided to ever speak to her again. She could not—would not—blame him if he cast her from his life completely.

Ellie would do the same to anyone who kept such information from her.

Sadly, his preoccupation with her injury and his own pain would not last; yet she found herself unable to resist taking in his perfectly tousled hair as he inspected her arm.

"Why ever would you allow yourself to be beaten for something you did not do?"

"How do you know I had nothing to do with the missing grain?" His eyes searched her face.

CHAPTER 12

"BECAUSE..." LADY ELLINGTON paused, her words laced with hesitancy. He couldn't think of anything she could say that would garner this much reserve from her.

Alex expected her to declare her support for him, speaking to his honesty and integrity—he'd shown her nothing else during their short acquaintance, going so far as to pose as a marquis, despite the risks.

"I am the responsible person."

Such simple words, leading to a hundred more questions and the pit of his stomach falling. If he could think past the pain, he'd find his legs shook.

"Why would you steal from your own stables?" Alex asked, puzzled. "You can take anything—and everything—and no one would dare deny you."

"It is not so easy." She avoided his stare.

"It is possibly the simplest thing." A far

easier thing would have been to step forward—before the dressage whip had hit him the first time. Damn it, but he would have accepted her intervention after the second blow.

Ellie continued to stare at the ground as her hand cupped her torn sleeve. "Be that as it may, why were you willing to take the whip for something you did not do?"

"Because that is my lot in life." How to explain the life of a parentless, crippled, stable hand without a farthing to his name—to her, a girl brought up in one of the wealthiest homes in all of London, used to fancy dresses, well-hung bedsprings in rooms with blazing fires, and food, every meal of every day. But he would give her an answer in the hopes that she'd give him something in return—anything, let her guard down for only a moment. "Taking that whip was my duty, just as stepping in when you were in danger was my role as a man." But there was that one night, not long after he'd come to London, when he'd heard Drake and Lady Ellington arguing and he hadn't stepped in, but instead allowed the man to curse her over and over.

"But Eckles is my servant," she said, lifting her gaze to his. "I can protect myself."

"You should not have to when I am with you." Had she never had someone look after her? Protect her from the world—and herself?

She only looked on questioningly.

"As your servant, I cannot allow any harm to come to you." He hoped she took his words for their most basic meaning—the repercussions to him if she'd been seriously injured while he was present would have him remanded to Newgate—and not the deeper meaning they actually held.

"Did you say that Cook has a salve?" He noticed her sudden change in conversation; his answer satisfying her at last, and he breathed a sigh of relief. "Do come inside so we may cleanse your back. You must be in a great deal of pain."

Surprisingly, he'd pushed his agony to the back of his mind the second the whip had licked at her arm. Even now, the throbbing, while excruciating, was kept at bay by the blood pumping through his veins. The pain was muted—surely to return with vigor the moment he knew Ellie was indeed out of harm's way.

With little effort, Lady Ellie led him from the stables, through the kitchen, and into the late marquis' private study—though he'd been gone over a year, the pungent odor of cigar smoke and fine bourbon still hung in the air like a thick cloud. The room was everything Alex had ever dreamed of in a home with inviting chairs, a large hearth, and more books than any one man could read in a lifetime. The wealth of knowledge in this room alone was staggering.

Behind the desk, many boxes were stacked, and Alex assumed they were the items Adams had promised to deliver.

Their surroundings made no impression on Lady Ellie—the room, its grandeur and stateliness, escaped her notice, glaringly pointing out another significant difference between the pair. But if that had been the last time he enjoyed this room, then he was a better person for it. If that night hadn't occurred, he never would have seen the true nature behind the false façade Lady Ellie donned to keep others out.

"Sit, please," she instructed when she returned to the room. He hadn't noticed she'd left, his mind dizzy with the increasing pain. Her arms were weighted down with a wash basin steaming with hot water, strips of material, and two jars, one clutched under each arm. And she looked beautiful, breathtaking, her hair wild around her crown, and her face flushed from activity. "I will have you patched up in no time."

"Allow me to assist you." With only a sharp look, she allowed him to take the heavy water basin from her arms. The searing pain from the weight of the basin nearly brought him to his knees, but he quickly set it down and returned to her side to take the jars. Spots invaded his vision and his head rang with dizziness. "Could you not have rung for a servant to bring all this—or asked me to fetch it for you?" he asked to distract her from the agony that must show on his face.

She moved to the basin before answering. "And have someone see your condition?" She kept focused on her task of dipping the lengths of cloth into the heated water, avoiding him where he stood next to her. "I did not think you would be overjoyed to have the other staff see you in such a manner."

Alex had already pondered his next move—he could not remain in his current position, for gossip moved quickly between London households. He would likely be branded a disloyal servant...and he cringed to think what would be said of Lady Ellington, plus, the new marquis would have no reason to retain a servant with his reputation now. It would not take long for word to spread to the Haversham servants. He could not risk Lady Haversham hearing of everything, nor Ruby blaming him for Ellie's injury.

"For your thoughtfulness, I am grateful, my

lady." Alex leaned forward, issuing a simple bow in gratitude for her compassion. He was rewarded with a fresh wave of pain slicing across and down his back as his lash marks tore open once more, the dried blood giving way to a new onslaught of red trailing his back, no doubt. "I think I shall sit upon the floor."

Alex lowered himself to the rug before the fire in an attempt to keep the crimson blood from marring any of the furniture, while keeping his shoulders as square as possible to keep the lash marks from opening further. Kneeling, he felt the ground was miles away.

"Allow me to help, if you insist on sitting upon the floor." She held out her arm for him to lean on and braced her other on the table holding the basin. "There," she smiled. "That wasn't so awful."

"You are correct, my lady." The heat from the blazing fire warmed his chest, yet the heat was nowhere near the intensity coursing through his back. "I will certainly need your assistance to stand again, as well. I hope you do not look upon me as the weaker man for it."

Her smile disappeared, replaced with a knitted brow of concern. "Your actions were foolish. You sought to look brave, but the consequences were too severe. You never should have allowed him to whip you. You are ten times stronger than he…"

"He is the stable master, and I am only a servant in his stable." He didn't know how to explain any of it to her because it seemed the height of recklessness to him. "I desperately sought to please the man—it is, or *was*, my only way to continue on at Drake House." *And be close to you*, he longed to say, but he wouldn't risk having her close herself off to him again. It was too soon.

He could feel her warm breath on his neck and everything stood still. He feared expelling his own held breath, for she would pull back. In that instant, there was only the pair of them before a small fire. Her tender, soft hands upon his back. And he was a man in love—with a woman far above him. Both refused to say a word, for they would have to admit how out of reach she was for him. An unspoken fact that neither was ready to admit aloud.

No sound of servants about their chores, no sounds of the wind outside pushing against the paned glass of the study doors—the crackle of the large log in the fire had even muted.

"This may sting a bit," Lady Ellington whispered as if even she could not stand breaking the silence. "I will work as delicately as I can."

"You are too kind, my lady," Alex said as she pressed a wet, heated strip of cloth against a deep gash. He hissed as searing drips of moisture etched down his back. "You were correct," he said through clenched teeth. "This might possibly be more excruciating than the lashes themselves."

He tried for a soft laugh to ease the dark mood that had settled around them, but it caught in his throat as a new sensation settled on his back, close to his shoulder blade—a light press of something warm, yet not ablaze. Closing his eyes, Alex concentrated on the new trail this gentle caress created as the sting faded—he felt nothing but the press of her lips on his back as she moved across his neck to his other shoulder, raining tender kisses.

Lady Ellington's lips worked in tandem with the cleansing strokes of the material she brushed across his aching back, washing away the dried blood and filth from his wounds.

"My lady?" He knew he should remove himself from the room—return to the stables and pack his things, and certainly not allow her to give him such liberties. She'd been injured in the stables, as well, and a part of him wondered if she were acting in a way she did not know—possibly from shock at the violent altercation she'd witnessed. "Please," he begged, though he could not bring himself to move away from her touch.

"Please," she whispered, "my name is Ellie."

"I fear it is improper for me to use your given name," he groaned.

"Am I not your master?" she asked. "To command as I please?"

"Certainly, my lady."

"Ellie," she corrected, her lips following an invisible trail along his shoulder blade. "And are you not a dutiful servant?"

"Of course," he paused, swallowing. "Ellie."

He could spend a thousand nights whispering her name—in time, he was certain to dream of lovelier words to call her, such utterings of the world's most romantic poets hadn't had the inspiration to put to paper as of yet...because they hadn't met a female form worthy of such things.

But Alex had.

And he hoped it would not also be his downfall.

He sat as still as possible, his hands clenched before him and his eyes shut in an effort to stop from taking her into his arms.

There was not a single thing Alex would do to corrupt the trust she showed him in that moment. Even as her finger lightly traced the thin lines marring his back, he stilled himself from pushing her caring hands away and crushing her to him. He should be the one caring for her, tending to her arm, trailing kisses along her shoulder to her neck and up to her lips.

Instead, he allowed her the freedom of touch—and taste.

He didn't know which was the crueler punishment—the lashings or enduring her gentle tending.

Control of either situation was not his.

One he was forced to relinquish, and the other he gave freely.

Finally, she withdrew her hands and lips from his back. A sense of emptiness—an unnerving aloneness—took their place.

Alex braved a glance over his shoulder as Ellie stood, moving to the sideboard. She uncorked bottle after bottle, gently smelling each. Her profile was illuminated by the fire in the hearth, making her red hair appear as flames framing her face and neck.

Satisfied with the last bottle, Ellie plucked the half-empty decanter from the shelf and regained her seat behind him.

"This may hurt more than the whip," she cautioned. "You may fare better if you take a swig before—"

"I do not partake of spirits. Besides, I can handle the outcome, I assure you." The touch of her lips had numbed him of every ugliness and pain in the world. He could handle anything at this point. However, Alex still braced for the sting, instinctually tightening his back, causing the wounds to open and ready for the alcohol to course down, killing any possible infection; but instead, her lips touched his neck once more.

"I am sorry," she whispered into his ear before pulling back.

She was no longer close, and the cool air cascaded over him, causing him to shiver.

And just as quickly, scorching heat flooded him as she poured the liquid over his back—the pain was nearly enough to take him under. He fought to keep his back still and his consciousness intact.

The waves of agony kept washing over him—and through him to his very core. His hands clenched into tight fists, his fingernails biting into the sensitive skin of his palms to alleviate or at least distract from the pain at his back.

"Bloody hell."

"The worst is almost over," she said. "I could never forgive myself if you took ill because of my cowardly actions. Only a few more moments."

True to her word, she recapped the decanter a moment later and set it aside. "I do wish Madame Marce were here. I am unsure if I am doing exactly as I should." Her tentative tone and light fingers pressing at his back did not reduce his confidence in her nursing skills, it only grew his view of her for undertaking a task that no proper lady should be exposed to.

"And how would the good Madame know so much about ministering to the wounded?" He wanted nothing less than to change the subject; in fact, he wanted her lips to return to his neck, his shoulders—anything but a return to formalities. However, he would respect what society deemed proper for them and not push her past what she was uncomfortable with; though he was certain no etiquette guide outlined the suitable way to act in the presence of a half-naked servant. He had no right to ask any of this of her. "She does not look the sort to be on the front lines of battle," he joked.

"Hold this," she instructed him to hold the end of the cloth tight to his chest as she wound his middle with a long, wide strip to bind the cuts and keep them clean. "There are many battles to be found, not all taking place during war."

"Whatever do you mean by that?"

"It is not my place to say." Ellie secured the end of the material with a pin before standing and taking a step back to admire her handiwork. "I believe this should keep the cuts clean— though I fear you will have many scars."

"A few more scars will not be noticed." He stood, adjusting the wrap where it folded over with his movements. Her eyes traveled down his partially bared chest and she looked away quickly; her deep blush only enhanced by the firelight.

"I should be getting back to the stables, my lady."

She turned and snatched the two jars she'd carried into the room with the rest of her mending supplies. "Before you go, take these. One is a cream laced with sage to be applied in the morning and another contains a tincture of laudanum if the pain becomes unbearable." Alex took the jars, committing to memory which was which. "May I check after your condition on the morrow?" She avoided gazing at his semi-undressed upper body by focusing on his boots.

"You have been very kind to me this eve, my

lady." He needed to tell her the dire circumstances surrounding their continued interactions. There was no guessing at how many servants had seen them enter the room, closing the door behind them—and their extended time alone. "But I think it best if I retire to the Haversham townhouse."

If he stayed, he could not guarantee that if she touched him again, he would be able to hold himself back from taking her into his arms, his injured back be damned.

It would mean the end for her—though she didn't realize it. She was one to take action in any manner that befitted her in that instant, impulsive to the extreme, but what about tomorrow or next year?

If he gave in and allowed them to traverse the rough waters of their desires, then she would be the one ruined, not him. It was she who would be tarnished; many men would view her as undesirable because of her association with him.

His future was what it was, but he would not willingly destroy hers.

One day, she would meet a man she loved—a man who could provide her with the life she deserved. That man was not Alex.

He would not steal the most cherished thing a woman could give the man she loved.

CHAPTER 13

"HAVE I DONE something wrong?" Loss filled
her even with him still present. She could not
comprehend why he'd seek to leave after she'd
laid herself bare, given in to her deepest desires
and touched him so. It was as if she'd taken a
dagger and opened her soul to him—and he was
content to walk away. "You must rest. I will have
a guest room prepared for you."

Although, this was his home—and she
should tell him.

Possibly he already knew. If her father
hadn't told him, then surely Mrs. Dutton had.

Had he been deceiving her all along? No,
Ellie knew him enough to know he was very
much unlike her. If he'd learned about his
lineage, she'd be the first person he told.

"You understand why I cannot accept your
offer," he replied, glancing about the room.

Panic set in as Ellie realized the heart of the
matter—she'd come on to him like a complete

wanton. A trollop, the same as her mother. She'd thought all these years that everything about her was tainted by her father's blood, but truly, it was her mother's that would push the only man she cared for to leave. She never should have taken such liberties with him, never should have set her lips to his neck or whispered in his ear. A man as honorable as Alex would never allow himself to fall into the clutches of a woman like Ellie.

She should apologize and beg for his understanding. His forgiveness. Tell him her emotions from the entire evening had gotten the best of her, that she regretted it all.

Ask him to return things to what they used to be. Master and servant.

But, she didn't regret a single action she'd taken after finally stepping in to stop Eckles.

"Lady Ellington, we have already been seen together more than is proper—and now with the problems with Eckles, I think it best I give up my position here. The servants will gossip and it will only be your reputation that is tarnished."

"But…" She searched for the words to convince him to stay. If he left now, it would be before she could tell him everything she knew—and chance him finding out from someone else. He should have connected the information from Adams already, but he was not one to think the worst of others, especially that Mrs. Dutton and she would keep something of this magnitude from him. Unfortunately, his broad chest and muscle-toned arms were making it difficult for her to concentrate. "My arm…it is hurting ever so much."

She wanted to flee the room and hide the second the words had left her mouth—they were the utterings of a feeble woman, and the opposite of everything Ellie had always worked to be.

She could easily tend to her own arm.

But she wanted him to stay—and she'd given him the perfect reason. He was a noble man, and he'd never leave a woman in need.

She fought internally, the battle between needing him close and her anger at him possessing all that was needed to take her home from her almost overwhelming.

"Let me see it." He set the jars aside and moved to inspect her upper arm where the strike had cut clean through her coat and dress sleeve below. "That man should be drawn and quartered for harming a woman."

Ellie smiled as he leaned in close to inspect the cut.

"What is so comical, my lady," he asked with a sharp look.

"It is only that I find I enjoy your overprotective nature, that is all."

"Overprotective?" he asked with all seriousness. "You could have been seriously injured or maimed by that man and you think to jest about it?"

"He did not set out to strike me," Ellie corrected.

"There is nothing amusing about you being injured—and naught that should distract from that man's guilt in this situation." His tone took on an angry flare and Ellie flinched, taking a step back from him, on guard at his sudden change in demeanor. "Please, let me tend to your arm—then I shall leave."

Pushing her sleeve up and her sense of foreboding aside, Ellie allowed him another look. She had nothing to fear with Alex; he was as kind a man as any she'd met.

Yet, her instinct to flee at his raised voice had her trembling—another lasting effect of the marquis' harsh treatment. One she need focus on more to move past.

Her arm was only mildly sore with blood dried to a rusty brown color that made her sleeve stick to the wound. It would heal within the week with a bit of cream and a clean wrap. She was surprised the whip had made it through both layers of clothes to nick her arm at all.

"The amount of blood and size of the stain is deceiving, is it not?" she asked, hoping to distract him from his deep musings. "It is no more than a minor scrape."

"One can never be too cautious when it comes to injuries of this sort." He studied her arm longer than was necessary. "Does this hurt?" He pressed on the area surrounding the cut.

"It throbs a bit."

"The skin is red, but not swollen," he said matter-of-factly as if he were used to tending the injured. "With a good cleansing it should heal without a trace." He dipped one of the remaining strips into the water basin. The saturated material was cool when it gently touched her arm, the water having chilled since she'd washed his back. Setting it aside, Alex took another piece and quickly bound her arm—his movements sure and confident.

"And how do you know so much?" Keeping him talking was the only way to keep him here—and stop him from leaving her. Maybe in time, she'd gain the courage needed to tell him all she knew—or thought she knew.

Alex stepped back, allowing her another view of his broad shoulders, trim waist, and muscular legs clothed by his breeches. The image of him standing with the fire at his back should cast from her mind all the violent confrontations and fights that had taken place in this room while the marquis was still alive; yet, Ellie feared if Alex left her here, she would once again become the scared child she'd once been—beaten down mercilessly by the one man who should have cared for her most.

Ellie refused to let that happen, she would not show that part of her to Alex—not now or ever. She was no longer the sniveling child who'd taken the harsh insults hurled by a man who'd had his own heart ripped from his chest.

The papers she'd spent hours poring over, devouring every word, would not change her opinion of her *father* and his miserable existence. That he had a reason for his treatment of her—and giving what should be Ellie's to the man before her—did not lessen the damage done in the past, no matter how it affected her future.

Though, she wondered if her father hadn't picked the more deserving person to continue the Drake lineage. Had the marquis suspected his daughter to be like him in all ways, in a manner certain to tarnish the title further?

She glanced to the cabinet behind her father's massive desk. It held some of the crates from the solicitor's office; meticulously handwritten notes on variously aged parchment, detailing the unconventional entailment of the Drake estate and title, including the indecipherable scribbling of a man losing the grip on his sound mind, and letters—oh, how many letters Ellie had unsealed and read—love letters, angry letters, newspaper stories detailing the marriage and death of Lord and Lady

Chastain. The rest of the records, crates, and boxes were stacked under and behind the desk. It had taken her time to drag everything there, making sure to return each lid.

There was more information than any one person could muddle their way through in a year, most of it making no sense as to how it translated to Ellie and her future. The only certainty that she'd come to grasp was that the Drake title had been given special notice by decree of King George III, and unusual circumstances surrounded the inheritance of the estate. Ellie hadn't found the papers in their entirety, only the hurried notes made by her father after arriving home from a meeting with Adams. The solicitor must not have included the original papers with all the crates and papers sent, seeing as it was viewed as a highly sensitive document and if it went missing, the Drake estate would fall into jeopardy.

Ellie doubted the papers' existence. If she ever met with Adams personally, she'd tell him just that, forcing him to either present the documents or demand a new successor to the Drake Marquisate be found; though she did not see her future faring any better with another man selected to inherit—but if the title lay dormant as it had since Drake's death, then she could continue as she was, without fear.

None of it made perfect sense to her, except Drake's provision that Ellie marry Lord Chastain—the son of the late Lord and Lady Chastain—to keep her place in Drake House. The papers had been dated no longer than a year before the marquis' death. He knew Ruby and Ellie were his blood, but he'd favored another to assume the title.

Not for the first time, Ellie marveled at how any of this could be seen as official. Certainly, the daughter of a marquis and his nightly companion was better suited to inherit than a man who knew nothing of this true birth and had been raised an orphan—even if she discovered Mrs. Dutton had confided his true identity to him.

"Your thoughts, my lady?"

Ellie startled, fearing her musings were written all over her face. "Ah, my apologies," she stammered. "I was thinking of matters that certainly would not interest you."

"And you know this how?"

She grasped for a topic he'd be uninterested in, settling on the grand ball her sister and Lady Haversham had insisted she attend. "Because it also does not interest me overly much, but I find myself obligated to accommodate my sister."

Instead of retrieving his jars and departing, Alex stiffly sat on the lounge closest to the hearth, its flames already receding, in need of more wood to keep the embers burning. "You have never been the accommodating type. Forgive my bluntness, my lady."

He inspected her from several feet away, making her feel like the undressed one in the room.

It should irritate her that he dared make such a comment; yet she was loath to push him away by unleashing a sharp retort.

"That I am not." She found his company to her liking.

"Then why do you feel obliged now?" he asked, settling a bit deeper into the lounge while keeping his damaged back from pressing against the material. "It is not as if you must answer to her or Lady Haversham."

"You say that, even when you owe so much to the pair," she commented, taking her own seat on the lounge, conscious of the mere inches separating them.

His brow rose at her insinuation. "There are no better ladies to owe my allegiance to than Mrs. Jakeston and Lady Haversham."

"But with that comes expectations…and obligations."

"Which are not always a terrible thing to owe."

She thought on that for a moment before responding. "Is not owing something to someone the makings of an unbreakable binding?"

"Some do not fear being bound to another, my lady." Could he know of the paper detailing the link between them? Part of her wondered if they still spoke of invisible ties and not physical ones. Ellie had learned from her association with Madame Marce that unseen bindings were sometimes stronger than any metal or corded ties, leaving lasting damage that was irreparable. "Now, what has you fretting so?" He expertly moved the conversation to a safer, more comfortable topic, sensing her unease.

"Lady Haversham is hosting a grand ball to present Ruby and Mr. Jakeston to society—" she confided "—and Ruby begs that I be at her side."

"Is it the grand affair, or the unanswerable questions being at her side will inevitably cause that worries you?"

Ellie looked to her hands, avoiding his hard stare—it was as if he truly *knew* her, beyond what she even knew of herself. "Both, I suspect," she admitted in a whisper.

"You can trust her." She didn't know if he

referred to Ruby or Lady Haversham, but trust was something she rarely afforded anyone. "She will not allow you to fail."

"I am not worried about failing." She turned to him. She truly wasn't afraid of failing as much as she was terrified of disappointing or embarrassing her sister. She may see herself a lady, but she hadn't been raised in privilege or bestowed the proper upbringing of one. She was more comfortable in the darkening evening of London's less reputable streets as opposed to the sophisticated drawing rooms of the *haut monde*. She'd been successful with duping her household, but the hawk-like eyes of London society would not be fooled for long. Maybe she could share a bit of truth with him. "It is my sister I do not want to disappoint. Our acquaintance is so new, and I haven't been the most gracious to her…"

"Yet, she loved you from the moment she met you," he said. "Long before she suspected that you both shared a father."

"How can you be certain?" Ellie asked, desperate for an answer that would ring true, one she would not be hard-pressed to doubt. Everyone seemed to have designs for her life and future. Even her own father—keeping her around only to marry her to this man…all in the hopes that Alex would agree to accept her. Ruby, her sister, was certain to demand something of her, as well; though she hadn't asked for a thing as of yet. She'd originally thought Ruby sought funds or a place to live, but with her husband's trading ships seeing success, and their contentment living with Lord and Lady Haversham until their own home was repaired, that didn't seem to be the case.

Next, she'd focused on her sister's insane need to help others, even when it had been made clear her assistance was not needed nor wanted. Ellie feared Ruby's need to help was born solely from a sense of obligation. Society deemed it appropriate that one care for their sibling, and Ruby was acting out in that vein. There was nothing Ellie despised more than pity, whether it was directed at her or she felt it for another. It signaled that either she was weak or another person was. And Ellie was in no way weak—she fought against her own helplessness every hour of every day.

Alex set his hand, warm and solid, on hers, stopping her fingers from wrinkling the fabric of her gown further as she twisted while she pondered. "I am certain because no matter how unaccommodating you are—how much you resist her kindnesses—she keeps trying. As Lady Haversham and Mrs. Dutton never gave up on me, so will your sister never forsake you, even if you beg her to."

It would be the simplest thing to believe him, take what Alex shared and accept Ruby and all she offered, but an even simpler truth existed. Ellie hadn't tried to overcome or change.

She'd never loved another.

It was possible it wasn't something she was capable of.

The thought of giving all she was to another in friendship or something more—baring her innermost thoughts and desires and giving them to another to hold and cherish without using them to hurt her terrified her.

A trust such as that was not something Ellie was capable of giving—nor receiving.

"You are certainly correct." Ellie stood.

"Thank you. Are you sure you must leave?" she asked.

He stood as well, wincing when he bent slightly to retrieve the jars from the low table once more. "It is the proper thing, my lady."

"Will you return to the marquis' house?" She needed to know she'd see him again, even if only to welcome him as her new lord.

"Do you wish me to return?" he asked.

Ellie took a step forward, her chin tilted up to meet his exploring gaze. She hadn't noticed how tall he was, the tip of her head barely reaching his chin. "I never want you to leave."

"If you need anything, you only need send word to the Haversham stables and I will come without delay."

How Ellie wished that were true, and that she had the right to ask more of him. She was already unable to return the kindnesses he'd shown her over the previous year; the many times he'd looked after her without her knowing. And now, she'd made it impossible for him to remain—no, that had been Drake's doing and the stable master's. She would not dwell on her own deceptions.

"That is kind of you, but I am quite accustomed to caring for myself."

"Then I will bid you farewell." Balancing both jars in one hand, he reached for hers with the other and brought it to his lips, no little feat as they still stood mere inches apart, but his lips halted before meeting her delicate skin, his breath caressing her hand ever so gently. In that moment, she longed to beg him to stay—not leave her or her home, but she kept silent, her own breath locked in her chest. "Until we have the pleasure of meeting once more."

Before she knew his intentions, he turned her hand and placed his soft lips on the sensitive spot at her wrist. The warmth barely touched her, but it was enough to brand the feel of him upon her. She had little doubt it was his revenge for the long moments she'd trailed her lips across his skin. As quickly as he'd taken her hand, he released her and was gone.

The door clicked shut after him—muffling his retreating footsteps.

But distance did not dampen the need growing within her.

CHAPTER 14

ALEX HEFTED HIS sack higher on his shoulder as he stared down the lighted alley leading to the stables at Haversham townhouse. That all his worldly possessions fit in a sack easily slung over his shoulder and carried the few blocks between Ellie's home and Lord Haversham's belied all he'd thought he'd accomplished in his short time away from Mrs. Dutton and the orphanage.

The Drake stables had been abandoned when he'd collected his meager belongings and slipped out without anyone the wiser, which suited him well enough. To say the other servants hadn't accepted him with open arms and warm smiles would be an understatement. He'd been a pariah among the household staff, except for the leering looks turned his way by the kitchen servants and sully maids as he went about his chores.

It was likely why he and Lady Ellington had

forged a friendship. They were both invisible, treated as if they didn't exist. Their bond was something that should not have ever been; he was a servant...a stable hand, and therefore unworthy to be in a lady's presence. She was the daughter of a marquis, no matter who her mother was. By right, she was a lady, and he should have kept his distance. She should be embracing her new role and taking her place in society—preparing for the eventual day when the heir to Drake could take his rightful place.

There were no signs the new marquis would throw her from her home, if so, he would have made his appearance long ago. It was possible the man wasn't interested in the new title and wealth. And Ellie would continue as a ward of the new marquis, and therefore, be safe. Alex would no longer have to worry over her welfare. It would be the marquis' duty to care for Ellie, not his. But did he want another to care for Ellie? Could he trust another to protect her?

Alex sighed, knowing he only avoided the inevitable, going round to the stables and begging Lord Haversham for a position either here or at Foldger's Hall. But that would mean admitting his failure—and questions regarding his departure from Drake House. It was something he was not ready to discuss and possibly never would be.

"Watch out, boy!"

Alex turned to see a flat-backed carriage, loaded with crates and trunks, maneuvering the sharp turn onto the lane leading to the stables. The carriage rolled past when he moved to the side.

For the first time since he'd arrived, he noticed the many lights glowing from within and the sounds of activity coming from the rear of the home. If it weren't close to midnight, it would have been attributed to the normal workings within an earl's household, but the lateness of day told him something else was going on.

"Sir," Alex called to the carriage driver. When the man glanced over his shoulder, he continued, "What is all the activity about?"

"Grand ball," he shouted over the sounds of the slow-moving wagon wheels on the cobbled lane. "Tomorrow night, boy."

He hesitated, racking his brain for anywhere else he could seek shelter, just for the night—to avoid causing any undue strain to the earl and his good wife.

But, as he turned, settling on the notion of spending his meager coin on a room, someone shouted his name, not from the lane leading to the stables, for the carriage still moved slowly back making sure not to jostle its contents, but from the house.

"Alex?" the voice called again. He looked about, judging his ability to slip into the shadows and disappear before Lord Haversham could catch him. "Come in."

"My lord," he greeted the man, his large stature framed by the open door, blocking the light from within the foyer. "Good eve. I do apologize for my lateness."

"Lady Haversham has been at work since before dawn—and swears she will not rest until everything is ready. I believe she is making up for the dismal Christmastide celebration," Lord Haversham confided, stepping back for Alex to enter the house. "Her words, not mine. I believe the festivities were perfect. My son was born, and both he and my love were happy and healthy. Not much more a man could ask for."

Alex entered the house, the butler immediately stepping forward and taking his sack as other servants hurried to and fro, their arms heavy with bolts of fabric, glassware, and potted plants.

"Have Mrs. Calhoun ready a room," the earl said without asking Alex if he planned to stay. "Good to have you, Alex. I know Mrs. Dutton will be happy to see you."

"Mrs. Dutton is here?" He'd sworn never to be a burden to the elderly woman again—but his failure was evident by his presence, and she'd demand an explanation. "I was unaware."

Lord Haversham chuckled. "Do not look so stricken by the news. I was unaware she and a few of the girls would be joining us in London before this afternoon myself, but Lady Haversham thinks the older girls will benefit from attending a true soiree."

"If I had known, I would have been here to greet her." Alex missed Mrs. Dutton more than he'd admit. His few days in the country over the holiday had been like being home, surrounded by the people who cared for him most—the children and servants at Foldger's Hall knew him better than anyone else. It had been hard to leave to accompany Lady Ellington back to London. The many offers of employment at Foldger's Hall or one of the Haversham estates had become increasingly hard to turn down as his lonely days turned to even longer, lonelier nights in the Drake stables. "But I am here to speak with you, my lord."

Brock, Lord Haversham, eyed him, seeming to understand the importance of Alex's arrival. "Join me in the study?"

"It can wait until the morrow—or after the ball, my lord." Alex looked about the foyer as servants nodded to him in greeting as they passed. "I will retire to the stables and help where needed." He only hoped his back would allow the extra work.

"You shall do nothing of the sort," Lord Haversham replied. "When you come to my home, you are a guest—not a servant. Let us retire to the study to talk privately. I can see something weighs heavily upon you. My dear wife would not forgive me if I allowed you to find your bed without helping you with whatever troubles you first."

Lord Haversham gestured toward the hallway leading to the study, and Alex started in that direction, knowing the earl would not allow him to retire until they'd spoken.

Closing the door behind them, Lord Haversham sighed. "I have not found a quiet moment in over a day. The bustle at Foldger's Hall was child's play compared to preparing for a grand ball...I will admit, I may be too exhausted to attend by tomorrow evening." He sank into a chair not far from the hearth, and Alex followed suit, lowering gently to avoid another spike in pain.

"I should have waited to call on you."

"Do not be foolish, Alex," Lord Haversham said. "Now, you'd better start talking before Lady Haversham discovers us and interrogates you herself—I can guarantee that will be more painful than this."

The man jested, putting Alex at ease. "I left my employ with the marquis' estate."

"Oh." Brock eyed him, confusion setting in. "May I ask why?"

"There was a disagreement between myself and the stable master." Alex owed the man at least this small amount of the truth. "I thought it best I seek other employment."

"How can I help?" he asked, without any further questions.

"Do you think Lady Haversham would be agreeable to having me at Foldger's Hall—or possibly your country home?"

"We've told you several times in the past, you are welcome at any house you choose. And we will be better for having you, my boy."

"I certainly appreciate the work, my lord, and your faith in my ability." Alex didn't know what it would feel like to be someone's boy, but in all his life, Lord Haversham had been one of the kindest gentlemen to him. The newest little lord was blessed to genuinely be this man's boy. "I will not keep you any longer. I do hope it is not overly taxing if I stay in the stables until I depart London?"

Lord Haversham placed his palms on his knees and pushed to his feet, groaning as he stood. "You will do no such thing. A room is being prepared for you—I will have a bath brought up, followed by a meal."

"That is not necessary." Alex rushed to take his leave, his leg stiffening as he made his way to the door. "I am used to the stables."

"Your leg ails you." It wasn't a question but a statement, and Alex was reticent to admit that he'd kept his knees locked to remain upright during the whipping—the result being an aching more intense than usual. "A warm bath will soothe your muscles and clean the barnyard smell from you. Lady Haversham would be peeved if her bed linens smelled of animals."

He knew the earl well enough to know he would not take no for an answer—and a warm soak did sound heavenly after his horrid night. "Very well, my lord."

Lord Haversham followed him from the room and called a maid to take him upstairs. "Do get some rest, my boy."

He clapped Alex on the back in good spirit, and Alex's legs buckled. He reached out for the side table to keep himself upright as sharp pain shot to every extremity of his body at once.

Relaxing his face to keep the agony from showing, Alex straightened and turned, unable to force even a small smile, knowing his grimace is shown instead.

"Is all sound?" Lord Haversham questioned, alarm settling as he took hold of Alex's arm, careful not to touch his back again. "What happened?"

"Do not fret, my lord." He pulled away and Lord Haversham's hand dropped to his side. "I injured my back is all. I will be better after a full night's rest, I assure you. There is nothing to worry over."

The earl continued to stare, and Alex held his look, refusing to look away. For a brief moment, Alex feared he wouldn't accept his explanation and instead rip the shirt from his back to expose the lash marks. Surprisingly, he only eyed Alex a moment more, shook his head, and called for a servant to immediately bring warm water for Alex's bath to his room. He turned to Alex once more. "You will send for myself or Lady Haversham if you need anything."

"Of course, my lord." Alex took the earl's proffered hand and shook, as if they were two equals, gentlemen meeting about town. "As I said, I will be back to normal by morning and ready to depart for Foldger's Hall."

"I would ask one favor, actually."

"Anything." There were no truer words, for Alex would do anything for the man who'd accepted him without a second thought.

"I request you wait to accompany Mrs. Dutton and the girls back to Foldger's Hall." Alex didn't readily agree, so the man continued, "It will be two days, at most."

"As long as you allow me to earn my keep while I am here."

"I am certain between Mr. Jakeston and myself, we can find something to keep you occupied."

Alex didn't ask what exactly that meant, but nodded and followed the waiting servant to his room, nodding to various people he'd seen on his previous visits to the earl's home along the way. Thankfully, they didn't stumble upon Mrs. Dutton or the girls.

Once inside his guest chamber, he laid his shoulder against the closed door and sighed. While he hadn't lied to Lord Haversham, he'd certainly omitted important details of his departure from Drake House. There was little he was willing to do about that. Maybe when Ellie's future was a bit more secure—and he was safely at Foldger's Hall—he would write to Lord Haversham and explain the entire situation...and pray the man would not think less of him for running.

For now, Alex had a few days to get through before returning to the country—putting the alluring Lady Ellington, thoughts of his past, and hopes for his future behind him.

He was an orphan.

A stable hand.

An honorable man.

Nothing more, and certainly, he'd allow himself to be nothing less.

And the only honorable thing for him to do was stay far from Lady Ellington. He could not do anything to compromise her in any way—or jeopardize her securing a beneficial future.

The room he'd been shown to had a distinct masculine tone, the bedding a rich brown with dark blue draperies covering the two banks of windows. From what he'd gathered as he'd been led to the room, he figured if he pulled the material back he'd have a scenic view of the Haversham gardens below, the large terrace that spanned the back of the impressive house spread beneath. His sack appeared small sitting in the bottom of the open wardrobe; only holding his extra pair of boots that Mrs. Dutton had sent him after he arrived in London over a year ago, his cherished book, The Task, wrapped in an old cloth, the jars from Lady Ellington, and a change of clothes. There was nothing else he could claim as his own. Even keeping the boots felt as if he'd taken much more than he deserved from Mrs. Dutton. She'd likely spent her entire quarterly salary on the fine pair, so exquisitely crafted, Alex hadn't found the courage to sully the shiny leather soles.

He'd always planned to sell them and return the money to the older woman. Maybe he would do just that before they left London, the market for such fine boots in the country would be hard to acquire.

Stepping away from the door, Alex untied the string at the top of his shirt and pulled it gently over his head. His body ached in protest when his back tightened. Standing before the full-length mirror hung on the wall next to the washstand, Alex admired Ellie's handiwork. Even now, the binding held strong, keeping the wounds together, no blood showing through. It was a shame he'd need to unwrap the material to bathe, but it would give him the opportunity to apply the salve.

He slipped the pin free from the material and slowly began to unwrap the binding—taking his first deep breath since she'd cleaned his back. Air flooded his lungs, and as they filled and expanded, fresh soreness overtook him. The cuts would take much time to heal, their scars likely to never completely fade. It would be a reminder to him of the hurt a person could cause— something he hoped never to inflict on another.

The last of the bindings fell to the floor at his feet and he took in the mangled sight of his back for the first time. It was a wonder Lady Ellington hadn't fled the room in tears.

She was a brave woman, much like her elder sister, Ruby.

Being alone as she'd been nearly all her life had made that a necessity.

And though she'd been the one stealing grain—if one can steal from their own stables— she hadn't deserved the lashing that had landed on her arm, nor was she responsible for tending to Alex's wounds. He was the one to care for her, not the other way around.

He hoped she was faring well at the Drake townhouse—all alone. He'd never understood why she hadn't offered Ruby a home after the marquis' death, or more yet, why Ruby hadn't insisted she stay with Lord and Lady

Haversham. It was certainly not proper for her to dwell all alone in that house.

But, as she'd reinforced numerous times, she was not his responsibility.

"Sir?" a tiny voice called from the doorway. "M'lord said ta bring ye water…"

The young maid's words trailed off as Alex whipped around. She looked stricken; the towels she'd carried now resting at her feet as she covered her mouth with both hands. It took him a moment to realize she cowered from the sight of his exposed back.

Would this be his fate—the sight of him causing fear and panic in others, his damaged body the only thing people saw when they looked at him?

"Do not go—" he attempted to calm the girl.

"My apologies," she stammered, backing out of the room. "Jenkins be here soon with ye bath water."

He slipped his shirt back over his head, not bothering to chase after the girl for he'd likely frighten her further. Grabbing the drying towels from the floor, he made his way over to the bed and sat.

As promised, a light tap sounded, followed by two footmen, each straining under the weight of the loaded copper basin. "Good evening," the man who must be Jenkins bowed to Alex after setting the tub close to the hearth. Neither man appeared familiar to Alex from his previous visits. "Your meal will arrive shortly. Is there anything else you require?"

"No, thank you." He stood, waiting for the men to depart before removing his shirt once more. The men seemed to tarry a bit longer than necessary. His only guess was that the maid had spoken of his injuries. Gossip spread quickly in large homes; you'd think the lateness of the day or business surrounding the ball would have prolonged the news from spreading, but that didn't seem to be the case. "You have been most kind to bring up the bath. Good night."

Alex was relieved when the door closed behind the men.

He was finally able to remove his shirt, bend carefully to remove his boots, and slip his trousers off. The warm water called to him as the steam rose, heating the room further—banishing his many memories of being cold and wet.

When he dreamt of his childhood, or when a particularly frigid storm blanketed London, it always brought back the deep, bone-chilling cold he remembered. He and Mrs. Dutton had moved frequently before she saved enough coin to found the orphanage. There were many days and weeks spent traveling the English countryside as they journeyed from one relation's property to another, seeking shelter and food. Alex was happy Mrs. Dutton never need live so meagerly again. Especially with Lady Haversham as her champion in recent years.

It would be wise to not burden her overly with this new predicament. It had been his fault she'd needed to move so often—and work so hard. If he'd been older...stronger...less injured...more capable, he would have been able to earn his keep, and Mrs. Dutton's relations would have seen the benefits in allowing them to stay.

He stepped into the water, slowly lowering himself to his knees and then sitting. The tub wasn't grand, only large enough for him to sit with his knees bent, but more spacious than any he'd ever been afforded before.

And the water…it stung for only a moment before it started soothing away aches and pains he hadn't been aware existed. He grabbed a small cloth that sat atop the pile the maid had left in the doorway, only to discover a wedge of soap that slipped out and into the water. With quick action, Alex retrieved the small piece and brought it to his nose—it smelled of something vaguely familiar. Lavender…and rose scents filled his nose.

Alex pulled the bar away and inspected it. He marveled at the smooth texture and intoxicating scent as he rubbed the wedge against the small cloth, suds immediately gathering.

Suddenly, he remembered his coming meal—and hurriedly completed his bath—washing his body, scrubbing his hair, and using a small kettle hanging from the side of the tub to pour water over his head. The soap moved down his body into the increasingly murky water, his back stinging as the lye in the soap hit his open wounds.

It would suit him perfectly to lounge about his bath all night, yet the water grew chilled and he must dress before his meal arrived.

He paid close attention to his back as he swiftly dried his body and fetched a clean change of clothes. It was important that he apply the salve to his cuts and re-bind his middle, though time was scarce before another servant came knocking.

Alex slipped his shirt over his head only seconds before a knock sounded again—this time, the person set their knuckles to the door with a resolute thud.

It was the simple, self-assured knock that had Alex scrambling to make sure his shirt covered his entire back. A quick inspection in the mirror told him one small cut was visible at his collar, but it was only the very tip of a lash and would not draw the eye. At least, he hoped.

"I be know'n ye in there, Master Alex," Mrs. Dutton called from the opposite side of the door. She likely didn't enter without permission because she feared he could still be in the bath, not that she hadn't seen him sans attire his whole childhood. But he was a man now, and he appreciated the semblance of privacy the woman afforded him. "Open the door immediately, lad."

Her patience wouldn't last, especially if the woman sensed he was avoiding her. "I am dressing, one moment," he called, preparing for her questions and concerns. The maid must have gone directly to Mrs. Dutton with what she'd seen.

"This tray be heavy," she said, her voice softening.

The many years she'd spent taking care of hordes of children had given her the ability to be the disciplinarian they needed, but also their shoulder to cry on. She would have made a wonderful mother, yet that had not been her fate—her husband passing at a tender age.

"Come in." Alex pulled the collar of his shirt higher to cover as much as he could, wincing when the pain shot through him at the movement. He turned with a smile to greet her. "Mrs. Dutton. I was going to call on you in the morning."

Her return smile pushed all other thoughts from his mind...he was happy to see her. She was the closest thing to a mother he had, and he never doubted she loved him more than most loved their own children.

"Me lad," she said, bustling into the room and setting his meal tray on the table closest to his untouched bed. "Glad ta see ye already taken a bath. I be send'n the footman up ta collect the basin, I will."

She paused, eyeing him from head to toe— waiting, her arms crossed over her chest.

Alex stepped forward, wrapping his arms around her rounded frame, tucking her head under his chin—the same as she'd done to him in his youth before he'd grown taller than she at age twelve.

The gesture was meant to let her know that things were not fine at the moment, but one day they would return to normal, if she'd allow him his silence.

"Who hurt ye, boy?" She'd called him *boy* as a youth when they'd first moved to London and a group of street urchins had taken to calling him cruel names on their walk to and from the market. True to form, as soon as she'd heard what upset him, the boys had disappeared from their walking route—fleeing inside when he and Mrs. Dutton rounded the corner. "I willna be bugger'n ye, but I canna be worry'n meself senseless."

"The situation has been taken care of." Alex would never want to be the cause of her needless fretting. "Please, do not worry. It was a misunderstanding—and it will never happen again."

She pulled him close, avoiding his back by clutching his upper arms. "I be so worried when I heard, an' I came rush'n. But ye a man now, an' don't be need'n yer old nursemaid make'n a fuss." Mrs. Dutton pushed him to arm's length before continuing, "Ye still be look'n healthy, lad. Your arms be stronger 'an when we visited at Christmastide."

"I have heard you may be seeing a bit more of me," Alex hinted. "And very soon."

"Have ye finally taken ta m'lord's offer?"

"I have done even better than that," he teased.

"Oh, lad, jus' tell it ta me." She swatted his shoulder before apologizing for doing such in his condition. "Will ye be here at Haversham townhouse or mayhap Mr. Jakeston's new home?"

"Even better…"

"Where, me boy?" Her enthusiasm got the best of her and she pulled him close, not waiting for his answer.

"I will be accompanying you and the girls back to Foldger's Hall."

He expected her to beam with joy—happy to have him close once more, but her simple response was, "No."

"No?"

She vehemently shook her head. "No, London is ye home."

"But I thought you would approve of me being close." Her reply confused him greatly. "London is no more my home than yours. We always dreamed of living in the country, around animals—mayhap have a garden."

"That be me dream, never yours, lad."

"It was our dream." He remembered many nights when they'd lain in their cots across the room from one another—the money run out for coal—freezing under their thin blankets and talking of the day they would once again be away from London's congested streets and murky air. "We said we would live off the land, away from the crime of the city. I could find work at a local estate."

"Ye need ta be here," she said, moving to sit before the hearth. "If'n ye be done with yer position at Mrs. Jakeston's relation's, then ye find another—with m'lord an' m'lady or Mr. Jakeston. They be know'n ye a hard worker. One day, ye be more 'an jus' a stable boy."

"But…"

"No use fight'n with me," she scolded. "Ye will remain in London proper."

Her refusal was perplexing; she'd cried for many nights before Alex had left for his employment at Foldger's Hall the first time because he would be so far away. Now, Mrs. Dutton had the opportunity to have him back and she'd said no.

"I can help you with the children, maybe tutor the young in their reading," he offered one last time. "It will help you greatly. I know how rambunctious they all are."

"No."

"Can I ask what changed your mind?"

"Ye did," she said, tears pooling in her eyes. "Ye be so much more 'an I ever deserved. Strong, loyal, a real gentleman."

"I learned all from you." Alex had made the mistake only once of talking down to one of the girls Mrs. Dutton had taken in. It was with a firm lecture—and a leather belt—that Alex had learned to respect females, even the youngest of the lot. "I have years of care to repay you for."

She bowed her head to hide her trembling chin as she sank back to her seat.

Alex was at her side as quickly as he could

move, ignoring the shooting pain in his back as he knelt beside her. "Do not cry." He gently rubbed her shoulder, hoping to calm her. Alex hated that he'd caused her tears. "Tell me what I need to do." At that moment, he'd promise to swim the English Channel if it meant her tears would be banished.

"Ye need ta let me tend ye."

Alex didn't try to dissuade her, but gladly pulled his shirt over his head. The cold air hit his back, cooling his heated skin. "It will shock you," he warned.

"I be see'n much in me life, boy." But when he turned and exposed his ripped back, she inhaled sharply. "Ah, me dear boy." Her voice broke as she struggled to keep her emotions from spilling over. Alex was relieved he didn't have to face her because the pain he'd see in her eyes would wound him worse than the beating Eckles had given him.

"There is a salve over there." Alex pointed to the jar, but neither made any move to retrieve it. "Ellie—er, Lady Ellington collected it before I left the Drake townhouse."

"She be a troubled lass," Mrs. Dutton said as she finally retrieved the jar. "But a good heart, she has."

Alex hadn't spoken about Ellie to anyone. At first, he'd pitied her lot in life, but as he'd gotten to know more about her and spent time with her, he'd discovered she wasn't at all what she appeared to others. She was fiery and tough on the outside, but that had been bred from many hard years with the marquis. Alex had witnessed it firsthand, her more delicate nature, the soft interior she hid from everyone—even her sister.

Mrs. Dutton smoothed the concoction over

his wounds—and neither of them said a word, lost in their own thoughts. He only hoped the older woman didn't blame herself for what had happened to him.

With quick work, she wrapped him and gave him his shirt to don. "Ye all patched."

"I am truly blessed to have you." Alex faced Mrs. Dutton, smiling. "You have always been so loving toward me."

"It be I who don' be deserve'n yer love." She broke into a fresh wave of sobbing. "I lied ta ye all these years."

His first instinct was to tell her she was mistaken. Mrs. Dutton, the woman who'd given up so much to care for him, must be worried over something trivial.

"What do you mean?"

"I be know'n who ye mum an' da be," she confessed.

"I suspected you knew all along," he tried to soothe her guilt. "But I have no doubt you saved me for a reason." In all likelihood, Mrs. Dutton had saved him from a life with unworthy parents—the exact details better left unknown. It was why he'd never questioned her about his past.

She shook her head once more and her lip trembled as she stared at her hands. At some point, she'd retrieved a dotted handkerchief from her pocket and wrung it to still her anxious hands.

"No, ye parents—" she paused, sucking in a deep breath "—they be dead. Their carriage crashed when ye was jus' a wee thing. M'lady made me swear 'n me late love's soul that I get ye ta safety—away from everathin ye knew. But the marquis, he never be giv'n up, so long as he be breath'n."

Bits of conversation—parts of sentences—important phrases from his meeting with Drake's solicitor came to mind. A carriage accident had claimed the lives of Lord and Lady Chastain—his mother born of French blood—how he looked the perfect mix between the striking pair.

"Are you saying I am Lord and Lady Chastain's son?" he asked.

"How do ye know of 'em?" Her question came on a whisper and she grasped his hand, tightly. "Did someone come to ye?"

"No—"

"Lad, ye marks didna come from that, did they?" Her serious expression returned. "I shouldna have let you work for that man."

"Stop, please," he pleaded. "Your words are only confusing me more. Did you know Lord and Lady Chastain?"

"I did, lad—ye must forgive me."

"Is there anything to forgive?" She'd been the one—the only person—to clothe him, feed him, and make certain he received an education, of sorts.

He was torn.

Alex had never asked any more about his parents, never questioned why they'd abandoned their son; so could he blame Mrs. Dutton for never telling him, when he hadn't asked?

"I was ye true nursemaid, ye see," she started, her eyes imploring him to listen. "Ye dear mum asked me ta take care of ye as a babe—an' made me promise ta look after ye if'n harm eva came ta her."

"How...but," he stuttered. "That would make me a duke."

...and the ability to give Ellie everything she deserved: a home, a name—and love.

"It be too dangerous for ye ta be spout'n that about." She squeezed his hand once more. "I be in the accident that took ye mum an' da. Ye was so wee—an' hurt real bad, but I kept ta me word an' we fled as soon as that lord, the marquis, helped us from the wreck."

"Why did we not return to my home?" All the information was too new to know if his questions made any sense. "We needn't have lived like beggars all those years—and I am certain to have others who have searched for me. The house is mine, is it not?"

"That it be, me boy. We couldna go back, ye mum made me swear ta keep ye safe—away from, well, jus' away. She gave me her wedd'n band ta coin, an' I promised ta keep ye safe." The sobbing intensified, and her shoulders shook as she released his hand and took to her handkerchief once more. It was almost two decades of sorrow, grief, and regret pouring from her. "I always meant ta tell ye, I promise. But..."

"But what?"

"There be too many people who woulda done ye harm," she sighed. "No one was ta be trusted. Ye mum made sure I be know'n that. She deceived people—it was how she came ta wed yer da. But then when she be see'n ye for the first time, she be tormented with it all. She be need'n ta make a better life for ye."

"Than why didn't she?" Alex asked, trying to make some sense of everything.

"There not be enough time. We be ready ta flee when the accident happened—she didna make it."

"Am I even now in danger?" he asked. "Has anything changed?"

"Truth be, I not be know'n. It be so long since everathin'." She looked to him, tears still slipping from her eyes. "I be hope'n the marquis called for ye 'cause he done made it safe for ye."

"My name is not Alex." He paced the room, attempting to keep his agitation at bay.

"No, lad—ye birth name be Peter. Ye hadn't been on this earth more 'an a few months a'fore ye was rightly, Peter Davis, heir to Lord Chastain, true gentleman, an' one day, a duke." Her accent faded some as if she'd practiced saying the name before, sounding as proper as she could. "When m'lady, Lady Haversham, sent word that the marquis be want'n ye ta come ta London ta be his stable hand—I be think'n he tell you the truth of it all. I worried meself sick, I did. Know'n ye'd never forgive me for keep'n it from ye all these years."

"Does anyone else know?" He paused to give her a chance to answer, but she remained silent. He should be furious, hurt, betrayed—but Alex couldn't even muster enough anger to raise his voice. "Lord and Lady Haversham?"

"No, Alex," she whispered. "I never told a soul...it wasna safe. I couldna be have'n 'em come'n for ye."

"Having who come for me?"

"All o' 'em—the horrid Frenchmen, ye grandsires, even the marquis. None be suppose'n ta find ye. An' when the wee ones started ta come, it be more 'an ye who be need'n me. Harm'n the other young'ns—or worse, doing ta ye what they did ta yer dear mum. They be treat'n her wee better 'an a mongrel; she be have'n ta do all they say. Until they pushed her too far an' she were gone."

There was much he was missing, but whether Mrs. Dutton was leaving it out or didn't know where to start with the telling of his life—and her lies—he wasn't sure. He tried hard to not be angry with her; though she'd made their lives so difficult, knowing in a fine part of London there was a home—an entire estate—that belonged to him. And he'd blamed himself the whole time.

"You allowed me to think they'd abandoned me—like I was rubbish." He knelt before her chair to see her face.

"It be the only safe way. That be far better'n what they woulda done ta ye if they found ye."

"If who found me?" he asked again.

"I not be sure who they all be—but ye grandsires for certain." She stood and paced before the dying fire, leaving him kneeling by her empty chair. He'd been hunched over for so long he feared tearing his wounds open if he straightened. "An' the marquis, he wasna supposed ta find ye an' me. I be question'n ev'ry day how he found ye."

Alex pulled himself into her chair. His face sunk to his hands and he scrubbed at his eyes.

"I be start'n ta think after all these years, they stopped look'n for us," Mrs. Dutton continued. "No one eva be look'n ta East End for the lost boy, neither they think ta look where'n a horde a young'ns be. I did ye mum proud, I did, keep'n ye hidden well. Me only relief was that ye da died in that carriage with her."

"And what did my mother—I do not even know her given name," he sighed. "What did she fear from the Marquis of Drake?"

"Lorelei, her name be Lorelei." Mrs. Dutton

smiled at a memory Alex longed to belong to him. "She didna fear the marquis, no. She be in love with the man, an' he be smitten with her, I suspect."

"Then why keep me from him?"

"She be try'n ta keep ye both safe. She loved the pair a ye more 'an herself."

"And my father, the duke?" He was overwhelmed, stricken senseless by the bizarre situation, all of it too unbelievable.

"He be a cruel man." She shook her head, as if she regretted her many choices in life.

"Who sought my mother?"

"Ye mum wasna what people be expect'n," Mrs. Dutton said, staring into the weak flames. "There be people who used her 'til she had noth'n else ta give—then they kilt her, they did."

"How much did Drake know of all this?" His mind was swirling with the knowledge of what could be in the papers delivered to Lady Ellington—the woman likely hadn't bothered to read any of it. If Drake knew anything about Alex's past, he must have written of it to Adams. "He never spoke of any of it to me before his death."

Mrs. Dutton turned to him then, imploring him to understand. "I not be know'n what m'lady said a'fore she went—bless her soul. I be worried greatly, take'n care a ye. When ye'd seen a doctor proper, we made our way ta me sister's house—I saved ye mum's ring as long as I could a'fore return'n ta London. It fetched a right nice sack a coin."

The words and explanations kept coming, though Alex hardly said a thing besides uttering the occasional question. He wondered if the marquis had known his true identity before offering him a position in his stables—more possibly, he didn't then nor at his death.

"I be sorry, lad." Mrs. Dutton apologized once more. "Ye must be ready ta find ye bed. There is much ta ready a'fore the grand soiree tomorrow eve. Good rest, me boy."

"I have many questions."

"I be know'n ye would." She shook her head as if she felt sorry for all he'd learned. "There be much time ta speak a everathin, but ye need ta rest now."

"It is as if I never existed, Alex—he is an imposer." And in turn, he'd misled those around him without knowing it. "Peter. Peter. Peter." He said the name with varying inflection. It didn't flow from his mouth, and yet, it was his true name.

A name did not make the man, but the actions and deeds of the man made the name.

"Doona fret all night. I loved ye, *still* love ye more 'an anyth'n. I be ready ta tell ye all I be know'n. Ye mum loved ye, too." She finally fled the little heat still radiating from the hearth and placed a quick kiss to his forehead. And with a tentative smile, she left.

Leaving him to spiral into uncertainty.

He should feel betrayed—the one woman tasked with caring for him had kept a vital truth from him. Had she told him, he could have sought out the Chastain townhouse—at least gaining them a place to lay their heads, but would anyone believe his farfetched tale?

Mrs. Dutton surely knew the greeting he'd get—and the burn to their tails as they were thrown from the house by whoever had claimed the Chastain title. It was better he kept his distance.

Lorelei.

Lady Chastain.

Lorelei Davis.

Alex wondered what her maiden name had been—certainly French, from all he'd learned thus far.

He needed to see Ellie, tell her everything. She was safe in her home; no one was coming to take it from her.

The farce, not a farce at all.

If the solicitor was to be believed, a man with no home to speak of was now a man with claim to two of London's finest estates.

CHAPTER 15

ELLIE PAUSED BEFORE exiting the carriage, expecting Alex's familiar smile to greet her. To her displeasure, a new Drake servant assisted her down. Unlike the footman, the drive outside Haversham House was familiar. The cold night air smelled of freshness, the storms from the past several days washing away the dirt and grime that came with London's busier residential neighborhoods. She also sensed something else on the evening breeze—excitement?

Not hers, certainly, but that of Payton and the twins. It was not often they received invitations to high society soirees. She would credit Marce with her cool reserve and elegant demeanor in the face of such a grand evening. The woman exited the Drake carriage behind her, stepping lightly to the ground as she surveyed the line of coaches behind them, waiting to deposit their own lavishly adorned occupants.

Ellie had alternated between severe reluctance in attending the ball and outright guilt for allowing Alex to walk out the previous night without explaining all she knew and confiding in him about the files delivered from the solicitor's office. She buried her shame by reminding herself that she didn't understand half of the information she'd read—and it possibly had nothing to do with Alex at all. Yet, all night, the marquis invaded her dreams, imploring her to trust Alex.

Alex was doted on by the woman who'd raised him, cherished and praised by Lady Haversham; and Ellie had no doubt that if he hadn't been hand-selected by the marquis, Alex would have been favorably accepted by the other servants.

"Come now, Ellie," Payton whined from the carriage. "Move aside and allow me to depart this blasted conveyance."

Marce slipped her hand through Ellie's arm and stepped to the walk leading to the front door where the Haversham butler already waited to greet them. "Do not fret, my dear. You look exquisite, I hardly recognize the red-haired mop that frequently raided my sweets as a child."

Ellie couldn't help but smile at the memory. "I have not been that young—and precocious— in many years."

"A return to youth is not always a bad thing," Marce confided, patting her hand. "I am grateful for your including us in your invitation."

"If it were not for you and the girls, I would be dreadfully alone, surrounded by stuffy, pompous men, and marriage-minded matrons with their insufferable daughters in tow." After her evening spent at Covent Gardens with Ruby and Harold several months before, Ellie had a sense of what to expect from other London entertainments—and it did not bode well for her sanity. "At least, I know Jude and Sam will keep us entertained if not another soul notices us."

"I do not fear that you, or my sisters, will have much idle time." Marce used her free hand to adjust the blue cotton at Ellie's shoulder, which did an admirable job of hiding the healing cut on her arm. "The four of you are likely to set the room abuzz with your lovely dresses—as long as you refrain from vulgarities, that is. Otherwise, the room will be ablaze with scandal."

Ellie, Payton, and the twins had endured an exhaustive lecture on their drive from Craven House to Lord Haversham's. Payton received a scolding for her tendency to whine and sulk. While Sam and Jude had been cautioned against posing as one to fool others. Marce had ended her long ramble by making Payton swear to stay clear of the card room and Jude to keep her hands visible at all times. As for Sam, she was advised to stay within eyesight of Marce and not to wander off with any man who seemed smitten with her.

Marce knew her sisters all too well, especially their bad habits.

Thankfully, Ellie had avoided garnering a final warning from the older woman, for she already knew the consequences if she stepped out of line. The effects of any misstep would be directed at Lady Haversham—her hostess—and Ruby.

"Oh, Ellie," Sam and Jude sighed as one as they all made their way to the front entrance, their carriage pulling away. "Your sister is so much better than ours!"

"That is certainly a fact," Jude said, ignoring the look Marce turned in her direction. "Marce has never taken us to—let alone hosted—a party this grand. She always insists we study hard and keep up with our pianoforte lessons. She is ever so boring."

"I can hear you," Marce sighed.

"We know," Payton retorted, sticking her tongue out at her eldest sister before speeding up and linking arms with the twins, leaving Ellie and Marce to walk behind the trio. "Oh, one day I shall dress in such finery every day!"

"She'll have to win many card games to make that happen," Marce whispered for Ellie's ears alone. "I swear that child will drive every potential match straight to the far reaches of France with her trying nature."

Marce shook her head in resignation, but Ellie spied the smile she hid. The woman loved her horde of misbehaving sisters, and would likely endure a lifetime of Payton's whining to keep her close at hand and dissuade others from harming her sensitive soul.

"And what about you?" Marce kept her gaze straight ahead, as if she meant it to be a question in passing conversation. "Is there anyone special you are hoping to see this evening?"

"Certainly not," Ellie answered, though she wished to bring Marce into her confidence and tell her all about Alex. "I am here because my sister demanded it."

"Demanded?" she quizzed. "I've only had the occasion to meet your sister once, but she did not seem the demanding sort."

"Requested intently?"

Marce slowed their pace to allow them an

additional moment of privacy before entering the soiree. "Can you do me one favor?"

Ellie halted and turned to the woman. "Anything."

"Do try to enjoy yourself this evening."

"I always enjoy—"

"You do not always enjoy yourself, or even don a convincing facade of pleasure." Marce scolded. It seemed Ellie's lecture was to be a private one, meant only for her. "Smile."

"That is all you request?" It seemed too simple.

"Yes." Marce regained her pace toward the door. "Your smile will light the room brighter than a thousand candles. Besides, a smile is the first step in achieving anyone your heart desires."

Ellie's heart didn't desire anyone, or at least that's what she'd been repeating over and over in her mind since the moment Alex had fled the study the night before. Marce seemed content in her life, so Ellie decided to take her advice anyways.

And with a smile so large her cheeks ached, Ellie greeted the Haversham butler.

"Good eve, my lady." He bowed to the group. "Sevins will take your coats. Right this way, Lady Ellington. Lady Haversham and Mrs. Jakeston are awaiting your arrival."

Ellie touched the elderly man's arm to stop him. "I do know my way about."

A puzzled expression covered the man's face, only to be replaced a moment later with a look of utter terror. "This is not an afternoon tea, Lady Ellington," he whispered, aghast. "I will announce your arrival."

She'd asked to escape having her name

called out as she and the Craven House ladies descended into the ballroom, though her sister would likely not follow through on her promise.

"Chins up, girls," Marce called in her singsong voice as she brushed her long, blonde hair from her shoulder. "And, remember to smile."

Ellie glanced nervously to both sides, feeling no security even though Marce and Payton flanked her on one side and Sam and Jude on the other, sensing how much she needed them. "I was a fool to agree to this," Ellie said.

"Lady Ellington," Lady Haversham called from inside the ballroom before their party could be announced. "And you must be Miss Davenport, and these, your sisters. Thank you so much for joining Ellington this evening. We are overjoyed to have you in our home." The woman, large with child only a couple of months before, stood adorned in what appeared to be spun gold, her slender form returned—it put Ellie's gown to shame.

"Thank you for including my sisters and me." Marce dipped a curtsy. "We are honored to accompany Lady Ellington on such a special occasion."

Lady Haversham reached forward, dragging Ellie into her embrace. "When Ellie spoke of such dear friends, Ruby and I knew we must have you all here...if only to guarantee Ellie's attendance, which would greatly please her sister."

Pulling back from her hug, Ellie watched as each girl showed her respect for their hostess by curtsying and giving their name.

"I suspected you would be more at ease if we entered the room from the side door—skip the receiving line." She winked at Ellie and turned to Marce once more. "Ruby has been anxiously awaiting Ellie's arrival. I fear she is a ball of nervous energy."

Marce laughed as if they shared some secret between the pair of them. "I do remember my first ball—it was rather overwhelming, to say the least." Next, she turned to her sisters who excitedly waited behind her, trying to peek over her shoulder to the grand room. "Girls, please stay close...and remember your manners. We would not like Lord and Lady Haversham regretting their kindness."

With that, Marce took hold of her gown skirt, raising it ever so slightly, and stepped into the room, her sisters following her lead, leaving Ellie with Lady Haversham, right outside the door.

They listened as the foursome's arrival was announced.

How Ellie wished she were brave enough to have her name called loudly and enter the room with her chin high. She wasn't ready for that, nor might she ever be.

"How is your arm?" Lady Haversham asked as they began to move down the corridor to a set of closed double doors farther down. At Ellie's startled glance, she continued, "Alex is here—and his back has needed some care."

"I am sorry about—"

"There is nothing for you to be sorry about." The woman gave her a gentle smile. "He is a grown man seeking his own way in the world. With that determination comes obstacles. He is a strong, steadfast gentleman. The exterior wounds will heal, I only hope his spirit does, as well."

They reached the double doors leading into the ballroom before Ellie could ask Lady

Haversham what she'd meant. The light strings of a song could be heard through the thick wooden doors.

"My cut was insignificant and does not call for your concern," Ellie said. "It is my fault Alex was injured—he was to be under my protection, and I failed him."

The woman had been nothing but kind and generous to Ellie since they'd met; she deserved the truth and some sort of guarantee that it would never occur again. Yet, it could never happen again.

Alex had vacated his position at Drake House—and left her.

"Rest assured, he does not see it the same way as you, my dear."

Ellie could only hope that held true over the coming days.

"Are you ready?" Lady Haversham gave her a reassuring smile and awaited a servant who opened the door, revealing the crowded ballroom beyond. "Shall we?"

She spied her sister, Harold at her side, standing a few feet inside the doors, greeting the long line of guests as they entered. Marce and her sisters had already made their way down the line and stood along the wall bordering the dance floor, Jude and Sam likely awaiting the dancing portion of their evening. The stately pair, gowned in varying shades of green with their fiery hair drawn high to reveal their matching slender necks, smiled at each passing gentleman while quietly speaking back and forth. Ellie felt compassion for the poor gentleman the pair targeted, for he stood no chance when the sisters turned their female charms on him.

Payton stood near the wall in the shadow of a potted palm, fretfully fussing with her gloves, switching between nervous and envious looks at the more outgoing guests in the room. While she was lovely in her own right, it was difficult to compare to the sophisticated air Marce gave off and the elegantly stunning duo that was the twins.

Marce expertly kept a close watch on the trio, while making sure her gaze did not meet those of the *ton* surrounding her. It hadn't escaped Ellie's notice, the awkwardness Marce faced being in the same room as many gentlemen who sought entertainment at Craven House; another horrid thing Ellie must apologize for at some point in the evening.

Taking her last long look at the room, Ellie smiled as she stepped around Ruby and greeted the couple. "Good evening, sister." She was rewarded with a quick peck on the cheek from Ruby and a tight hug from Harold. "Brother," Ellie said as she slipped from his embrace.

"Your dress suits you admirably, dear sister. Does it not, my love?" Ruby beamed. "That particular shade of blue compliments your skin marvelously."

"It is a gown," Harold mumbled in response to his wife's overzealous words. "And her skin looks the same shade of cream mixed with freckles as it did last week."

Ruby swatted at her husband's arm, irked. "Men!" she declared, as if Ellie knew what sentiment should mean. "If it were a bottle of French port, you would notice the tiniest scuff on the bottle."

"Right you are, my wife, but then again, your dear sister looks exquisite in anything." He exaggerated looking about the room to the two farthest corners, bringing his hand to his forehead as if shielding his eyes from the glare of the sun. "Oh, speaking of scuffed bottles, do not look now, but my eyes behold such a creature—awaiting its rescue."

Ellie laughed as she followed his line of sight. The drink table stood near the terrace doors for guests to retrieve refreshments before stepping outside for fresh air or quiet conversations.

"My dear, young sister," Harold bowed in her direction. "May I request your company on my adventure to liberate the port kept yonder by foul natives?"

Restless to be away from the receiving line, lest Ruby ask her to stay, Ellie placed her hand on Harold's proffered arm. "I kindly accept your offer," she said, playing along.

"Harold, you rascal," Ruby sighed. "You will search for any reason to be away from your wife."

"There is not another place I'd rather be than by your side, my sweet." Harold placed a kiss to Ruby's crown. "But what sort of gentleman would I be if I did not offer our guest refreshments?"

"Oh, be gone with you," Lady Haversham chided. "Ruby and I will manage well enough without you. I see my dear husband has wandered off, as well." She craned her neck to see Lord Haversham speaking intently with a portly gentleman close to the dance floor.

"Do promise to return quickly."

"I shall, do not fear." Harold led Ellie toward the refreshment table at a leisurely pace. "Thank you for coming, Lady Ellington."

He was known for his jests and easy nature, so his formality took her off guard, as it was something she was unaccustomed to.

He nodded to an older couple as they passed, and Ellie couldn't stop from asking, "Do you know all these people?" The room was filled to bursting with more guests entering every minute. She'd lived in London her entire life, but only counted a handful of people as anything more than mere acquaintances.

"Barely a single one, my lady," he chuckled. "I doubt Lord and Lady Haversham know half of the people in attendance."

"Then why are they all here?"

Harold led her along the edge of the ballroom, on the opposite side from where Marce and her sisters congregated. "To be seen. To overhear the latest gossip. To spy this lord or that about town with his mistress on his arm."

Ellie pulled away sharply to get a look if he were jesting.

"Now, now." He held her securely, drawing her back to his side. "Society is a funny flock."

"Flock?"

"Mob. Horde. Gang." They neared the refreshment table as Harold rattled off words. "One thing I have realized since moving in Lord Haversham's circle is that members of the *ton* move in large groups. They attend the same parties, meet the same crop of debutantes, and spread the same gossip year in and year out. They all graciously accepted Lord Haversham's invite into his home to survey the fresh meat."

"Fresh meat?" Ellie understood the nature of people—she'd been around London streets long enough to know that like-minded people tended to attract one another, either for safety or for fear of being left out, but her mind swam at his continued train of conversation.

"Simply put," he continued as he handed Ellie a flute of sherry before accepting his own from the servant before them. "They have all gathered to see what scandal Lady Haversham may present them with this night."

"But Ruby said the ball was to introduce you and her to the *ton*."

"Very true, yet all still hold their breath, for age-old gossip and shame are not easily erased from society's mind."

She sipped her drink before continuing, the sherry bubbling in her nose. "Lady Haversham is one of the most gracious and kind women I have met."

"Which makes her past all the more titillating to her guests."

Ellie breathed a sigh of relief. If everyone was focused on Lady Haversham, then none would notice the bastard child walking amongst them. No one would denounce her as an impostor for daring to enter the front doors of a grand London home—that of an earl, no less.

"I will freely admit I was taken by surprise how readily you accepted Ruby's invitation to attend."

"I find I enjoyed myself at Foldger's Hall and decided to show my appreciation for Lord and Lady Haversham's thoughtfulness. Do not share that with Ruby, I beg of you."

"Certainly not." He shook his head, gravely. "Your confidence and ability to experience a bit of enjoyment will remain safe with me."

"Thank you, Mr. Jakeston." She'd originally decided to attend the ball to ask after the current Lord Chastain, to judge his mettle before making her decision to willingly hand over the Drake estate or…there truly was no other option left open to her as a female—and bastard child of the late marquis. But since reading through all the papers from the solicitor, and discovering all she had, Ellie wasn't sure of her reasoning anymore. "I find the need for a distraction every now and again, besides, how often am I given the opportunity to wear such a lovely gown?"

"Very true." Harold led her toward Marce and her sisters. "After your year of mourning, I am certain you are embracing a more colorful wardrobe." They stopped before Marce, and Harold bowed. "It is lovely to make your acquaintance once again, Madame Marce."

Marce tipped her head in his direction, a wicked smirk capturing her lips. "And you, as well, sir. I do hope you have been taking better care of your wife than last we met."

Harold's eyes grew as round as tea saucers at the mention of their last meeting—and Ellie had to squash her urge to laugh.

"I most certainly am."

"That is good to hear."

"I will bid you both a wonderful night." With a quick bow, he hurried back to Ruby's side where she continued to greet guests—he was likely more agreeable to his hosting duties than being stared down by Marce, who'd once thought the worst of him.

"You are rotten, Marce," Ellie scolded, finding it hard to keep her own mirth from spilling over. "He must be dreadfully frightened of you."

"As well he should." Marce plucked the flute from Ellie's hand and drank the remaining sherry. Marce had met Ruby and Harold before the pair had wed when Ellie's sister had been struck in the face during a foolhardy plot to enter White's Gentlemen's Club. Ellie had delivered them to Craven House in hopes that Marce would have something to reduce the swelling and bruising to her sister's face. "Enough stalling. It is time all four of you find dance partners. The floor—and your cards—should fill quickly."

"And what about you?" Ellie knew little about Marce's personal life beyond caring for her sisters and Craven House; yet she seemed at ease in the crowded ballroom, certainly more than Ellie or Marce's sisters. "Will you find a partner?"

Marce peeked at Ellie from the corner of her eye, keeping her attention on the rest of the room. "When shall I do that?" she asked with a soft laugh. "While I am keeping Payton from the card tables...or ushering Jude away from the exquisite painting in the hall...or better yet, after I dissuade Sam from attaching herself to the first man who shows her any interest? No, Ellington, I will be content to secure a successful evening for the four of you."

"Are we so much trouble?" Ellie had invited the sisters because she owed them much for the kindness they'd shown her over the years.

"Ellington, you do not worry me as much as my wayward siblings," she confided. "And I hope it stays that way. I suspect, with both Mrs. Jakeston and I looking after you, you will do just fine."

"I do not need a—"

"I know," Marce interrupted. "You are not in need of a nursemaid, but how about a friend?"

Ellie had never thought of them as friends,

only an obligation Marce had agreed to many years ago—a promise to her mother, Madame Sasha, to look after Ellie, but the thought of calling her a friend was comforting. After Alex had left, Marce seemed all she had. Just as Sasha had been a friend to Ellie's mother—now, Marce was to her.

"I would enjoy that," Ellie replied. "Another question, how does one find a suitable partner?"

CHAPTER 16

ALEX STOOD IN the shadow outside the Chastain townhouse. No lights shone from the windows facing the street,; the draperies tightly pulled across every windowpane faded from the sun. The alley leading behind the house was clear of growth, but no carriage wheels or hoof prints marred the ground.

Pulling his coat tighter to ward off the coming night, he stepped forward, approaching the front door. He'd loitered outside long enough for the afternoon sun to set and evening twilight to take over. He'd seen no movement inside, nor any deliveries arriving on foot to the kitchens. No one came or left the property.

After the excessive activities about the Haversham townhouse he'd witnessed—and barely survived—today, it was odd that a duke's residence, in the height of the season, appeared abandoned.

He'd come seeking answers—explanations.

But an empty house taught him nothing.

He'd debated most of the night and all day about what to do; he'd discarded the idea of paying the solicitor another visit because Ellie was in possession of all the papers pertaining to Drake, though he didn't know if they also held information regarding Chastain. Similarly, he'd thought of returning to the Drake townhouse, though he knew distance was the best thing for now. He'd worried about Lady Ellington most of the night—in between dwelling on his own circumstances.

The evening grew late, and Alex had promised Mrs. Dutton he'd return early enough for them to sup together before bedtime came. For him, not her. Mrs. Dutton was certain to be kept awake by Jillian and Beatrice, for they attended the ball Lady Haversham was hosting. The girls were likely to be awake most of the night gossiping about their first London soiree.

With sure steps, he reached the front door of the Chastain townhouse, knocking before his nerves ran out.

His three sharp raps on the door echoed inside—but no footsteps answered them.

After a few moments, he knocked once more. If no one answered, he'd have naught else to do but return to Lord Haversham's, no more the wiser for his time spent out, but his time was limited. Alex had only two days at most before he'd escort Mrs. Dutton and the girls back to Foldger's Hall. He'd thought long and hard over Mrs. Dutton's insistence that he remain in London, but he needed his own time and space to figure out what his life held next.

One thing he knew for certain, he would not take Ellie's home.

230 | *Christina McKnight*

He certainly did not deserve the Drake estate.

And he hadn't learned enough about his mother and father to know if it were safe for him to claim the dukedom—or even if a child presumed deceased could prove their right to inherit. It was something he would need to speak with Lord Haversham about.

It was daunting to think about how much his life had changed in the last several hours—from an orphan to a lord.

Finally, he heard something from within. A person was shuffling their feet.

A key turned in the lock—the sound of grating metal against metal—and an elderly man opened the door just wide enough for one eye and his nose to be visible.

"May I help you, sir?" he inquired, his voice raspy as if he hadn't spoken aloud in many years.

"I am here to see Lord Chastain." If his father was deceased, and Alex was clearly not living within Chastain walls, then someone must have been noticed as the heir to the dukedom.

"He is not in town." The man made to close the door, but Alex's hand shot out to stop him.

"Do you know when he will return?" When the man's eyes narrowed but he remained silent, Alex continued, "Please, I must speak with him. Will he be in London before the season ends?"

"I have not seen Lord Chastain in almost two decades, sir," the man said, his raspy tone subsiding. "If you see him, please kindly ask him to visit this townhouse. I would not know what the man looked like today—you could be him, and I would not be the wiser. Now, if you will allow me to close the door, I am late for my bed."

Alex stepped back, granting the man's request to shut the door.

After the key had been turned in the other side of the lock, Alex listened as the man retreated inside, the sounds of his shuffle fading.

Alex pushed his hands into his pockets and turned back to the street. It was a short, brisk walk back to the Haversham townhouse, and when he arrived, the drive was filled with waiting carriages. To avoid the crowd, Alex slipped round the house and entered through the kitchen, teeming with servants busily filling trays with sandwiches.

"Good evening." He nodded to Cook and departed the room quickly, taking the servant's stairs to the second story and his chambers. Thankfully, he passed no guests along the way.

Lord and Lady Haversham had kindly invited him to take part in the ball, but he'd quickly turned down their offer. For once, no one questioned his decision—and so, he'd taken his meals in his room and departed to Chastain house when the opportunity arose.

However, the day had garnered him no new information.

Though that was not exactly correct.

He paced the room, pondering the man's odd response. Could it be that no one had claimed the dukedom after his parents' deaths? Did the servants still await his miraculous return?

It had been over a year since the marquis' death, and his estate had kept the same way.

He pulled the drapery aside and stared out into the night—lit by the many torches scattered on the garden's paths below. Several partygoers walked the paths or huddled in groups or couples, while others sat on the many benches positioned about the garden.

Adjusting his view, Alex looked to the terrace below him where yet more guests milled about. He wondered if anyone remained inside, for so many had sought the outdoors.

A flash of the palest blue caught his eye at the side of the terrace—standing alone as if only a spectator to everything going on around her. Detached.

Her hair—the color so vibrant that even in the soft glow of the terrace torches it shone brightly where it hung about her shoulders.

No one paid her any mind where she stood unmoving, looking out at the darkened gardens.

It had been less than a day since they'd parted ways—and he missed her deeply.

It had given him comfort to know she hid in the rafters watching him work.

It had filled him with hope that she'd taken to caring for Ember, the fiery kitten he'd given her at Christmas.

It had given him confidence in her safety when he'd been close to watch over her, as no one else seemed concerned about her.

He realized his duties for her had given *him* purpose.

Lady Ellington would not miss his presence, nor find herself at a loss following his departure. Alex hadn't a doubt that both he and Eckles had already been replaced at Drake townhouse, as servants came and went frequently in some households.

He would miss her temper, her cunning, her bravado.

Her sharp-tongued retorts would fall on deaf ears.

He only hoped word hadn't spread of the incident that occurred in the stables—and their time alone in the study after.

The blame would be his if scandal marred her reputation.

As he watched, she turned as if to re-enter the ball, but her eyes traveled up—finding him on the floor above.

Alex didn't know if he should step back into the shadows and pull the drapes closed or nod in greeting.

It was possible a glare covered his window and she could not see him standing at the large opening, keeping an eye on her even though she was no longer his responsibility.

Instead of looking away, she kept her gaze locked on his.

It was as if they were standing together, not separated by glass and distance.

It was Ellie who broke the spell they were both under. She smiled—a shy and almost reluctant smile—then nodded toward him and gestured to the gardens beyond the terrace.

An invitation?

Certainly, she was not requesting they meet during Lord and Lady Haversham's ball. He looked down at his patched shirt and worn trousers; they were clean yet not appropriate for any London entertainment, even if he weren't attending as a guest but instead, undertaking a secret rendezvous with a lady.

Before his courage failed, he nodded. They had much to discuss.

She quickly moved down the stairs and into the garden.

Making his way down the servant's stairs once more, Alex thought over what he knew of the townhouse layout. He hadn't even been in the house except to meet with Lady Haversham on his afternoon's leave—normally joining her in the salon, which faced the front of the house. The only other room he knew of was Lord Haversham's study, its double doors surely opening to the side of the terrace, not far from where Lady Ellington waited.

The hall outside the study was deserted. Alex took the opportunity to exit the stairwell and slip into the study, the pain in his back almost completely forgotten. His luck held. It was as empty as the hallway had been.

Alex navigated the room, lit only by a small fire in the hearth, and hurried to the double doors on the far wall, clicking the lock free and exiting into the twilight. No torches had been lit on this side of the house, keeping the guests to the ballroom, terrace, and gardens.

"Alex?" Ellie called from the darkness. "Is that you?"

"Of course, it is I." He took the two steps leading down from the small side terrace to the foliage-lined path below. "Is all as it should be?"

"I am never certain how to answer such questions," Lady Ellington stepped forward and into the pool of light coming from an open window above. "I am here at this ball in a beautiful dress among many happy people. Everything should be glowing with joy."

"Yet, you are not happy?" he asked. She stood a few feet before him, her gown appearing even more breathtaking than it had from above.

"No."

He wanted to share with her all he'd found out; confirm no one would be throwing her from her home anytime soon, and if that did happen, there was a place she was welcome to live if being with her sister was not what Ellie wanted.

"I have heard one should be dancing long into the night at their first ball." Or, at least, that's what he'd overheard when he'd passed Lady Haversham's drawing room earlier in the day—the woman had been giving Beatrice and Jillian a lesson in ballroom decorum: what to expect, how to greet a lord when introduced, and what dances were popular. There had been much laughter from both the girls and Lady Haversham. "Did Eckles return?"

"Heavens, no," Ellie shook her head as she spoke. "And yes, Marce and her sisters are quite enjoying themselves, delighting in all the attention a group of unknown, mysterious young women garner from the eligible men of the *ton*."

"And you are not?" He'd always suspected her antics were to gain the notice of either the late marquis or her sister; now he wasn't sure of anything. "I am sure your dance card filled the moment you stepped in the room." A twinge of jealousy spiked within him at the thought of another man laying his hands on Ellie—or her feeling comfortable and secure with another.

"It would not matter if someone were interested enough to gain an introduction and ask for a dance."

"Why not?"

She tucked her head—and he was sure if there were more light, he'd see her cheeks red with embarrassment.

"Come now, Lady Ellington," he coaxed, stepping forward and taking her hand. "You tell me your secret and I will share one of mine."

Her gaze popped to his, as if she were taken aback that he could have a secret; yet she stayed silent.

"Am I so dull a person to not have a secret?" he teased.

"I cannot dance." She squeezed his hand as she confessed.

Alex kept a serious expression for it obviously worried her enough that she'd spend her first ball hiding in the shadows with him. The woman was skilled at so many things most young women were oblivious to; he'd even overheard Mrs. Jakeston detailing Ellie's ease for pickpocketing—but dancing was the shortcoming she was ashamed of?

"You are versed in climbing a ladder in full womanly garb, riding astride, sneaking in and out of your home without notice, and did not so much as flinch when struck by Eckles' whip." He listed every point he admired about her—those that came to mind in those quick seconds anyways. "But dancing is something you cannot master?"

"I have never been shown," she retorted. "If I had had a proper tutor, I am certain I could out dance any woman in Lady Haversham's ballroom."

"That is the hellion I know." He laughed. "I can teach you."

"I should have known my stable hand would be as versed in dancing as he is in poetry."

He kissed her hand and bowed slightly to her. "I have more secrets than you know, my lady. May I have this dance?"

She looked about nervously, but a hint of a smile touched her lips. "There is no music."

For the first time, he thought of how truly alone they were. Not even a whispered tone from the ballroom could be heard.

"What?" He cupped his ear with his free hand. "You cannot hear that sweet melody?"

"What if someone stumbles upon us?"

"Not a guest within these walls knows either of us," he whispered, pulling her toward him. "A scandal cannot start if the parties involved cannot be named."

After Lady Haversham had become Mrs. Dutton's benefactor when Alex was almost nine, the orphanage saw many tutors come and go, teaching the children to read, write, and figure numbers. As the years passed, and the coin continued to come, Mrs. Dutton enlisted tutors for the piano, decorum, and dancing. The children, many injured and abandoned by those who should have loved them, learned many of the finer things society's children were taught. By age thirteen, Alex had mastered and memorized many of England's most known poems, had banished the accent that cast him as a boy from the East End, and was proficient enough to perform a cotillion or scotch reel, though he'd never danced with a partner as lovely as Lady Ellington.

But his lessons in both the cotillion and scotch reel would be of no use to him now, as there were no other dancers to complete their square—and he desperately wanted Ellie closer than either of those dances allowed.

"Have you ever seen a waltz danced before?" He prayed she hadn't because, while he'd seen one of his tutors teaching the younger girls for fun several years ago, he'd never danced one himself.

He breathed a sigh of relief when she shook her head.

"It is called a gliding dance," he shared. "So all one needs to know is how to glide—there are no complicated steps or formations. Only you, your partner, and the music." At least, he hoped that was all there was to it. "We clasp hands like this." He adjusted his hold on her hand. "And I set my other hand on your hip, like so." He stood facing her, settling his hand lightly on her hip.

"And my other hand goes here?" It landed at his hip, mirroring Alex's hold on hers, and she looked up at him for reassurance.

"Yes, or it is used to hold your gown off the floor so as not to stumble."

She moved her hand from his hip to her skirts. "What is next?"

"We move." Alex took two steps back and one to the side, unsure if a certain number was customary. At first, her movements were hesitant and jarring, but soon she settled into his lead as they moved in a small circle, in and out of the dim light shining from above. "It is not so hard."

"That is because you are a noble teacher, Alex."

His breath caught. She'd said his name before, but this time, it sounded different—more intimate than ever before.

"Will you tell me your secret now?"

"Beyond my tutoring in dance?"

"I am certain that was not your grand secret."

Their eyes met, both of them smiling. It was something neither of them was prepared for—a moment of pure amusement—neither was hiding from anything. It was an openness they'd shared on a few brief occasions: that first night in the marquis' study, the broken carriage at Christmastide, and the previous evening as she'd tended to his back.

"Do you remember when we spoke of my parents over the Christmastide holiday?"

"Of course." Her movements began to slow as if she suspected the magnitude of what he was about to share with her.

"I know your mother is Lady Chastain—"

"I learned they did not abandon me—"

Their words collided, and he focused on what he'd thought he heard her say, pushing his own words aside.

She stopped, and her hand fell from his, almost causing him to stumble. "You knew?" He wasn't in danger of stumbling over his feet, but his words were another thing entirely. He should have felt some sense of despondency when Mrs. Dutton had broken the news his parents were both deceased, yet he'd never expected them to return for him, so there was no loss to experience. Only a sense of closure.

"I wanted to tell you." She paused, taking another step back and out of the square of light they'd been standing in.

"But you did not." Suddenly, she was closed off to him.

"It is only…" She began to pace—three steps, turn, three steps, turn. "I…"

"Tell me." The moment they'd shared had been broken so quickly; Alex wished he would have saved his secret for another time and that she would have done the same. She'd paced like this the night in the alley when she'd asked him to participate in her scheme to fool Adams. Ellie was nervous about something—anxious, worried. "Come now," he prodded, his anger rising.

Suddenly, she stopped and faced him, her

entire body tense, and he knew he'd regret forcing her tongue. Her hands dropped to her sides and she held his stare. "I know your father was a duke—and your mother born of French nobility."

"How long?" Her admission sucked the air from his lungs, causing him to take several shallow breaths. "How—no, it cannot be—certainly you..."

The more he stumbled over his words, the taller she stood.

"Do you take pleasure in this?" he asked. "The poor stable boy without a name?"

"No, I—"

"And to think I pitied your circumstances, actually felt torn up inside at the cruel way your father treated you," he seethed. At the mention of his pity for her, her eyes clouded and her face grew red. He'd pitied her at first, that night he'd heard her father call her all sorts of horrid, vile names, but that emotion had evolved into something more genuine and lasting over the last year. But she had deceived him, made him out to be the senseless stable hand she'd always treated him as. "However, the pair of you are a matched set. You are his protégé—a likeness of the marquis, mirror images."

"Pity me?" she hissed. "No, stable hand—it is I who has always pitied you."

Alex wasn't sure what injured him more—her words or the realization that she'd known about his past and hadn't trusted him enough or thought enough of him to tell him. She'd allowed him to continue living as he had, a nameless man. She, above all others, should understand the significance of a name.

"And you made me your little puppet—

sending me on a fool's errand. Did you laugh the entire time I was playing the lord? Of all the things I thought you capable of, this was certainly not one of them. You are the most selfish, self-serving person I have ever laid eyes upon." Alex should walk away. Allowing this argument to proceed gained them nothing but more wounds; yet he felt betrayed by the one person he'd never thought to hurt him.

"You would have left me if you knew."

"Left you?" Alex threw his hands wide in defeat. "And you think you have the right to make the decision on what I know and do not know?"

"It was unfair—"

"It is more than unfair, Ellington." He sighed. "It is the actions of a true coward. A person who is so blind to those around them they cannot even see the damage they do to themselves and others. You are incapable of trusting another, even me. You truly believe everything I say and do is overshadowed by some nefarious motive. You are the only person here who lives in a constant state of obsession— dwelling only on your self-preservation at the cost of *every* relationship around you."

"Maybe I chose the correct path." Ellie crossed her arms over her chest, rebelliously.

"This—" he gestured to her exquisitely gowned body as he took a step back, putting distance between them as his voice rose "—this young, vibrant woman will turn into a lonely, angry woman faster than you think. And you will only have yourself to blame. I cannot do this any longer."

Alex needed space, time to breathe—work through the stark reality that Ellie had betrayed him without a second thought.

How long would she have allowed the charade to continue?

CHAPTER 17

THERE WAS NOTHING for Ellie to do as Alex continued to withdraw from her and he finally turned and walked away, his heavy footfalls echoing on the steps back into the house. Everything he'd accused her of was true; she was selfish, she sought self-preservation before anything else, and she was incapable of trusting another person. It had never mattered how earnestly Alex had worked to prove himself, that he'd never intentionally hurt her.

Ellie *had* felt remorse for keeping what she'd learned from him. But she'd justified her actions, rationalized her fears of what he'd do if he knew.

The consequences of the situation hadn't sunk in for her. Alex was gone—but he wasn't allowed to leave her; at least that's what she'd told herself over and over. *He* was the one person who would never leave her. She'd hurt him with her insults and actions many times, but he'd never abandoned her. She'd thought him incapable of deserting her—until this very moment. How had she not seen this coming?

And worse yet, to find he pitied her.

It would have been simple to remain in his arms, swirling about the shadows to an unheard melody, act surprised at his news, but that would have only made things all the worse later when he discovered she'd known all along.

One thing she'd never doubted was that Alex was a smart man—he would have discovered everything given enough time.

He wanted her trust—and at the moment, Ellie knew there was nothing she could do but hope he could forgive her. It would have been wise to beg for his forgiveness, offer him all the papers to read; yet she'd kept that from him. A part of her was not ready to part with her father's handwritten notes and letters—from them she'd discovered an alternate side to the man she'd always seen as pure evil. A man that had been broken before Ellie had even been born. It would not change the way he'd treated her, but it did show a marquis Ellie could have loved if she'd only known or been given the chance.

But, like Ellie, the late Marquis of Drake hadn't trusted easily, not even his daughter.

Ellie would be without a home if Alex couldn't see past her mistakes to the reasons behind them.

Suddenly, the light above her went dark, as if the room's occupant blew out the candle sitting by the window's edge. Looking up, Ellie saw someone had drawn the draperies closed— signaling not only the lateness of the night but also that it would be wise if Ellie returned to the ballroom. Someone would have noticed her absence by now. If not Ruby, then Marce for sure. And they would have questions Ellie would not—could not—answer, at least not tonight.

She rounded the corner of the house, heading toward the terrace doors when a cold blast of wind hit her, chilling her arms and cheeks.

The walk to the terrace proved her suspicions correct; the night had grown late—and cold—and guests had either taken their leave or sought refuge in the ballroom, away from the frigid night air.

Her meeting place with Alex had been sheltered from the elements, providing them a moment of privacy—away from the prying eyes of the many *ton* members. Alex had been right when he'd said their chance of creating a scandal was nonexistent, for neither of them was known to anyone inside the ballroom except the few people who genuinely cared for the pair. And none of them would seek to cause them harm or embarrass Lady Haversham.

She and Alex could have spent hours alone outside those double doors, dancing and laughing—but instead, she'd ruined their moment.

Music still floated from the ballroom as couples danced across the floor in an elegant way Ellie would never master. As she scanned the room, she noticed Ruby standing by the open door to the card room, her head tilted toward Mr. Jakeston's as they engaged in some deep discussion. In direct opposition, Marce stood on the far side of the room speaking with a man who stood a bit too far away—and too rigidly—to be conferring about anything more personal than the weather.

Payton, Jude, and Sam were among the *ton*

members swirling about the dance floor, Lord and Lady Haversham in their midst. The whole ambiance of the room was intoxicating, and she understood why so many spent their entire London season going from one entertainment to the next. Before her Christmas time at Foldger's Hall, Ellie had spent an evening at Covent Gardens with Ruby and Mr. Jakeston. She'd spent the entire evening trying to irritate her sister. Her antics now seemed childish. Every decision she'd made since her father's passing had been childish—and selfish.

But this night could have been different—if only she hadn't looked up to see Alex in the window above. She could have enjoyed her time with Marce and her sisters, maybe even had a pleasant conversation with Ruby, but instead, she'd said the one thing guaranteed to push away the only man she cared about.

"And where did you run off to, may I ask?"

Ellie leapt in fright. "Do not sneak up on me, Pay."

"Oh, do not change the subject." Payton stood beside her, her arms crossed over her chest. "I have been drowning in boring conversation about the weather and the pianoforte—all while you were off doing heaven knows what."

"You are wrinkling your gown," Ellie commented to distract the girl. "And I do not answer to you."

"Well, you can sure wager that Marce will not take your snide words."

"I am certain your sister will take more harshly your comments about gambling."

"I haven't been so much as tempted to peek inside the card room," Payton retorted. "Besides, the stakes are those that can be found in gambling hells all along the East End streets. I prefer a payout much grander than those found in London ballrooms."

"Again," Ellie pointed out, "something Marce will not be happy to hear."

"I will be married soon enough, and my sister will no longer have control of my comings and goings."

"And you think a husband will be any less strict with his wife?"

"If my winnings help earn my keep, then he should not take issue with where it comes from."

Ellie only shook her head as she walked away, leaving Payton to her own delusions. Ellie suspected any man Payton married would keep the girl under lock and key—as men did. The marquis had kept close tabs on Ellie her whole life, and they were only father and daughter.

She hadn't been around many married couples, but Ruby and Mr. Jakeston seemed to travel together for most things—and the same could be said for the Havershams. It was certainly so the men could keep watch over their wives.

Which was exactly the reason Ellie had no designs on marriage. She'd had an overabundance of years under the marquis' control to willingly tie herself to a man who had the rights, by law, to treat her like chattel. Many women may love their husbands enough to allow them control, but not Ellie.

Ellie made her way to Marce, where she stood alone watching Sam and Jude as their next dance partners collected them.

"How is your evening fairing?"

She certainly would not share her

impromptu dance with Alex beneath the stars, nor their argument after, but she did owe the Madame some answer. "Not as horrid as I'd feared."

"I am pleased to hear that," Marce said with a small laugh.

"Who was the man you were speaking with?" It was a sight Ellie rarely saw. Marce was much the recluse in her own right, though she hadn't turned to drinking as the marquis had. "Is he a friend?"

"Long ago, I considered him a close friend," Marce answered matter-of-factly. "But something changed a few years ago when his father passed away—and I've rarely seen him since."

Ellie spotted the man as he paused outside the card room for a quick word with Mr. Jakeston before entering. He was a dashing figure with a well-tailored coat, his neckpiece certainly tied by a manservant accustomed to fine knots. He stood taller than Harold with hair as dark as the night.

"He is handsome."

"And you will stay far away from him—his soul is as dark as his hair," Marce vehemently said. "If you ever see that man near Craven House—or any of my sisters—you will alert me immediately. Do you hear?" Marce grabbed Ellie's forearms as she spoke, squeezing tightly to get her point across.

"Of course," Ellie agreed, gently pulling her arm from Marce's constricting hold.

"Thank you," Marce relaxed at Ellie's agreement. "Are you ready to depart?"

Ellie looked to Ruby. They hadn't shared more than two words all evening. "I should speak with my sister before we go."

"I think that wise, please thank her for extending your invitation to include myself and the girls." With a nod, Marce started toward Payton, who stood where Ellie had left her, glaring in her direction. "Please, send for me when you are ready," Marce called over her shoulder.

There was much Ellie longed to share with Ruby, but the timing was all wrong. She needed to sort everything out in her own mind before dragging her sister into the mess she'd created.

The marquis had implored her to trust Alex.

Now she knew why—not only was he to inherit the Drake estate but also, Ellie must marry him to keep her home.

And that was exactly what had kept her from being honest with Alex from the very beginning. In her mind, it had nothing to do with trust and everything to do with her father dictating her life.

There was too much information to process: Alex's true identity as a duke and a marquis, Ellie's home being given to another, and her father's last decree for her to marry the man who would ultimately be responsible for taking everything she cherished from her. Not to mention the many pages of letters written to a long-lost love—Ellie hadn't thought the marquis capable of that particular sentiment. Anger, yes. Contempt, certainly. Violence, without a doubt.

But love?

Heartbreak.

Sorrow.

He'd never once ever so much hinted that any of those emotions lay within him. When, in fact, they had slowly eaten him alive—taking his ability to empathize and be compassionate long before Ellie could remember a man not drowning in self-loathing and regret.

If she were as selfish as Alex had accused her of, she'd tell Ruby everything, lift the full burden from her shoulders and place it squarely upon her sister's.

And repair the damage Ellie had done to her relationship with Alex.

It was important for Ellie to figure out her problems without encumbering Ruby and her new husband. Neither deserved to be dragged into the mess Ellie had created.

If that were her being self-seeking, then Ellie was fine with that. She at least wanted the opportunity to fix things herself before begging for Ruby's assistance.

Ellie hadn't a chance to really look at Ruby previously. Her sister was outfitted in a dress of fine silver, her hair piled atop her head to expose her long neck—something Mr. Jakeston had long jested had drawn him to his wife. Teardrop pearl earrings hung from her lobes, matching the strand around her neck. She was the height of elegance, a lady through and through. Ellie wished she'd been blessed with an ounce of her sister's naturally regal nature.

"Sister," Ellie greeted. "Thank you for the kind invitation."

Ruby smiled, and Ellie understood why her husband was ever so smitten with her—beyond her kind heart. "You will always be welcome. Harold and I will soon move into our new home, you are welcome to live with us." When Ellie shook her head, Ruby continued, "Or visit—as often as you would like."

"That is most caring of you, but—"

Her sister sighed, cutting Ellie short. "Will the day ever arrive when you treat me as family and not an acquaintance you have met in passing?"

Ellie had come a long way since the day she'd met her sister. The girl who'd openly pickpocketed in London's busiest district was gone. The girl who shouted, argued, and threw insults like a common man had disappeared.

Yet, her distrust had proven more difficult to overcome.

"I am trying, Ruby." She should admit that she didn't know how a family treated one another, but that would likely be one more thing Ruby would try to fix—and Ellie didn't believe another could repair her. The hurt was inside Ellie and not caused by those around her. If it were possible to reverse the years of damage, Ellie had to accomplish the feat alone. No one could fix what was wrong on the inside but her—for she was the only one who knew the vastness and depth of the damage. "But I can try a bit harder."

Ruby pulled her into a tight embrace, and Ellie hugged her back. "It meant much that you came tonight. I know this is not the sort of activity you enjoy—and neither do I seek all this undue attention—but it made it bearable to know that we did it as a *family*."

"No one knows who I am," Ellie confided. "Let alone that we are relations with a scandal-ridden past."

"I know who you are—Brock and Vi do, too," Ruby said as she pulled back, pushing Ellie to arm's length. "Besides, the nature of one's ties to another are not any more solid if known by all and sundry. I love you, no matter your sometimes disagreeable demeanor. And I am certain you will get used to my meddling ways. We accept each other for who we are—and that is what family does. We love despite our flaws."

Ellie prayed it was that simple because her flaws were many.

She wished for the hundredth time that she could tell all she'd learned to her sister, if only to have someone to share the burden with, but tonight, at a ball thrown in her sister's honor, was not the time nor the place to air their many family scandals.

"Good night, dear sister," Ellie said with a quick squeeze of Ruby's hand. "I will visit as soon as possible."

Instead of sharing all her troubles with Ruby, Ellie would leave the ball and return to her empty home, which would likely not be her home for much longer.

CHAPTER 18

ALEX RUBBED HIS hands up and down his face again. Nothing made sense—Mrs. Dutton had lied to him his entire life, and now Ellie was doing the same. He'd rather have two honest people in his life than an English countryside of manor homes with titles attached.

He hadn't made it any farther than the stiff-backed chair inside the double doors of Lord Haversham's study before he'd collapsed. The thought of bumping into a servant or guest in the corridor had kept him to the dim room—it was also quiet, allowing him time to think without fear of discovery. Mrs. Dutton would come searching for him shortly, he knew, but he was reluctant to give up the few moments of solitude he'd found.

To his dismay, it hadn't brought any clarity to his situation.

While he'd acted angry with Ellie for her deception, truly, he was hurt more than anything.

He'd risked his safety playing the marquis—and the whole while he'd only been assuming his true self.

There had to be more Ellie wasn't telling him—there simply must be. He had not imagined their closeness over the last few months—or her tendency to let her walls down when alone with him. That she hadn't trusted him enough to tell him sooner hinted to the depth of her impairment. She appeared solid and sound on the outside, but she was hurting on the inside—possibly past the point where he or Ruby could help her. What other reason could she have for staying guarded even with all they'd been through together?

Alex would never understand her reasoning for moving through life as she did. There was a world of people and things to experience; however, she preferred to hide, wasting valuable time without actually living.

He'd gone to her almost the moment he'd learned the truth about his past—she'd been the only person he'd longed to tell, yet she hadn't done the same. He need face the harsh fact that she might never feel as he did. She'd rather live a lie and keep the Drake townhouse to herself than risk him claiming what was rightfully his. The thought of pushing Ellie from her home had never crossed his mind. But he'd be lying if he didn't admit he found the idea of sharing the home—and their future—very appealing.

However, Lady Ellington had made it clear she wanted nothing of the sort—with him.

He would respect her wishes, but he would not allow her to keep hidden all the papers that could very well prove who he was—Lord

Chastain, a duke. Alex knew very little of his parents. Mrs. Dutton hadn't been with his mother long enough to know much of her past, besides what she'd shared shortly before her death, but she was a woman he longed to know—to somehow piece together the choices she'd made and the actions she'd taken to make sure her son grew up alone and without benefit of his real name.

Those files held secrets of his past.

And now that he'd learned the truth, he refused to live the life of a pauper and shirk his responsibilities.

If what Mrs. Dutton had said were true, Alex's mother hadn't taken his destiny from him, but enabled him to grow up without fear, allowing him a future where he was strong enough to take control of what was rightfully his when he was fully capable of all that came with it.

"Ah, so this is where you've been hiding." Lord Haversham stood in the open doorway. "Mrs. Dutton sent round a servant to ask if you'd returned from your earlier outing. She is worried."

"Not as worried as I'll be if I have to drink one more watered-down sherry," Mr. Jakeston said, pushing past Lord Haversham to enter the room. "Lucky man, you are. Wish I had the chance to hide." He saluted Alex with his empty flute.

"Good evening, my lord," he said as he stood. "And to you, Mr. Jakeston. I was out on the terrace—for a bit of fresh air. I was returning to my room—"

Lord Haversham held up his hand to stop him from speaking. "I am not your guardian or caretaker. You are a man and only a few years until your majority—a guest in my home—your comings and goings are none of my concern. Unless you want them to be, that is."

"Drink?" Mr. Jakeston called over his shoulder as he retrieved a tumbler from the sideboard and uncorked a bottle of clear liquid. Alex could only picture Ellie, kneeling behind him as she poured the fiery spirits down his exposed back. "Brock and I are having one—you must join us, Alex. I can tell something weighs on you."

Alex only shook his head no, cringing at the way Eckles had demeaned himself after over imbibing—though Alex knew the difference between a casual drink and tipping a bottle until it was dry.

Jakeston poured a healthy portion into two matching glasses, ignoring Alex's answer to his question then filled his own flute with a blushing red sherry. Someone must have stoked the fire while Alex had spoken with Ellie outside, for the hearth roared with renewed life.

"Come, sit with us." Lord Haversham dropped onto the lounge across from Mr. Jakeston, stretching out, his eyes closing. "Oh, I highly recommend the life of a father, but wish the hours were not so long. Why do children not understand the necessity of sleep?"

Mr. Jakeston handed Alex his drink as he sat in the last open chair. "A child cannot be as tiring as renovating an old, decrepit house. We have been working for months, and I fear the property is no more livable than it was the day I handed over every shilling I had for the deed."

"You know you are welcome to stay as long as it takes," Lord Haversham answered without opening his eyes. "Besides, Vi and I are very grateful for Ruby's help with the babe."

"It may come to that, I fear."

"Then you need to start importing your own sherry because you have about finished all that I have," Lord Haversham chuckled.

Alex sought comfort in the banter between the pair. It reinforced that not everyone was deceitful—and that true relationships built on honesty and care did exist, even though the two closest people to him had proven to be neither of late.

"So, tell us what ails you," Mr. Jakeston prodded as he sipped his drink, his lips stained a light ruby red. "You can distract us old men from our boring, mundane existence."

Alex planned to call on Lord Haversham for advice, but he hadn't had the time to think through all the options open to him, nor the opportunity to read through the files sent from the solicitor's office. They very well may not give him any new information about his past, but they'd give him the knowledge of how he'd come to inherit the Drake title and vast estates—leaving Ellie homeless and, if her many stories of the marquis' cruelty were true, penniless, as well. Not that Alex would condemn her to that fate, even with her recent actions—he had no use for anything associated with the Drake title; even if the laws provided he keep the title for appearances, she was welcome to use the property and wealth that came with it at her own discretion.

He'd grown up with nothing, so even if the Chastain estate were bankrupted, at least he'd have a roof over his head—everything else he would deal with as needed.

"Are you going to make us question you like a gaggle of nosey women?" Lord Haversham asked, sitting up. "Take a drink and get to talking...we cannot escape our wives for long."

"I..." Alex paused, bringing the tumbler to his mouth. The liquid burned the entire way down his throat but warmed his insides. "I am unsure where to start. Not enough time has passed for me to understand everything."

"Start with what is worrying you most at the moment," Mr. Jakeston offered. "You appeared fairly desolate when we entered. What were you thinking about?"

"Can a man live his life without accepting his responsibilities?" The question was vague, giving both men a chance to give advice without the burden of what truly ailed Alex. "I am not running from it, mind you. Only wondering if the option to ignore its existence is plausible."

Both men laughed. Lord Haversham's a deep chuckle while Mr. Jakeston's was on the melodious side.

"Did I say something comical?"

"You ask us about accepting responsibilities?" Mr. Jakeston stopped laughing long enough to ask. "I, a man raised to take over as vicar on the Haversham estate, who spent years arguing with his father, gallivanting about London with Brock—and fairly ignoring his mother's many requests to return home."

"Oh, I think I can beat that," Lord Haversham sobered. "I spent almost ten years risking my life in battle to avoid dealing with the death of my twin brothers and avoiding my distant father, who died alone because I was too selfish and angry to stay in England."

"Yes, Lord Haversham is correct," Mr.

Jakeston confirmed. "We know nothing about responsibilities or ignoring them."

For the first time since Mrs. Dutton and he had spoken the night before, Alex felt a bit of pressure lift from his shoulders. If Lord Haversham and his friend had spent years running from their obligations, yet, now lived such fulfilled lives, then maybe Alex could, too.

"If you could go back in time, would you accept your obligations immediately or do exactly as you did?"

Lord Haversham scratched his jaw in thought. "That is difficult to say for certain. I had much pent-up rage and my need for vengeance was overpowering. I would not have been able to forgive Vi for her hand in my brothers' deaths—and I cannot, at this moment, picture my life without her by my side."

"Much like Brock," Jakeston said after draining his flute once more, "if I had taken to my father's insistent call to take my future as a vicar seriously, I would not have been in London nor would I have met Ruby. If I hadn't wormed my way into her search for her father, then she likely would not have tied herself to a man such as myself."

"Oh, do not sound so dire, Harold. What woman can resist a man so in touch with their sensitive side? Speaking of, Lady Haversham inquired today on how your needlepoint is coming along."

"I am seriously reconsidering my living arrangements," Mr. Jakeston mumbled. "Either way, you can only run for so long—and sometimes avoiding your responsibilities only makes it more difficult to handle once you decide the right time has come."

"Maybe if we knew a bit more about your predicament then we could better offer you advice."

Alex felt he owed the men something—maybe not the whole gravity of his situation, but more than he'd offered thus far. "I have recently learned who my true parents were."

"That is wonderful news," Lord Haversham said with a joy Alex didn't feel. "That should give you a bit of security."

"I wish that were the case, my lord. But with that information came the brutal news that the woman who raised me had kept their identity secret my whole life." Alex didn't know if he could hold a grudge against Mrs. Dutton for long. "But in her defense, she was doing exactly as my mother had requested of her."

"Mrs. Dutton does not have a malicious bone in her body," Lord Haversham confessed. "She is one of the most selfless woman I've yet to meet. I am certain she did what she thought was best."

"I do not doubt that to be true," Alex agreed. "But our lives could have been less difficult had she been honest with me."

"And would you have gone against your mother's wishes?" Mr. Jakeston asked.

Neither men knew anything of what he spoke about—not his parents' deaths, his right to the Chastain estate, or his claim to Drake's title. He'd kept more from them than what he'd shared, yet the men had given solid advice.

"I do not know what I would have done with the information, but I do know I would have valued the choice."

"Sometimes choices are not as great an option as one thinks." Lord Haversham stood to refill his glass. "With knowledge comes the unequivocal need to make a decision—to do something. The age-old adage that ignorance is bliss comes to mind."

"That is very wise, my lord." Alex set his tumbler on the table beside him, the fiery liquid not something he enjoyed when other fiery things were much more to his liking. "I suspect it was best that I found out now as opposed to discovering the truth at a tender age."

"See, Harold," Lord Haversham proclaimed, slapping his knee with his free hand. "We are wise. Alex, is there any way you will repeat that sentiment to our wives?" Both men laughed once more, finding Lord Haversham's request quite comical.

Alex wished he were secure in his own identity to be as carefree as the pair before him. Though he couldn't help but think if things had been different, he would have been raised their equal—and not a servant.

It was Ellie who'd given him his first glimpse at who he actually was. Draped in the fine clothes a few days prior had felt right, truer than the stable garb he donned each day.

"I should find Mrs. Dutton before she sends out a search party to locate me. Thank you for taking time to speak with me." He needed to be gone from the room before either man asked a question he wasn't ready to answer. "I bid you both good night. I have much to think over—and someone to see first thing on the morrow."

He was almost to the door when Lord Haversham said, "Do not let the woman go long thinking you will not forgive her."

They no longer spoke of Mrs. Dutton, though Alex hadn't a clue how they knew of any other woman consuming him. His thoughts—

and theirs—going to the one woman, Ellie, who overshadowed every doubt in his mind.

"That suggestion is welcome—and do not fear, I cannot go long without her in my life."

CHAPTER 19

ALEX SAT IN the same cramped office as he had a few days prior, new crates and stacks of files filling the spots where Drake's papers had previously resided. The office had been locked tight with no lights showing through the windows when he'd arrived an hour before; but Alex had been at a loss for where to find answers.

Mr. Adams had mentioned knowing Lady Chastain, Alex's mother. It still shocked him to realize he had a mother—he'd grown accustomed to the idea that others had mothers, but Mrs. Dutton had been as close as he'd ever gotten to one.

Once the notion had taken root, Alex had had to learn more, by any means necessary, before he spoke with Ellie or Lord Haversham.

And so, he'd departed Haversham House and pounded upon the door of Mr. Adams' office until the man had stumbled down the stairs within, still in his night clothes and wiping sleep from his eyes.

If the man had been surprised to see Alex at such an ungodly hour, he hadn't mentioned it as he'd ushered Alex into his office and disappeared to make himself presentable.

That had been...

Alex glanced at the tall clock against the wall for confirmation.

Near thirty minutes before.

There was nothing left to do but wait—and hope the man could impart more information than Mrs. Dutton possessed.

"Aw, my lord," Mr. Adams greeted as he walked into the room. "It is nice to see you again."

Alex leapt to his feet, for a minute forgetting his place as he stopped short of bowing his head in respect to the man. "Mr. Adams," Alex said, retaking his seat. "Thank you for seeing me."

The man pulled his hand through his messy hair, as if flustered at the thought of a duke who was happy to gain an audience with *him*. "I apologize for missing you the other morning, but your housekeeper assured me you would be notified of my visit."

"Ah, yes." Alex pressed his palms into his thighs, searching for another train of conversation without appearing the vulture he felt. "I appreciate your swiftness in delivering all the papers. It is just...I have a few more questions."

"Certainly, my lord." Adams felt about his cluttered desk as he spoke; his fingers finally locating this spectacles. "I am at your disposal. As you likely noticed, all estate accounts are up to date, and the roof situation at your country estate was mended as soon as I was told—"

"Hmmm, no," Alex interrupted. "I have no concerns over my estate matters."

The man sat up a bit straighter in his seat, as if preparing for damning news.

"I am here in regards to my mother—and father," he added as an afterthought. Alex knew that once his petition was filed to claim his estate, his father's home would give him a wealth of knowledge about his father, the late duke, but Mrs. Dutton had said his mother was not from England and was only married to Lord Chastain for a short time before their passing. "You said you were acquainted with her, am I correct?"

"Why, yes, I did say that, didn't I," he mused. "Sometimes I speak of things I know nothing about."

"But you did know her?"

"Of course, but I fear not as well as you'd think."

Alex was desperate for anything the man could tell him; even the color of her hair was a mystery to him.

"I certainly have no more information than your father's servants could have imparted over the years."

Alex needed to stick as closely to the truth as possible, for Adams was unaware he hadn't been raised as the future duke. "My parents were not long married before my birth—and their passing."

Adams bowed his head as if saying a short prayer or feeling mortified he'd made Alex speak of his parents' deaths.

A deep ache started in Alex's gut, muting the pain that still lingered in his back. He ached for something—*someone*—he'd never known. His mother had been stolen from him.

"I only wish to know more about my mother, that is all," Alex admitted. "The servants did not know her well." He kept his voice level, as if they spoke of shipping trends or a cold and wet storm front approaching. Something about allowing this man to see how vulnerable Alex felt unnerved him.

"There is not much to tell," Adams paused, looking off as if trying to remember something of import about the late Lady Chastain. "There was much talk when she arrived in London, but she married your father, the duke, quickly—at his country manor."

It was already something Alex hadn't known.

"They must have enjoyed a whirlwind courtship, for they married, and no more had they returned to London than your mother was with child." Adams smiled. "But that certainly put the Marquis of Drake in the foulest of moods. I think he was smitten with your mother and felt slighted when she chose your father over him."

Without realizing it, Alex sat on the edge of his seat, leaning in toward the solicitor as he hung on every word the man uttered; he begged his body to regain its position further into the chair. "Yes, I had heard that she had not been in London long, but the servants, they did not know the exact place of my mother's birth."

Adams could not be further from the truth with his thoughts of a whirlwind courtship between Lord and Lady Chastain. Mrs. Dutton had made that very clear. His father, Lord Chastain, had been a very angry man.

"On that account I fear I cannot be more helpful, I do know it was somewhere in France, as I said before." Adams eyed him, and Alex hoped the man only saw a son longing to know his parents, which was accurate. "There was much gossip about your mother after her passing—rumors flew and the papers even reported she and her parents were sent by the French to spy on our country."

Adams laughed in an attempt to lighten the mood, but his words aligned exactly with what Mrs. Dutton had hinted at. Was it possible the scandal pages had the correct information?

"Yes, that is outlandish," Alex laughed along. "I cannot imagine what made them report such nonsense."

"Oh, it was something about her parents fleeing the country—and a Frenchmen found stabbed to death in a London stable. I guess they assumed one dead Frenchman must be connected to all other people of French birth in our city. It was absurd...and hurtful to your parents' memory."

"Most undoubtedly absurd." Alex regretted missing the chance to speak with Drake before he'd passed away, but didn't understand why the marquis hadn't spoken to Alex about their connection. It was a link to his mother that he'd never gain back, someone who knew her—truly knew her—on a level far deeper than servant to mistress. "And what about my mother's relatives? Someone must have escorted her to London."

"Oh, yes." The man's eyes lit as if he remembered some long-lost obscure fact. "The comte and comtesse. Your mother was of French nobility, though the English tend to overlook foreign nobility. They left London following Lady Chastain's passing—disappeared into thin air, they did. I believe their hasty departure also lent a mysterious air to your mother. The marquis spent many years searching for them— and much money, too. He brought me letter after letter sent by private carrier to France. If he received any response, it did not come through my office."

"But eventually, he stopped coming to you to post the letters?" Alex asked. His mother had been the daughter of a French count—and more than likely a spy; it had Alex asking himself, why? Why London and why Lord Chastain? It would make sense if she went against her parents and married for love, but that wasn't the case according to Mrs. Dutton.

"Yes, a little over ten years ago, if I remember correctly," the man confided. "That was about the time he brought me several boxes of miscellaneous papers and letters. He instructed me to safeguard them until you came for them—and then our meetings became fewer and fewer, until one day he instructed me to handle his affairs as I saw fit."

"Is that common?"

"Nothing with the late marquis could be classified as common." Adams cleared his throat before continuing, "Do forgive my forthright reply, my lord. Is there anything else you wish to know? There is not much more I can tell you."

"My mother, what did she look like?" It made no sense, but for some reason, Alex needed to hear about his mother from another man's view; not Mrs. Dutton, who saw her as little more than a girl too young for the responsibilities forced upon her. "Can you tell me?"

Red crept up from the man's collar and

spread across his face. "Ah, well, you see," he stammered. "I only caught sight of her once and it was from a distance, but she had hair of the darkest black and eyes that fairly glowed when she looked at you—not that she ever turned them on me, mind you."

"Of course not," Alex agreed with the man, hoping he'd keep talking.

"But I can certainly see why every man spoke of her as if she were an angel sent from heaven—I remember her being ever so tall and regal. She was destined for great things, before—" He immediately cut off his next words, but Alex knew the solicitor was about to say *before she died*. "Oh, well, unpleasant business and all. Is that all?"

When Adams stood, Alex knew their meeting had come to an end and he'd learned all he could from the man, or all the man was willing to share.

Alex followed suit, thanking the man for meeting with him before departing. The day was still early, certainly too premature for a morning social call, but Alex needed to speak with Ellie and find out what information, if any, the boxes held about his mother—and her ill-fated life.

ELLIE LOOKED AT the heaps of papers and stacks of files taking over the room. Not a thing beyond what she'd already known had been learned in her many hours of reading. All the night had produced was a sore back and aching eyes.

She wanted her bed—but first, she need

prepare everything to be delivered.

"I want it all put back in the crates and trunks it came in," Ellie instructed the two footmen who stood in the doorway. "As quickly as possible, if you please."

She was exhausted beyond reason, and she still wore her gown from the previous evening. She'd no more alighted from the carriage from Lord Haversham's before she'd set to work immediately.

And the pretty frock she'd spent an exorbitant amount of her stashed coin on was ruined—dirt and ink marred the delicate blue material, unlikely to be scrubbed out.

"I have organized as much as I could." She pointed to a rather high stack, which leaned precariously to the left as if to topple at any moment. "That over there should go in the black trunk. The rest in the smaller crates."

"Yes, m'lady," the footman said. "And we be take'n it ta Haversham House."

"That is correct." Ellie paced the room as the men started loading the many crates, thinking of what she'd decided. There had been two discoveries made during the long night. One, if she gave Alex all the papers, he'd have no other choice but to forgive her.

The other was that she couldn't live without him.

And if, after handing all the crates over to him, Alex still wished her gone, at least it would put her mind at ease knowing she'd done the right thing—in the end.

The two men packed everything faster than she'd been able to unload it all, which was favorable because it didn't give her time to change her mind. If she wanted to be like her father, she should burn every paper in this room—deny any of its existence and continue the charade as mistress of her father's home. But if she wanted to prove she was not the selfish, cold-hearted girl Alex thought she was, then she needed him to have everything, allow him the chance to decide for himself if he would throw her from her home. She wouldn't blame him for the decisions he made, one way or the other.

Ellie had made many decisions of late, and none of them for the best. But this—sending all the papers to him—was right.

If last night hadn't happened, Ellie didn't know if she'd have ever shared with him what she knew. And that was exactly her father's child.

The realization scared her more than the possibility of having everything she cherished stripped from her.

Her days following in her father's destructive path were over.

A future, fated to be alone, drinking herself into oblivion without anyone who cared nor noticed. It was certain to be her fate if she continued as she was. She would fight with all her might to make it not so.

Alex losing faith in her was the one thing she could not live with, even if he chose a path without her—she would not let him go thinking she was the monster she'd proven herself to be. She'd never thought to consider another's opinion of her, but she cared what the damn man thought.

If she were honest, she more than cared what he thought of her.

All she'd done over the last year had been for him, despite everything ingrained in her by her father. Alex had pushed her to realize that who she was would never be based on her past, but on the future she sought to have.

Ellie wanted Alex back at Drake House—permanently, even if that meant becoming his wife. How much better could she prove she trusted another than to give him full control—over her home and her body?

"It be ready, m'lady."

"Have it all taken immediately to—"

"What is going on here?"

Ellie looked to the open door.

"Do not touch anything." Alex stood just inside the room, his hands on his hips, blocking the footmen from leaving, as he looked her up and down; Ellie wearing her wrinkled and now stained gown from the previous night. "I said, what is going on here?" She'd thought him angry in the gardens, but he had both footmen stumbling back now, setting the crates they carried back on the floor. "The pair of you—go!"

"Alex, I was—"

"You were just what?" his voice thundered, filling the room as he stepped aside to let the footmen leave. "Discarding any proof of my true identity?'

"No," Ellie countered, shaking her head. She walked toward him, her hands outstretched to calm him. "I was sending everything—"

"Back to the solicitor's office...to be thrown into the Thames...maybe you have located a cavern where they will never be found." Alex eyed the many crates now stacked neatly. "I can only imagine the lengths you would go to keep things from me."

His accusations ignited her fury. "Enough!" He took a step back at her shout, uncertainty clouding his face for the first time since he'd entered the room. "I was having it all prepared to be delivered to you—at the Haversham townhouse."

"And you expect me to believe—"

"I do not care what you believe," Ellie raised her voice further. "It was never my intention to keep any of this from you. I only needed the time to allow the muddled mess to sort itself out in my head."

"Why could we not figure everything out together?"

"Because I am the only one losing in this situation." Her voice rose with each word. "While you have everything to gain."

"I would never take anything from you," he said. The words should have reassured her, but anger still laced his tone.

"That is not your choice to make."

"Of course it is."

"It is not!" Ellie moved to the largest trunk and flipped the lid open, rifling through the top couple of folders in search of the one piece of paper that dictated her entire future. Finding it, she held it out to him. "This is what condemns me to a future not of my choosing—or yours."

He grabbed the paper from her without looking at it. "No one can command you to live a life not of your liking, my lady."

"We shall see if that changes." She crossed her arms over her chest. "Read it."

A puzzled look settled on his face and his shoulders stiffened as he read. He glanced up at her several times before re-reading her fate, as if he didn't believe it—couldn't believe it.

"The late marquis—your father..." he said breathlessly. "He did not know me. Why would he—"

"The man was—and still is—a mystery."

"But, he requires you to wed a man you barely know."

"We know each other a bit better than that," she said.

"Yes, but he did not know that would occur." Alex held the letter out to her. "Burn it—burn it all now. Free yourself."

"It would do no good," Ellie sighed, refusing to take the paper. "It is likely the solicitor has copies of everything in this room."

"I would never take your home if you refused to marry me." Alex set the offending paper on a small table and sat. "How could the man put you in this position?"

"He loved your mother," Ellie confided. "He thought he was doing right by her by securing your future."

"At the expense of his own child's happiness and well-being?" Alex shook his head. "I did not know either of my parents, but I am confident my mother would not have wanted that promise from him."

"I can speak for neither my father nor your mother for I didn't know him any more than I knew her." Ellie sunk to the lounge next to him. "But I can confirm it is all there for you to read. Every handwritten letter and note declaring his undying love for her, and his merciless search for you."

"You were truly sending it all to Haversham House?" Alex leaned back into the lounge, the tension draining from his body, only to stiffen again as his back made contact with the rough material. "After all the hurtful things I said."

Ellie hadn't wanted to fight with him, nor

push him away, but marriage? She still could not picture being wed to any man, let alone Alex.

"Can I ask you a question?"

"Certainly," Ellie answered, slouching into the cushion behind her, matching his pose. "I do not see where it could hurt."

"Do you want this house?"

"It is all I have." It was the only way to answer his question, but there was much more to ponder than that. "I have known no other, though it holds much grief."

"Then I shall never ask you to leave it." He slapped his hands against his knees, as if all their problems were solved with his simple question and her uncomplicated response. "I should be going."

"But you must stay," she said with alarm.

"No, that is not possible." He stood, stretching his arm out and squeezing his hand closed and then opening it again. "This may be your home, but it is not mine."

"You can return—I beg you."

He only shook his head, denying Ellie her only request. "I have a home—and a title—and it is past time I accept them and the responsibilities that come with it."

"You are leaving me?" She hated the desperation in her tone. The thought of needing anyone as much as she needed this man before her scared Ellie. "I am sorry. That is unfair of me." She looked down to her hands, clutched in her lap.

He leaned forward, using two fingers to tilt her head up so their eyes met once more. "I am not leaving you—I am going to make myself worthy of you."

"How can you be so selfless?" she asked,

holding his stare. "I have hurt you repeatedly—spoken to you less than respectfully. And still you do not cast me aside."

Alex sank to his knees before her, his hand still holding her chin. "At first, it was my duty to care for you. My loyalty as your servant—but then a promise made to your sister. The more I kept an eye on you, the more I saw a woman trying desperately to claw her way out of the mold her father had cast for her."

"I did not know I was in need of change, how could you see it?"

"Your care for others."

"I have tried hard to not let that weakness overtake my good sense."

"I don't see it as a weakness, but then why spend hours watching me from the rafters of the stable?" he asked.

"I—well…"

"And Ember?" he prodded. "There was no reason for you to bring the cat back to London. I made it clear that it would be taken care of in the stables at Foldger's Hall."

Ellie tried to pull her chin from his grasp, but he held firm. It was difficult to think clearly with him so close, all she noticed were his eyes, his lips, and the set of his strong jaw—making intelligible thoughts hard to align.

"You can speak with honesty, my lady."

"Ellie," she breathed. "My name is Ellie."

"Ellie," he pronounced her name slowly, letting each letter roll off his tongue.

"I do not want to suffer my father's fate."

"Which was?" His face was mere inches away, the warmth of his breath cascading across her cheek.

"I am not so sure now," she admitted. "I

knew I did not want to be cursed to live alone forever—angry and broken."

"And now?"

"I am certain I never want to be brokenhearted."

"Is your heart in danger, Ellie?"

More than either of them knew. Instead of saying those words, Ellie leaned forward and pressed her lips to his.

And she knew in that moment, her whole future was in danger, for she loved the man before her, and she was willing to give up her home and her heart to have him.

CHAPTER 20

ALEX SHOULD RELEASE Ellie—step back, allow her space to think, but instead, he wrapped his arm around her, pulling her closer as their lips met. Her breasts pushed against his chest while her hands found their way to his neck and caressed upward through his hair.

Her touch was pure, raw pleasure.

Something he'd never realized his life was lacking.

Alex ran his fingers down her back as their mouths danced, the soreness in his back faded, his desire for her overpowering all his senses.

Every thought of walking from the room, discovering his place in society, and returning for her when he could provide her with something more than a dry stall in a stable, fled his mind.

He only needed this woman—nothing else.

Ellie pulled away, her eyes searching his.

"Please," Alex moaned. It was his turn to beg. "Do not…" He had no idea what he asked for, only that he knew he needed more—of her body pressed against his, of her fingers running through his hair, and certainly more of her.

Anything to keep their troubles at bay and Ellie in his arms.

"You are not still cross with me for keeping all of this from you?"

"I do not remember a time I was angry with you, Ellie." Or how he could have been mad at her at all. They were both pawns in a much larger scheme—one that had been fated to happen long before either of them were old enough to speak. He pulled her forward once more and set his mouth to her jaw and pressed light kisses up until his lips pressed close to her ear. "I only want you to be happy," he whispered.

And if her happiness led to his happiness, all the better.

But he'd respect her wishes if what she wanted didn't include him, though he would not likely give up on her easily. He knew what happiness looked like; and it included fiery red hair and green eyes.

"I am unsure what happiness is." Her words startled him, and it was he who pulled back this time, his eyes searching hers. "Alex..." she paused, pressing a quick kiss to his lips. "My life has been filled with strife. Hurtful words and actions...deceitful intentions. That is what family is to me. Heartache and hurt."

"I can show you—"

"You deserve better than anything I could bring to your life."

"How do you know that?"

"Look what I have done to Ruby," Ellie said with exasperation. "She's only shown me kindness—and all I've given her in return is another person to worry over. I do as I please, when I please, no matter how it affects others. Most of the time, I do not even think about how my actions hurt others. I cannot be the type of person you seek to have."

"I am beyond tired of people thinking they know what is best for me or what I want in life." He stood to clear his head, pacing toward the door and back again. "I am through with hiding. I didn't know it, but I have been pushed into hiding since I was a babe, carted about the country when it seemed someone might have discovered Mrs. Dutton and me."

"I am sorry—" She looked about to burst into tears.

"You have nothing to do with my past," he reassured. "And now I find I could have had enough funds at my disposal so as not to have spent all those nights freezing, wrapped in the meager blankets Mrs. Dutton could afford. We could have eaten more than stale bread and plain broth." Once the words started flowing, he was unable to stop them, though he was likely to confuse Ellie with his ramblings. But she need know all before their relationship went any further. "I spent years blaming myself—and the burden I felt I had brought to Mrs. Dutton, for our constant moving about. If only I were able to earn my keep, if only my leg and arm were not so damaged, if only my parents hadn't abandoned me. Mrs. Dutton could have sought out real employment. She could have married again, had her own family. She wouldn't have been cast out by her relations, year after year. She would have been afforded a warmer coat if she hadn't been concerned with saving to buy a growing boy new shoes, larger breeches—shirts without the elbows worn through."

"You were never to blame," Ellie said from her place on the lounge. "You were a child—and Mrs. Dutton loves you so."

Alex felt this anger return, not at Ellie, but at the situation people had forced upon them both. "That does not matter to a boy—I was not raised in a traditional home, no man was present in my life, yet I still knew the import of taking care of those around me. All the hardships Mrs. Dutton endured were because of me...and the promise she made to my mother."

"She is a good woman. Whether she made the promise or not, Mrs. Dutton never would have let you go without care." Ellie stood, coming toward him and halting his pacing. She looked so different than a few months before, as if she'd matured in more than just her attitude. She stood a bit taller, more confident. "A person cannot help but be the best person they can be when around you."

"Have I made you a better person?"

The question seemed to confuse her more than their talk of happiness.

"I do not know, but I find I *want* to be better—to my sister and to you, *for* you."

They both spoke of things unfamiliar to them. He'd kept his insecurities to himself for so long, never speaking to another about the responsibilities he felt fell to him, and the suffering he felt was caused by his presence. His injuries had occurred in his infancy, but Alex took responsibility for the effects they'd had—if he'd only worked harder at a younger age to strengthen his limbs...

It occurred to him that he took on others'

obstacles as his own—caring overly about those around him—while Ellie seemed to have disconnected herself from others as a child. In the years Mrs. Dutton had spent time doting on him, Ellie had had the opposite experience.

The marquis had avoided his daughter, kept her hidden from others, but at the same time, deprived her of having anything outside his home. She received the worst of his outbursts—or so Alex had heard.

"The worst fate, for me, would be to never be any more than the daughter of a strumpet." She looked Alex straight in the eye when using the harsh word. "It was the insult he spent years hurling at me without thought. Did he not realize I would have happily been the daughter of a loose woman, if only to be accepted as *someone's* daughter?" She didn't wait for any response from him. "He thought himself alone, forsaken after your mother died, but what he didn't realize was we had each other. My mother was taken from me—and his one love from him—that fact alone should have bound us to one another. Brought us close, but instead, it created a sea of distance neither of us were willing to swim across to reach the other." She shook her head, looking away from Alex for the first time since she'd come to him. "I think to myself, if I'd only tried harder...if only I'd held my tongue and not stroked his fury so often...if only I had known the kind of child he would have been proud to call his. Sadly, no matter what, he'd never wanted me—or my mother."

"That cannot be entirely true." Alex's heart broke to hear the things she said. He wondered if he would have preferred a childhood raised by a father with no love, or if he'd actually fared better than Ellie as an orphan.

"Do you know how many times he referred to my mother as anything other than a harlot, a jezebel, or a woman of loose morals? Do you know what age I was when I learned my mother's name?"

He was at a loss for words, but knew she needed to speak hers—something she'd never been given in the past. He only took her hand and led her back to the lounge.

"I was seven the first time Marce came to me," she sighed. "It was shortly after Mrs. Bee— the marquis' housekeeper and the woman who cared for me—passed away. I was playing in the gardens, using sticks as dolls, when a woman— maybe ten years older than me—climbed the wall and dropped down by me. I would have screamed had I not been overjoyed to have someone talk to me—actually see me." She leaned against him, staring across the empty room toward the far bank of windows, their drapes flung wide to allow in the morning sun. "She sat with me for hours and no one noticed. She told me grand tales of faraway lands. Soon, she told me of my mother, who she was and what had happened. That her mother, Sasha, and my mother were friends. After a few months of visits, she snuck me from the marquis' house and took me to Craven House to meet her sisters. She showed me the exact path to take; one that kept away from busy streets and skirted less desirable areas along the way."

Ellie's need to keep others at a distance was something Alex could understand, but not why she continued to place him at arm's length.

A faint smile touched her lips and she appeared to be miles away—in a time not so harsh. "I know you wonder why I continue to frequent Craven House, even with its reputation, but the women—I may not be able to call them family—but they are the closest thing I have ever had to friends. Until you."

She looked up at him, and his breath hitched. "You are the loveliest creature I have ever beheld." Ellie's face reddened with discomfiture. "You are not the recipient of many compliments? I cannot believe that."

"I am not, Alex," she confessed. "Besides you—and my sister—no one takes much notice of me."

"Then I shall count myself lucky your intense beauty has been kept hidden this long," he continued. "After Lord Haversham's ball, I am certain men will come clambering to gain your favor."

"I hardly think so." She shook her head in disbelief. "I was barely in the ballroom."

"But you did dance, at least one dance?" he baited.

"I danced one perfectly exquisite dance in the arms of a man who is most suited to leading a woman about a dance floor." Ellie peeked up at him through lowered lashes, her embarrassment turning coy. The woman may have attended her first London soiree just last night, but she had long ago mastered the coquettish look of a blushing debutante—he only hoped she saved all her talents solely for him.

He raised an eyebrow in question.

"He was a perfect gentleman, if you must know."

"That is refreshing to hear."

"I enjoyed myself so much, I did not notice the chilly night air." She teased him now, bringing back to mind the short time she'd spent in his arms the previous night. "I only wish I hadn't ruined everything as quickly as it began."

"You did not ruin anything," said Alex reassuringly. "It was simply a shock."

"Does it set your mind at ease to know I only put the pieces together two short days ago?"

He'd thought she'd known far longer—it was one of the reasons he'd reacted so intensely. "I thought you sent me to the solicitor's office on a lark, knowing the whole time who I was— laughing at my expense."

Alex couldn't believe he'd admitted his deepest fears from the last day. If she'd been capable of deceiving him so, with no guilt, it wasn't likely she'd ever change, but he understood now why Ellie had held on to the secret for the short time she had.

"I would never." Tears clouded her eyes once more. "You must believe me, I debated every moment between when I suspected everything and the time you confronted me. It was the worst thing I could have done—when all I longed to do was go to you and disentangle everything together."

CHAPTER 21

"THERE IS STILL time," he whispered.

Ellington could not believe the compassion and forgiveness the man next to her was capable of—she'd known his protective side, the part of him that tried his best to guide her. She'd taken his actions as a need to bend her to his will, as her father would have. But never did she dream anyone could show her this level of kindness. It was his right to have the servants remove all the papers to the Haversham townhouse or Lord Chastain's residence and never speak to her again. Or worse still, cast her from the Drake townhouse for her deceitful actions. Alex was free to expose her for the fraud she was, spread her name and misdeeds before all of London as repayment for her horrible decisions.

However, he sat next to her, caressing her hand as she kept the tears at bay. All the while attempting to solve everything for her—without regard for his own circumstances.

How had she been so very wrong about him?

How had she doubted his intentions and motives?

How had she thought to live without him?

How had she ever believed there was any other future for her than by his side?

"Everything is so overwhelming." Ellington had thought of little else since her father's passing, except for a way to keep her home—not that the property was in any way sentimental, but it was the only thing she counted as hers. For this short year, she'd been in control of something—and no one had done anything to take it from her.

Drake House was the one thing she prayed no one *could* take from her. It was her independence, and without it, she would be beholden to another. A fate she wouldn't take to kindly. "What can either of us do?"

"I need only speak with Lord Haversham," Alex said. "I am certain he will know where to begin and a way to sort everything out. Also, Mr. Adams should know any recourse we may have."

"And the marquis' demand that we wed?" Part of Ellie yearned for Alex to yield to her father's demands, for it would make everything come easier—though it would be a selfish act that would benefit only her, when before, he was the one to gain.

"Ellie," he said, pulling her close once more. "I will never force you to do anything."

"But you have every right—"

"No one has the right to force you into a future not of your choosing, even your father—and especially not me." He turned to fully face her, holding her stare. "This is your home. It will always be your home. I will perish before I allow anyone to take it from you. If you refuse to marry me, it does not change what is already mine—and I will never take what is yours."

A man who did not seek to claim all and conquer anything denied him? One such as Alex did not exist, she was certain. "I do not deserve such kindness." It was everything and nothing, all in one simple sigh.

"You deserve much more than my kindness..." He let his words trail off.

Ellie sensed he had much more to say, and she wanted him to continue more than she needed air to breathe, but she feared next would come his declaration of an exception to his kindness. Possibly, '...much more than my kindness, but I shall claim what is mine,' or something else heartbreaking, something certain to take away all she'd begun to hope for once again.

The moment she started to truly believe in his words and trust in him, it would all be stripped away—promises that were never his to make.

Her father had made it so.

"Why can you not believe how I feel about you?" he asked.

She'd puzzled over that very thing many times. It wasn't only his feelings toward her that Ellie was unable to reconcile, but Ruby's and Marce's, too. "My life has not been one of care, hugs, and kind words." Ellie needed him to hear everything, and then, if he hadn't turned away from her, maybe she could have faith in him. "I do not doubt you—or that you believe every word you say, but have you ever wondered if we are not in control of our fate?" She paused but quickly continued before he shot down her thoughts, counting off the many ways their future seemed out of their hands. "Your mother made it necessary for you to spend your life hiding, my father kept me as little more than a servant in his home...and now, by some cruel twist, we are to wed, but what name shall we list when the bans are read? Am I to call you Peter? I do not know a Peter. And will you list your intended as the daughter of a marquis? How can you do that and leave my mother's name—and scandalous past—from the gossip rags?"

Ellie stopped to catch her breath as ten more poignant questions begged to be asked.

But she kept silent when Alex only smiled, not answering a single one.

"These are not questions that need answers today—or even ten years from now."

She knew once she told him everything he'd be gone—of course, no answers would be needed in ten years because he'd have long forgotten her by then. Likely moved on and matured into the duke he was meant to be. Ellie would not be surprised to learn he'd taken his seat in Parliament and spent his off-season traveling between his estates, mending his buildings, and tending to the people who depended on him for their livelihoods.

"Because none of it matters."

"Of course, none of it matters," Ellie repeated, hoping verbalizing the words would make them true; that in ten years, she'd forget all about the kindest, most generous, bravest man she'd ever met. That she could lie to herself and say he hadn't made her a better person, if not now, than in the years to come. That she'd remember him and smile.

When, in truth, her fate lie closer to her father's if Alex walked out of her life. She would only remember him with her heart breaking anew each time he came to mind.

She couldn't look at him any longer. The tears pooling in her eyes were on the verge of betraying her—and she did not want his pity. Ellie wouldn't stall his departure by using female tactics. It was not fair to either of them. Alex, in his extreme need to be good and kind, would stay by her side, though he'd made it clear it wasn't what he wanted. And she would only delay her own heartbreak, all the while knowing the longer he stayed, the harder it would be to let go—of him, the way he made her feel, and the future she couldn't stop herself from envisioning.

"Even if our love results in both of us being shunned by society and thrown from our homes," he whispered into her ear, her breath hitching, "at least we will have each other. We will make our own home. Now, would it be so awful to embrace the destiny the marquis planned for you—for us?"

She'd once thought a life tied to a stable hand the worst fate of all, living in horrid conditions with little guarantee of food or warmth, but in this moment, she'd be happy to walk out of the marquis' house, never to return, and allow whatever power ruled above to drive her fate, if only she could have him.

"I have spent my life doing the exact opposite of what made my father happy," she admitted. "However, I only see now that I was aligning myself with his fate in life, instead of carving my own path." It was the harshest reality yet for her. Ellie had thought all these years she was living—doing everything—in spite of him. She replayed what Alex had just said. "Did you say, love?" She lifted her face to stare straight into his eyes, knowing he could not hide from her there.

"I HAVE LOVED you—spent my life searching for you—for so long I cannot remember." Her eyes swelled with tears at his words. "Do not cry." He took her chin, lifting her face so she could look at him, and placed a gentle kiss near each eye, the taste of her tears moistening his lips. "I did not realize until recently what had been missing from my life. I'd always thought the gaping hole I knew lay inside me was due to my lack of family, but I have always had Mrs. Dutton and the children, and more recently, Lord and Lady Haversham. My heart still yearned for more. So I worked hard, strengthened not only my weakened limbs but also my mind. Yet the emptiness persisted to grow inside me until I feared falling in—and disappearing forever."

Pulling back from her, he saw her eyes were closed. Not clinched tightly as if to keep him out, but with her lashes lightly touching, her chin tilted up, and her lips—normally drawn in a straight line of displeasure—slightly open as if waiting for his words. Or his kiss.

"But you...being with you is slowly closing it, or maybe it is your presence that is filling me, making me more complete than I've ever been," he continued. "I'd started noticing the hole disappearing when we spent time together at Christmastide, and then when I vowed to keep better watch over you. For it could not be anything more than the sense of usefulness and satisfaction I felt at protecting you, but it is so much more than that."

Ellie's eyes remained shut, closing off her feelings, but she didn't pull away.

"Truly, everything began to change after our first moments together in the marquis' study. Do you remember?" he asked, fearing she wouldn't answer. The night likely brought back horrible memories for her—as she'd stumbled upon him after a nasty fight with the marquis.

"You made me smile," she said on a sigh. "The first one in a long time."

"It was that and your kindness at keeping my secret that began all this."

"I had only just found out I had a sister." Her eyes never opened, but the corners of her mouth turned up in a faint smile. "The marquis and I had gotten into a particularly harrowing argument only moments before—he'd hurled the foulest insults that day. I was ready to collect my things and escape into the night, but then I heard you."

"Reading the marquis' favorite tale and sitting in his prized chair."

"Yes." She leaned into him ever so slightly he wasn't sure if he only imagined it. "Your tone lulled the fury within, banished the hurt—if only for a brief moment."

He longed for more than only a brief moment, he wanted a lifetime with her.

"Your gall and straightforward nature were refreshing." She opened her eyes then, and he was lost. "I never had to examine your words or actions for hidden meanings or wonder what you hoped to gain from me—but I did. And I am eternally sorry for that. I have treated you horribly during our short acquaintance."

"It is much more than an acquaintance." He saw it as much more than that—and if Ellie didn't, he was doomed to follow the heartbroken path Drake had.

They'd spoken of many things—their troubled pasts, their less than desirable sires, and what they both deserved for the future; but none of this mattered if she didn't return his love. It was that one thing that would overcome any obstacle in their path.

"You have changed my view on many things," she said. "Though, I knew in my heart I stayed guarded. My father was incapable of showing his love, but that does not mean I suffer the same shortcoming. He was talented in finding my weaknesses and using them to hurt me, but you and Ruby do not deserve that treatment from me. So much time could have been saved—many relationships given hope to flourish—if I hadn't built the wall to keep the marquis out. All I succeeded in doing was keeping those who truly do care about me at a distance."

Alex allowed her to work through her own thoughts, settling on wrapping his arms around her as she spoke. Once everything was out, then they could work as one to put the pieces back together—and see what that revealed for them.

"If only I could go back, knowing what I know now." She relaxed into his embrace, something he'd never witnessed her do. "I would try to comfort my father. I would not have pushed Ruby away, maybe even accepted her offer of a home, but that would have taken me from you."

"And you do not wish to be parted from me?" It was all he needed to know.

"Never."

Alex pulled back quickly. Ellie's red hair framed her smiling face, the emotion behind that one smile traveling all the way to her eyes. It was as if a great weight had been lifted from her, allowing her to express her true self—and with it, came Alex's bliss. He'd never thought it proper—or sane—to hinge your happiness or contentment on another's actions or emotions, but he knew he'd never truly know either without her.

Genuine happiness.

Ultimate passion.

Lifelong love.

It all rested on Ellie.

He should feel ill at ease and worried, but this was different. She was changed—a new glow surrounded her not caused by a lit fire or the setting sun; it came from within.

CHAPTER 22

ELLIE RESISTED THE urge to kiss him for only a brief moment, fearing he didn't understand all she wanted. She would not be content if their moment ended in anything less than a kiss.

Leaning forward, she pressed her mouth to his.

And something inside her came alive. It was almost as if she could feel the blood heating in her veins and pumping through her entire body at an alarming rate. The closest sensation she'd felt to this was when the tip of Eckles' whip had licked at her arm, but this was all pleasure with no pain.

Unlike their previous kiss, this was not one of desperation or influence. The kiss was not in payment for any favor or future request. It was not one of them seeking to force dominance over the other or a petty plea for control.

When she moved her lips across his, Alex did the same, creating a rhythm from the unknown, much as their dance the previous evening had. They moved to an unheard melody, in complete harmony.

Neither hesitated when he pulled her onto his lap, his arms wrapping securely around her while Ellie's hands grasped his shoulders. Not because she feared she'd fall from her seat, but because, for once, she didn't trust herself. She quickly slid her tongue across his lower lip, parting their mouths for a moment. Her fingers tightened their grip as she struggled to keep her hands from moving to the front of his shirt—and unbuttoning the row until she reached where they disappeared into his pants.

Moving her hands over his shoulders, Alex stiffened as she touched down the back of his neck to his back.

"I am sorry—" She hadn't time to finish her apology before he pulled her to him, Ellie's breasts pushed tightly against this chest.

She'd never allowed another such liberties with her person—never had she relinquished her control over a situation. It was startlingly refreshing and raw at the same time. The thought of stripping herself naked before him, putting her vulnerability on display and trusting him not to abuse it, was all she wanted in that moment.

No matter the question, she would answer.

No matter the request, she would honor it.

No matter the consequences, she would risk it all.

There was no more hiding—from the world or him.

This thing—this connection with another, especially him, was something she hadn't known, nor ever dreamed of having.

But she did want it—Ellie wanted him.

And no other man would do.

If they survived this moment in each other's arms, laid bare before one another, then surely they could endure all future obstacles meant to test their commitment.

"Alex."

"Yes…"

"Did you mean what you said?"

"Yes," he answered quickly, giving her no doubt that he knew exactly what she asked. "But we can speak of such matters at a later time. For now, I would enjoy setting my lips to yours once more."

"You are ever the gentleman, Lord Chastain."

The smile dropped from his face, and she suspected she'd made a grave error in addressing him by his newly discovered title. But his hold on her didn't loosen, nor did his stare leave hers, leaving her to wonder if she'd made a terrible mistake or not.

Finally, he spoke, "I rather adore the sound of that, but only from your lips." To solidify his point, he lowered his head and placed a delicate kiss to her parted lips. "Now, we have much to handle."

"We?" she squeaked, fearing he meant their discussion from earlier and his suspicions that she was sending all the crates to be destroyed.

"Of course." He set her from his lap back to the lounge, creating a distance between them that Ellie hoped they could close again. But he took her hands in his and brought them close for a kiss. Still clasping their hands, he smiled. "Your father—and my mother—have made quite a mess of things, and we must sort it all out."

"Everything does appear chaotic and, at the

least, distorted for even us to comprehend. I cannot fathom anyone believing our wild tale. A stable hand who is really a duke—with claims to a Marquisate—and the child of a trollop who is intended to be his bride. Are *we* so much as agreeable to any of this?"

"Would you suggest we walk away and leave it all behind to fend for ourselves?"

"Of course not," she said. "But it all seems rather daunting."

"And when have you been one to shrink from a challenge or allow another to create something that you cannot overcome?"

Ellie laughed, a light, airy chuckle that she felt better for, the gravity of the situation a bit less now that she knew she wouldn't have to face everything alone—or fear losing her home. "I do not intend to allow the marquis to win."

"Ellie," he sighed, his face serious once more. "This is not about winning or losing. This isn't a competition nor your father's last bid to ruin your future."

"Then what is all this?" She pulled her hands from his and waved them at the many crates still stacked around the room.

"It is about giving us the future my mother and your father should have had—together."

Ellie shook her head in denial. She could not accept that her father had done any of this for *her*. Drake had spent years belittling her, punishing her, oppressing her—he denied everything she asked for, even his time and attention. And now, to learn he'd *planned* all this? There was little possibility that was true.

"It is about love." He released her hands and brought his to her cheeks, halting her shaking head. "Possibly, it was his vision for us to meet, connect like he and my mother had, and allow that feeling to take over. He did not know me, nor do I suspect he truly knew his own daughter and her ability to thwart any plan another had for her."

Ellie let his words wash over her, unable to grasp the enormity of everything.

"What he did not count on—or maybe he knew all long—was that we'd have the genuine, instant connection he'd planned for us. Maybe he thought by bringing me here, we'd meet and you'd disobey his every command and fall in love with me out of spite." He paused, as if his comment could have been the marquis' devious intent all along. "Either way, he ensured we would find one another—eventually."

"And you do not see his actions as cruel and controlling?"

"We cannot allow the past to dictate what comes next for us."

"What *is* next for us?" She'd waited as long as possible before asking the question, but the time was upon them.

"Certainly, a grand wedding—attended by all those we hold dear."

A wedding? "You would still consider marrying a bastard?"

"Only if you are agreeable to wedding the son of a suspected French spy."

"We are most assuredly an unlikely pair."

"Not true."

"How so?"

"When love is involved—as it is with us— nothing is unlikely. There is only one thing left for us to do."

Ellie wasn't sure she could handle anything else—at least before she was able to achieve a few hours rest, allowing her mind a brief respite. She hadn't slept at all the night before, and still wore her gown from the ball.

"We must call Lord Haversham here to discuss everything we've learned. He will know how we can sort this all out." He stood, bringing Ellie to her feet, as well. "As the mistress of Drake House, please have Lord Haversham summoned." He placed a quick peck on her cheek before releasing her hand and turning his attention to the many crates that held both of their futures within. "I think I would like to read some of the letters you spoke of."

ALEX STOOD IN the center of Drake's study, crates and trunks open around him with papers stacked on every available surface.

Running his palm down his face, he stared at the mess he'd created in the short time since Ellie had left to summon Brock and change into a fresh dress. He'd been happy for the privacy at first, but then he'd longed to have Ellie at his side as he discovered so much about his own mother, set to paper by a man who'd clearly loved her above all others. The marquis had searched for Alex for decades, never giving up, even jeopardizing his own health and relationships.

It was a great love, yet almost inconceivable to others.

Alex was torn. He wanted to celebrate the discovery of his past, but in rejoicing his good fortune and knowledge, it in a way told Ellie that her father's harsh treatment of her was forgivable because of the outcome of her situation. He did not agree that the marquis had any right to be cruel to his daughter only because she had been unexpected and unwanted. Her existence should have given him cause to give thanks, for the Drake bloodline would live on through her. She'd been a helpless babe when she'd been left on Drake's stoop, the unwilling participant to her father's less than savory activities; however, he'd treated her like it was all her fault.

And she'd lived her life believing that.

It would be a battle for Alex to break through that belief and free her to love him. It would be a slow process, but one Alex was certain to conquer—there was no other choice for him. If she left him, cast him aside, there would be no point in fighting for what was rightly his— his name and title.

It would all be meaningless without her.

Even more than meaningless, it would be undesirable to undertake it all without her by his side.

Without knowing it, he'd become dependent on her: her appearances in the stables, her continually challenging behavior, and her quick wit.

Pacing the room, he thought through all he'd read in the last hour: years of meticulous letters, documentation, and other notes kept by Drake, with some correspondence between Adams and the marquis. Everything was outlined, in detail, about Alex's 'suspected' kidnapping, Drake's efforts to locate him, his continued harassment of certain French officials as to the whereabouts of Lady Chastain's parents—Alex's grandparents. It was disturbing that the couple had volunteered their child for service, but then left her when things went awry. Drake had written of his suspicions that the couple had taken Lorelei's babe with them, but there had been no evidence of it or them since. The truth was, they'd left not only their daughter behind but their grandson, as well.

During the course of his reading, Alex had come to the conclusion that his mother had, in fact, saved him; given him to the one woman who'd raise him properly without entitlement or risk to his life.

A tap sounded at the door.

Alex turned with a smile, ready to greet Ellie on her return, but instead, Lord and Lady Haversham, Mr. and Mrs. Jaskeston, and even Mrs. Dutton entered with Ellie coming in last.

It was Christmastide at Foldger's Hall all over again, but this time, it was he who was overwhelmed and not Ellie.

The only one missing was little Neill, Lord and Lady Haversham's newborn.

As soon as the door shut, all parties went in separate directions. The women—Lady Haversham and Ellie's sister—flocked to Ellie's side while the men came to him.

"I hear congratulations are in order," Lord Haversham said with a large grin. Thankfully, he resisted patting Alex on the back in celebration.

"True enough, my lord," Harold announced with a curt bow. "A duke, huh?"

"How do you know?"

"I be confess'n everathin, me boy." Mrs. Dutton stood close to the door, the only one not inserted in a group; obviously still fretting over her years of loyalty to Lady Chastain. "It only be right ta tell m'lord what I done."

Alex only held his hand out in response, a silent plea for her to join him—and the group.

Mrs. Dutton frowned at his gesture, not

coming to him and refusing to meet his stare.

Suddenly, Ellie was at the older woman's side, whispering something in her ear—and her frown turned to a toothy grin as Ellie slipped her arm through the woman's and guided her to Alex.

No one spoke during this, or at least Alex didn't hear anything, too intent on the two women he loved more than his own life.

Mrs. Dutton—the woman who'd kept him safe and raised him to be a humble, caring man—and Ellington—the woman who held his heart and soul.

Little did he know in his youth that Mrs. Dutton had been raising him to be the perfect mate for Ellie. To be the man who showed her that not every person was out to manipulate or hurt her.

Alex would be forever grateful to Mrs. Dutton for making him a man strong enough to overcome any obstacles to be with the woman he loved.

And he did love her—a soul-shattering, bone-deep love. The emotion wasn't as foreign to him as it was to her.

"Me boy?" Without thought, Alex stepped forward and wrapped his arms around both women, bringing them close. "I be sorry for keep'n ye hidden for so long."

"You did exactly as my mother asked," he said. "And I will never fault you for that."

"There you have it, Mrs. Dutton." Ellie pulled back and stared between the pair. "Alex is incapable of thinking the worst of situations and people."

"Oh, Ruby," Lady Haversham sighed, making sure she was loud enough for all to hear.

"We certainly had these two figured out long before they did."

Ellie's gaze whipped to Ruby with question. "What does she mean by that?"

Her sister swatted at her dearest friend's arm. "I suspect I haven't the faintest clue what she speaks of. I hear motherhood can make the mind go dull."

Both women giggled and retreated to the two chairs farthest from the men and closest to the windows. Their heads leaning together as they whispered happily.

Alex didn't know what Lady Haversham had meant by her comment—and he didn't care.

He cherished the realization that the people around him were happy and content.

And he longed for that for him and Ellie. A day when they could sit and talk about everyday things such as the weather, when they would travel to the country, and whom they would dine with. It was the most mundane idea—one that would likely send Ellie running—but it would be heaven for him. A life filled with everyday responsibilities, without fear of hunger or cold.

"You both are incorrigible, and your husbands should keep you on a shorter lead," Ellie huffed, still holding tight to Mrs. Dutton. "Why they encourage you both so much is beyond me."

Alex chuckled. His Ellie would never allow life to be stagnant or retreat into dullness. He was never more certain of that until she moved from Mrs. Dutton's side to stand before the two giggling women, her hands on her hips. Little did she realize Ruby did the same thing when she was peeved.

"Ellie," he called. "We have much to discuss

and my lord and Mr. Jakeston are not here to waste time."

"Vi was shocked to receive your note asking us to visit," Lord Haversham said.

"Correct," Mr. Jakeston confirmed. "The pair about pulled us from the house without waiting for the carriage to be brought round."

Alex looked between the pair, once again sensing the need for a friendship close to theirs. "Can we sit? There is much to discuss, and I'm unsure where to start."

"Of course." Lord Haversham moved to the massive desk, sitting in one of the vacant chairs, leaving one for Jakeston and the seat behind the desk for Alex. "We have all the time you need."

Alex rounded the desk, sidestepping a crate, and eyed the large chair. He'd seen the marquis in it only once when he'd taken the wrong hall and passed by the partially open study door. The man had been sitting in the chair, staring off at nothing. Now, he wondered if he'd been dreaming of Alex's mother—and he wasn't sure how he felt about that.

"Go on, me boy," Mrs. Dutton prodded. He looked up to see every eye in the room on him. Ellie nodded in encouragement, a rare smile settled on her lips. "It be yer chair, me certain a it."

"This is nothing I ever longed for."

"That is why you are the perfect man to claim the title as your own," Ruby said from across the room. He and Ellie's older sister got along well, but he'd never stopped to think if she'd approve of him as a husband for Ellie— he'd been little more than a servant his entire life. "You are impeccable for so many roles."

"Thank you, Mrs. Jakeston." He sat in the

chair as everyone in the room beamed at him. "You are all very kind to come and help us sort this mess out." The chair he inhabited had always looked huge sitting behind the desk, certainly too large for any one man to need, but he found that the chair fit him perfectly, hugging his sides. Testing his injuries, Alex leaned into the soft back. Not a single twinge of pain greeted him—maybe it was his fate.

Everything moved quickly from there as refreshments were sent for, the women mingled by the windows, and Alex—with Ellie by his side—explained everything they'd read in the marquis' paperwork.

Even baby Neill was called for—as Lady Haversham was filled with worry, leaving him for so long.

Not long into the conversation, Mr. Adams, the solicitor, was sent for. Lord Haversham knew there was much they needed to do for Alex to claim the Chastain title and estate, but he figured that Adams would know more.

A tap sounded at the door as Alex and Mr. Jakeston were sorting papers, setting the many private letters written by the marquis aside for Ruby to read. Ellie had also taken the papers detailing the marquis' plan that they wed, shuffling them into the top drawer. He understood she wasn't ready to tackle that discovery just yet...and maybe she never would be.

However, Alex would not give up faith in the design that Drake had conjured up all those many years ago. He'd let Ellie know that his feelings went far beyond friendship. That was all he could do for now—and hope the passion they'd shared with only a couple of kisses meant she felt the same.

Time. Ellie needed time—and possibly space. He would give her all she asked for.

"My lord." Adams stepped into the room and gave Alex a deep bow before turning to Lord Haversham and finally Mr. Jakeston in greeting. "Wonderful to see both of you again."

"I was happy to receive word requesting an audience, my lord." He pushed his round spectacles up the bridge of his nose where they'd fallen when he bowed. "As I said, there was much the marquis bid I give you when the time came. I am only regretful I was unable to attend to this matter immediately after his passing."

CHAPTER 23

QUICK INTRODUCTIONS WERE made round the room and a chair was brought for Mr. Adams, as Ellie tried her best to blend into the background. This was all happening so fast, and Ellie wanted nothing more than to be alone with Alex. There was much left for them to discuss— she hadn't the opportunity to tell him how she truly felt. Then she'd gone and done the worst thing imaginable by slipping the papers discussing their betrothal into the desk as if she were ashamed or opposed to the match. Although a mere few days prior, she would have been vehemently in opposition to marriage of any type.

Alex must think her the worst sort of person.

"Lastly," Alex took her hand and stepped around the desk. "May I present, Lady Ellington?"

She glanced to him, her nervousness certainly showing on her face, but it quickly vanished. Alex smiled back at Ellie as if it were his greatest honor to present her.

"I think we have met before, but it is certainly nice to make your acquaintance, Lady Ellington," Adams bowed.

She knew the solicitor was likely to expose her and Alex's ruse—for the only place she'd met Adams before this moment was when he'd delivered the crates housing her father's personal records.

"The marquis spoke of you frequently during our meetings," he said with a wink.

"He spoke of me?" Ellie whispered, unsure if she were relieved at his confidence or shocked her father had spoken of her.

"Of course," Adams continued. "I even caught a glimpse of your red hair once—I think you could not have been older than six or seven at the time. Your father was very protective of you."

Ellie wanted to scoff and make a snide retort regarding her father's intentions, but she wisely kept silent. Her smart mouth would not help the situation before them, nor speed things along. Besides, it was time she was her true self, no longer hiding her nature behind a sour disposition to keep others from hurting her. It was no longer necessary to hurt another before they were able to hurt her.

The realization was freeing in so many ways.

She was free to be whom she'd always dreamed of being.

"It is lovely to meet you," Ellie said instead. "I would like to thank you for preserving my father's correspondence so thoroughly."

"I…well…" Adams stuttered as if embarrassed to receive such high praise. "I am just grateful the marquis trusted my abilities. I rarely saw him in recent years, but gladly stored any papers he sent round to my office."

"We are very thankful," Alex said, allowing Ellie to sink into the chair next to his behind the desk. It created a barrier of sorts and gave her a sense of protection from everything going on around her. Alex also returned to his chair, taking her hand in his, their clasped fingers hidden by the desk. He squeezed hers, reassuringly.

They were a pair—first and foremost, it said.

With him close, Ellie would never have anything to fear.

"I am certainly happy to see that the marquis' presumptive and forward thinking is agreeable to you both." The man smiled. "I suspected my lord, may he rest in peace, had lost his senses when he'd asked me to draft the papers."

"What papers?" Harold asked.

"That is not what we called you here—" Ellie started.

"Lady Ellington and Lord Chastain's betrothal, of course."

"Their what?" Ruby shot to her feet and was next to her husband in a second. "What do you speak of?"

Adams stared from Alex to her, to her sister and back again, his eyes as big as saucers, knowing he'd once again made a grave mistake. "I...ummm...certainly..." he babbled as he retrieved a crumpled handkerchief from his pocket and dabbed his perspiring forehead. "I seem to be botching much with the Drake estate. I will not look unfavorably on either of you if you select a new solicitor."

Ruby and Harold stared at the man, mouths gaping. Lady Haversham had also joined the group around the desk and tightly clutched her husband's arm, her other hand covering her mouth. Mrs. Dutton seemed to have lost all her senses as tears spilled over and fell down her face in heavy waves, her emotional status hitting a vulnerable peak at the new turn.

Ellie had no idea how they were to explain things to everyone when they weren't sure of her father's motivations themselves.

Suddenly, a deep laugh filled the room—it took her a moment to realize it came from Alex.

"Oh, this is rich." He chuckled. "Your faces..." Alex looked to the shocked faces around the room. "Imagine if the marquis' decision hinged on this moment. A rare moment of truth, shared by so many people at one time." All the while, he held Ellie's hand firmly in his.

"What be so funny?" Mrs. Dutton asked, her tears never slowing.

Ellie wanted to ask the same question.

"This is rather shocking, even for my father." Ruby eyed Alex, and for once, Ellie noted their severe resemblance. "I will not allow him—or his silly papers—to force you into any marriage."

She wanted to leap from her seat and hug her older sister. It was her simple decree convincing Ellie that Ruby did indeed care for her bastard, wayward sibling. Or possibly, she always had, but it was Ellie who'd needed to see her actions more clearly.

"Ruby." Ellie gave Alex's hand a quick squeeze before releasing it and standing. She had much to say to him and she owed him so very much. "Your support means the world to me— and I can only pray it continues after Alex and I are wed. Our relationship matured at some point from friendship to affection, and I can assure you I will have no other as my husband than him." Ellie kept her eyes trained on her sister, afraid to behold Alex's reaction to her declaration. She feared she'd read too much into their kiss and his talk of love.

"I think that is wonderful." Ruby made her way around the desk and took Ellie into her arms. For once, she relaxed into the embrace, seeking any comfort her sister could spare. "Harold and I will be honored to have such a fine man in our family."

Tentatively, Ellie glanced toward Alex, judging his reaction to her words, but his face was a complete mask—neither showing elation nor fury. He was unreadable as he sat stoically at her side, and she feared she'd made a terrible mistake.

"Alex..." She held her hand out to him when Ruby released her. There was a hint of a question in the single word—a plea. She'd made her feelings known, and she only waited for him to rebuff her—it would only hurt all the more in front of the group who'd gathered.

Adams would witness her disgrace firsthand and need no further information...Ellie had tried, and it would be Alex—or Peter, whatever he chose to be known as—who'd rejected her. It should give her some sense of comfort with him knowing she'd not willingly went against her father's final wishes.

She forced a smile to her lips, preparing to push off her words as meaningless utterances by a distraught female. Certainly no one would think her serious.

The blow would be severe, but Ellie was

strong. Strong enough to live through the years of mistreatments and punishments dealt her way by the marquis. Her heart would mend faster than her pride, she was certain. The shame of her affections being rebuffed was what worried her—what else could it possibly be? She'd only discovered the depth of her love for Alex recently. They could not have dug so deep into her reality so quickly. Within a fortnight, it'd be much like this entire day hadn't happened.

She'd still have her home, if Adams allowed it, or she'd leave to live with Ruby and Harold. Her days would return to normalcy—there would no longer be her visits to the stables nor extended hours spent at Craven House, but she would at least have a room to call her own. It truly wasn't any less than she had now. Maybe Ruby would agree to her bringing Daphne—if the expense weren't too great a burden to the couple.

Ellie had grown rather attached to her maid, but she'd be easier to give up than Alex.

She pushed the offending thought from her mind when it threatened to dispel her smile and bring on tears.

She could be happy.

She *would* be happy—without him.

It was obvious she had no other choice.

Suddenly, her shoulders where shaking and she feared her anguish had broken through her smile and her body was visibility trembling, but hands held her upper arms. The pressure insistent but not so much that it hurt.

"Ellie," Alex said, his face only inches away. "Have you listened to a thing I've said?"

No, she didn't want to listen; she only wanted to flee the room—the house entirely—

and leave everyone behind.

She blinked rapidly and focused her gaze on his face—so stunningly handsome. Why had she never realized how truly, strikingly beautiful he was? It wasn't until one was faced with the possibility of losing something that they finally found clarity.

"That paper does not matter..." His words faded once more as the thoughts fought for control over her mind. Of course, the papers didn't matter—he would not agree to marry her. Why would he? She was a bastard. She was without a mother.

And he, Alex, was to be a grand duke.

Society—and every marriageable debutante—would be at his fingertips.

He would have no use for her. She was a liar, a coward, and not worthy of the love of a faithful man.

And she'd fooled herself into thinking it was she who didn't need him.

"Do you not have anything to say?" Alex asked, moving his hold to her hand. "Your hand in marriage will make all that's to come bearable—I want it all with you by my side or none of it."

It was her turn to stare, her jaw slack. "Did I hear you correctly?" she mumbled.

"Ellington," Alex started over, and she was grateful for it because she'd blocked every word, fearing them. "Will you honor me by taking the title of Lady Chastain—forever more to be my wife? You shall never want for a name or a home again."

"But..." Ellie couldn't seem to put all her thoughts into cohesive sentences. "Why me?"

"Because I love you," he said without

skipping a beat. "Because I can only be myself when I'm with you. Because I will never tire from keeping watch over you. Because I never want to go another day without you by my side. Must I go on?"

"Do put this sorry love struck pup out of his misery, dear sister," Harold proclaimed from a few feet away. "Brock says you must accept before drinks can be poured in celebration."

"And Harold is a sourpuss when he is denied his sherry," Brock chimed in.

Ellie looked at all the expectant faces surrounding her—each holding their breath, but their smiles fighting to break through, if only she'd give the answer they all hoped for.

Thankfully, it was the only answer she had to give.

"Of course, there is no need to go on." Ellie raised her hands, setting both to frame his face. "You are everything I have ever dreamed of in the man I never knew I needed—nor wanted, but now," she paused, taking a deep breath, "you have inserted yourself so completely in my life that I fear I would perish without you. It is I who was unable to be myself before you. It was I who cherished the many hours we spent in our travels between London and Foldger's Hall. It is I who will care nothing for the next sunrise if you are not close to share it with."

As each syllable left her mouth, everything and everyone in the room receded until it was only her and Alex.

It had been that way for the last year—since her father had died.

She'd kept watch on him, and he'd done the same.

"I love you, Alex." Ellie pressed her lips to

his, only pulling back a hairsbreadth before continuing. "No matter if we live in a grand house in London proper or a stable owned by another, I will be with you. I will follow you to any place that makes you happy because the only way I know to be happy and content is in your arms."

Ellie wasn't certain when Alex wrapped his arms around her or when everyone in the room started their loud cheering, but one thing she was confident about was her decision to take this man for her own.

No longer did someone hide who they were—and in turn, Ellie was convinced never to hide who she was from anyone again.

She was born a bastard child.

She was motherless.

She had the cruelest father known to all of London.

But she was loved by the purest man in all of England.

EPILOGUE

ELLIE STARED AT the miniature painting of a mother with her child—the only remnants of Alex's past and the mother he never knew. She was beautiful with an elegant, swanlike neck, eyes filled with light, arms holding her baby protectively to her chest. Her smile wasn't meant for the artist drawing their portrait nor for any person who'd eventually see the masterpiece, but for the little babe, wrapped in a soft blue blanket, who stared up at her.

Lady Chastain—she was a woman of immense strength and fortitude, as they'd learned from her father's many letters and all that Mrs. Dutton had shared with them in the past several weeks.

And now, Ellie was to be the next Lady Chastain, a duchess.

A true name—Ellington Davis.

She slid her finger across the image once more; the slight ripple of the artist's brush strokes told her it all wasn't a dream. This woman had once been happy, through her death she'd saved her child and given Ellie a future— with a man deserving of her love.

A man she'd surrender everything for.

A man who'd cherish her forever more.

She only seldom wondered if her own mother could have found such contentment with Ellie in hand, if she'd lived long enough.

The two things that had frightened her the most hadn't come to pass. Drake House was no longer her responsibility, but she had a new home, and with it, the man she loved.

All it had taken was giving up something she had held as solely hers, but with the sacrifice, she had gained more than she'd ever thought possible.

A forever home.

A true name.

A place that was hers and hers alone, to share with Alex. No one could take that from her.

The last several weeks had been filled with many changes. With Lord Haversham's help— and her father's meticulous note keeping—Alex had petitioned for his place as the Duke of Chastain. Harold and Ruby had moved to Drake House until their own townhouse renovation was complete. Ellie was happy for their company, since Alex had moved to the Chastain townhouse.

He insisted it wasn't proper to start their betrothal shrouded in scandal.

But that did not stop Ellie from slipping from the townhouse and stealing to Chastain House to surprise her intended. He may be worried about scandal and societal acceptance, but Ellie had never been one to heed other's rules.

Setting the portrait back in its place on Alex's tall chest of drawers, Ellie moved to the large bed that dominated the room. She'd spent many hours in this very room since Alex had taken up residence in the sprawling townhouse, its decor reminiscent of a long-ago time. Much the same as the Drake townhouse.

It was as if the day Lady Chastain died—the same day Mrs. Dutton had whisked Alex away—time had stopped in both households.

The duke had passed with his wife, leaving the marquis alone.

Except he hadn't been alone. He'd had his daughter, Ellie.

Ellie was ready for time to resume—to live the life Alex's mother had had stolen from her.

"My love." Alex stood behind her, slipping his arms around her waist and pulling her back toward him to comfort, as if he knew her every thought—which many times he did. "I was not expecting you this afternoon. Do we not have rather grand plans in a few hours?"

"We do," Ellie sighed, continuing to lean into him.

"Well then, why are you not slipping into the perfect gown, teasing your hair into a flawless knot, or donning scandalous undergarments?"

Ellie giggled. Not long ago, she would have scoffed at the thought of herself giggling like a schoolgirl over a silly comment, but with Alex she could be all the things she'd longed to be but hadn't had the opportunity. She could laugh when the mood struck. She could dance light-footed about her dressing chambers. Just the other morning, Daphne had caught her mistress singing—not a soft humming to herself, but the chords of a popular theater song sung loudly for all to hear.

She would wonder if she'd gone daft in recent weeks, but she knew the true cause of her great pleasure was the man behind her.

And the least she could do was show him great pleasure in return.

"I thought I'd help you dress for the day."

"Dress?" Alex asked, his brow furrowing. "I have yet to bathe."

"Oh, I am certain I can help with that, as well," she teased, raising her hands to unbutton his shirt.

"Ah, well, my love." His arms fell to his sides as she took hold of the buttons lining his shirt. "Do make quick work of it, we have a wedding to prepare for. And do not think you will be seeing me in all my wedding finery—it is bad luck, after all."

"I think you have marvelous luck, my lord." Ellie reached the last button then took hold of the clasp of his trousers.

"Ah, I stand corrected," he said with a smile. "I have earned the love of the most beautiful woman in all the world. I am preparing to bathe and dress to meet you before all our friends and family—to proclaim my commitment and love to you. I must say there is not a luckier soul alive than myself."

Her hands faltered and she looked up into his smiling face, certain hers glowed with warmth.

"What is it, my love?" he asked, his smile vanishing, his brow furrowing in concern.

Ellie shook her head, wanting to tell him it

was nothing, but his expression begged her to share—and Ellie was determined to never keep anything hidden from the man before her ever again.

"I am not used to having such endearments directed at me." Insults by her father, yes. Indifference from the servants, certainly. But these continued declarations of love? It was too much to hope for that they would continue ever more.

"I have many years to make up for—to prove to you all those years should have been filled with love and adoration." He spoke to her greatest fear, banishing it from her mind.

This man, Alex, did love her.

And she, the woman who'd spent her life hiding, was ready to start living—with him beside her.

"Now, woman, let us hurry" His voice held a tender note. "I will not be late to the happiest moment of my life."

AUTHOR'S NOTES

Thank you for reading *Hidden No More*
(A Lady Forsaken, Book Five).

If you enjoyed *Hidden No More*,
be sure to write a brief review at any retailer.

I'd love to hear from you!

You can contact me at:
Christina@christinamcknight.com

Or write me at:
P.O. Box 1017
Patterson, CA 95363

www.ChristinaMcKnight.com
Check out my website for giveaways, book
reviews, and information on my upcoming
projects, or connect with me through social
media at:

Twitter: @CMcKnightWriter
Facebook:
www.facebook.com/christinamcknightwriter
Goodreads:
www.goodreads.com/ChristinaMcKnight

Sign up for my newsletter here:
http://hyperurl.co/CMNL

For more information about
A Lady Forsaken Series, turn the page!

A LADY FORSAKEN SERIES

This is historical Regency romance at its best. Get lost back in time with the lords and ladies of the "A Lady Forsaken" series and fall in love with the historical romance genre.

Shunned No More
Forgotten No More
Scorned Ever More
Christmas Ever More
Hidden No More

AVAILABLE IN PRINT AND E-BOOK

For a special bonus short story conclusion to the A Lady Forsaken series, turn the page!

LOVED EVER MORE

LADY ELLINGTON'S HAND shook as she accepted the bouquet of blue flowers, bound together by a simple bow of yellow ribbon, and brought her eyes to meet her sister's. In Ruby's eyes—shaped exactly like her own—she saw unconditional love. Her sister's eyes brimmed with tears of joy and wonder—and zero reservations. Ellie had been a fool to think Ruby had ever wanted anything more than love and kinship from her. Over the last year, she'd spent so much time and energy pushing the woman away for fear her newly found elder sister meant her harm.

She tilted her chin up a notch to halt her own tears that threatened to escape.

"Do not cry, my dear sister," Ruby whispered as she placed a quick kiss to both of Ellie's cheeks and pulled her close for a hug, entirely forgetting the bouquet between them. "Alex, errr...Lord Chastain will make a wonderful husband. And I will be proud to call him brother."

How to tell Ruby that Ellie didn't fear Alex's suitability as a husband?

Ellie set the flowers on the dressing table at

her side.

In fact, Ellie had never doubted her betrothed—not his love for her, not his commitment to her family, and certainly not his suitability as the man she'd be honored to have at her side for all eternity. No, it had been herself she doubted.

Namely, that she could ever be a woman worthy of love—his love and that of others. She would always be faithful to Alex, of that there was no hint of doubt, but could she curb her need to be in control? Drop her guard enough to allow him in? If she'd been asked only a few months before, Ellie would have said it was impossible. Vulnerability was something her father, the Marquis of Drake, had taught her was unacceptable; however, that notion of impossibility was being dispelled, eroding away little by little as the days passed and Alex continued to love her. His patience and understanding knew no bounds. When she pulled away, he sensed she needed her space. When she held him too tightly, he allowed her to anchor herself to his solid footing and hold on life.

He knew himself so completely; it gave Ellie something firm to cling to.

Similar to what Ruby was offering Ellie at that precise moment—a chance to think through all the thoughts, doubts, fears, concerns, and expectations, without pressing Ellie to put them into words.

Sharing her thoughts and feelings wasn't something Ellie had ever excelled at, but in the coming months, it was something she need master. No longer would she need keep her fears hidden or her happiness contained. No longer would she need be terrified that another would use her innermost feelings against her—ripping from her any chance at a fulfilled life.

She was loved…every part of her. The good that came from somewhere deep inside, and the bad inherited from her father. She was not completely her father's child, nor was she wholly blessed with her sister's compassionate nature.

Ellie squeezed Ruby's fingers where they were intertwined with her own, signaling she was back in the present.

This was where she needed to be, where all her past days, and horrible, lonely nights had led her. It was more than she could have ever imagined for herself.

"You are to be wed this morn," Ruby sighed, her head tilting a bit as if daydreaming. "Everything is perfect…especially you."

Ellie's vision blurred as the tears returned. Blinking rapidly, she kept them within.

"I suppose I have tarried long enough." Ellie released her sister's hands and quickly brushed the unshed tears away before retrieving her flowers. She stepped before the dressing table mirror to inspect herself one last time. "Please, let everyone know I will only be a moment more."

Ruby's wide smile behind her in the looking glass was infectious, and Ellie realized she smiled, as well; though her unease kept the expression from reaching her eyes.

"You are the bride," Ruby said sternly. "As such, you can take as much, or as little, time as you need—not a soul will speak out of turn about it, or they will have me to contend with—and I suspect your ever-vigilant bridegroom, as well."

"I have spent my entire life making those who care about me wait. I will not be doing that today," Ellie confessed.

With a nod of approval, Ruby made her way to the door and closed it quietly behind her when she departed.

Ellie focused on the woman before her in the mirror. It was the girl she'd spent so many years running from, but at the same time, it wasn't.

Her naturally unruly and untamable fiery red hair had been brushed and pinned into submission, piled high atop her head in large curls, flowers matching her bouquet secured within.

With her locks gone from around her shoulders, her neck was exposed—allowing all to see her porcelain skin, unmarred by the sun's rays. Two sapphire-blue teardrop earrings hung a mere inch above her shoulders with a matching, handcrafted necklace tight about her throat.

When Lady Haversham and Ruby had suggested blue as the color that would perfectly compliment her skin tone and hair, Ellie had thought them wrong, but one look at her reflection said they'd selected precisely the right shade.

Not far below the sapphire of her necklace was the lace trim of her gown—a creamy white dress that hugged her form from neck to waist. Only at her hips did the material flare ever so slightly to allow her the ability to walk. Her dress was another piece of whom Ellie was—or at least, whom she was becoming.

A duchess.

Lady Chastain.

No longer would she have the freedom from scrutiny she'd relished while growing up under the marquis' guardianship and removed from the view of society. Gone was the child who'd delighted in pilfering a man's billfold as he walked down Bond Street. Missing was the young girl who'd found great amusement in rebuffing any person's attempt to befriend her. And exiled forever was the woman who'd built her life and future knowing she'd travel it alone.

Before her stood a woman who didn't recognize herself but was eager to become acquainted. A woman who now scoffed at her former solitary ways, favoring an afternoon in her sister's company or an evening meal with her betrothed over most anything. She'd even taken to visiting Craven House more regularly— reading with Samantha, playing cards with Payton, and discussing household management with Marce in preparation for taking over the running of Alex's home—their home.

Ellie longed to claim that she'd grown and changed all on her own—but that would be a falsehood. And she was done lying to herself and those around her.

It was the unconditional love from those surrounding her that had thawed her heart. It was precisely because Alex—as well as her sister, the Havershams, and the women of Craven House—had never given up on her. They hadn't allowed her to retreat into herself after her father's death. They'd fought to show her that she was more than her father claimed she was. And though his blood ran through her veins, she was not the bitter, angry, cruel person he'd been.

She was different, unique, and wholly herself.

Free of the weight laid upon her shoulders by her father.

And because of that, she was free to love— with her whole heart. Something she'd been shocked to discover, since she'd always felt a deep, cavernous void where those emotions should be.

And so, she'd chosen to do exactly that—love with her whole heart.

And as she'd seen that dream come to pass, the void in her chest—where her heart resided—seemed to fill to the point of bursting.

What she hadn't realized at the time, was that choosing to allow love into her heart and her life was the easy part. It was everything that came with it that was difficult. So many emotions had assaulted her since that day. Suddenly, she was not living for herself or in spite of her horrid father any longer, no, there were people who depended on her. Not for support or to provide them with anything; instead, they were dependent on her happiness. They truly wanted her to be content and cheerful.

She was living each day to prove to those around her that she could find joy in life—for the first time.

And that...that was far more difficult than living only for herself; making decisions that only affected *her* future.

The most overwhelming part of it was that Ellie *was* learning to be happy, to find joy in the little things, and to appreciate every moment with her family and friends.

It also meant she needed to discover who she was and how that realization played into her altered path through life. No longer would she allow herself to be the petulant child of her past. Pickpocketing in Hyde Park or Covent Gardens was far too risky. Ruby and Alex would be the ones hurt if she ever came to harm—and she could not bear disappointing them.

And Marce…dear, sweet Marce, she had all the trouble she could handle in the form of her four siblings: Garrett, Judith, Samantha, and Payton.

A soft knock sounded at the door, bringing Ellie back to the present once more. Glancing at the clock on the mantle, she noted several minutes had passed since Ruby departed to finish preparing for the nuptials.

"I will be right out." She smiled at her reflection in the mirror, her happiness reaching her eyes a bit more this time. "I need to fix a pin in my hair first."

Ellie glanced around the room—a large, sparsely furnished room. The walls had been freshly painted only a fortnight before in preparation for the new mistress' arrival. Her. She'd been told the room had once belonged to Lorelei, Alex's birth mother, but the woman hadn't a chance to renovate before she'd passed away in a carriage accident along with her husband, leaving the Dukedom without an heir until Alex had been found.

The entire house had fallen into disrepair due to extreme neglect, but thankfully, neither the Chastain nor Drake titles were lacking in funds. The renovations on both of their London homes would be complete before the year was over.

"My lady?" Daphne, her lady's maid, said, stepping into the room and quickly closing the door behind her. Ellie met the girl's eyes in the mirror she still faced. "My lady, you look stunning."

"That is very kind of you to say," Ellie replied. She didn't feel stunning—not in the least. If anything, she felt the imposter. She'd been outfitted in a gown far grander than she merited. She'd moved her worldly possessions into a room that had belonged to a woman far more deserving than Ellie. And she was about to take a man to husband who deserved any woman but the one he was prepared to wed.

"Should I call for Lord Chastain?" Daphne asked. "Or maybe Mrs. Jakeston?"

"That is not necessary." Ellie's smile pulled tightly across her face. Her lady's maid saw right through her ruse of joy, but Daphne had enough sense about her to act as if she hadn't seen her mistress's uncertainty. "I only need a few minutes. This is all so overwhelming."

"It is to be expected, my lady."

"Did my sister send you in here to make sure all was well?" It would not be the first—nor the last—time Ruby had enlisted the help of others to break through the walls Ellie had constructed around herself. When Daphne shook her head, Ellie was prepared to take her denial as fact since her maid hadn't pushed to call for Alex or Ruby. "I think I am ready."

Daphne nodded and pulled the door open for Ellie.

Her slippered feet moved across the room toward the open door. Once in the hallway, she turned to Daphne for guidance. Ellie hadn't had the time to learn the layout of her new home yet, nor had she any idea where everyone was gathering. It was another thing that Ruby and Lady Haversham had insisted upon. All she knew was that it was to be an outdoor ceremony with a meal to follow in the grand dining room: roasted pheasant and duck with platters filled to the brim with cheese, freshly baked breads, and fruits. Cook had prepared a variety of soups and delicate desserts, as well.

It was all to impress their new duchess.

Why couldn't Ellie smile graciously and accept everything that was being offered her?

The simple answer: she felt like an utter fraud, an imposter...the bastard child of a marquis and a woman who had made her living by her loose morals.

A woman with that type of ancestry was never meant to be a duchess.

In a sad way, her father, the Marquis of Drake, had likely been preparing her for the future. One where a woman such as herself was always relegated to the fringes of society — present but never fully acknowledged or accepted.

"This way, my lady." Daphne slipped her hand through Ellie's arm and guided her down the hall toward the sounds of laughter and much talking. The smell of deliciousness became stronger as the sounds of people grew louder. Ellie suspected they were only a corner or two away from the main gathering.

Her feet slowed, each step becoming more difficult to take than the last.

Once she had reached the gathering, all would move at a hurried pace. She'd be greeted by her sister and friends, she'd move to stand at Alex's side and face Vicar Jakeston, and before Ellie could catch her breath, she'd be swept into the arms of the waiting people — congratulations all round. Afterwards, merriment would commence, and everyone would toast her and Alex's future — one of happiness, many children, and a long life together. They would eat until their stomachs were full and aching, they would dance until they were once again hungry, and then she and Alex would retire to their chambers. Daphne would greet her with a large, knowing smile as she hurriedly prepared the new duchess for her new husband—a pristine white night shift with a low scooping neckline had been commissioned for this special occasion. Alex would tentatively enter her chambers, or likely summon her to his adjoining chambers, and their bodies would meet after so many weeks of longing for one another—though they'd shared a very private and intimate moment only that morning.

Things would be different. *Everything* would be different.

Once they were wed, it would be about them, as a pair, and coming together to secure a mutually beneficial future for themselves and any offspring that may result from their union.

It was all very specifically worded in the marriage settlement that had been negotiated by Harold, Ruby's husband. It was, after all, the proper thing to do.

Ellie had little faith in the ability of people— no matter their social status—to create and maintain a strong bond for a lifetime.

One only need look as far as her mother and father—and debatably, even more damaging, were Alex's own sires.

That their lives were intertwined as far back as Ellie's and Alex's births mattered naught.

That many—Mrs. Dutton and Lady Haversham specifically—saw the pair as destined and fated to be also mattered naught.

Especially if Ellie could not commit to putting the greater good before her own needs and wants.

A husband…children…plus, her sister and her husband.

It was all too daunting to take in.

"Shall I fetch you something to drink, my lady?" Daphne had halted beside Ellie, and if it weren't for their linked arms, Ellie would likely crumble to her knees. Her maid's question came to her as if through a great wind tunnel, the words sounding far away, yet they echoed in her head. "Lady Ellington?"

She wanted to run. She wanted to strip the beautiful gown from her body and don the plain knee-length dress with apron from her youth. She wanted to hide among the many rooms at Drake townhouse, invisible to all.

It should not be too painful to explain to her sister—and Alex—that she'd made an enormous mistake.

She wasn't prepared to be a wife. A duchess. A mother.

In fact, she was highly unsuited for any of those roles.

Ruby would not force her to wed if she knew her sister was not for the match.

Though if her sister asked for Ellie's honesty, the match was perfect.

Alex, her betrothed, was perfect...in every way.

Which only made Ellie's flaws all the more glaring.

It was Ellie who was far from perfect.

She only wondered if her flaws were visible to those around her. Her sister seemed agreeable to overlooking her shortcomings. The women of Craven House had known her since she was a girl in plaits and had acclimated to her sometimes dour disposition. Even Lord and Lady Haversham seemed to only smile and nod when Ellie's mood turned disagreeable.

How could they all fail to see that what she truly needed was someone—anyone—to recognize the fire within and draw her away from the flame?

There was only one who, no matter how disagreeable she was, no matter her dour mood, no matter her snide comments, would pull her close when all she sought was to run away.

Alex.

Ellie owed him more than to be jilted at the altar, awaiting a bride who never showed, and the embarrassment of explaining everything to the guests who'd traveled to attend.

This man—her betrothed—would lay down his life for her if she so asked.

And up until this very moment, Ellie had been the type to ask exactly that, if only to prove to all that the person's loyalty would flee once faced by such a possibility. It would have given her perverse pleasure to see another's true colors and lack of intention made known to all those watching.

"Mrs. Dutton." The alarm in Daphne's voice pulled Ellie out of her thoughts.

Ellie blinked rapidly, focusing on the many servants before her—all frozen in place as they watched their soon-to-be duchess. They stared intently, and she realized she had two choices: she could fall apart and flee, or she could square her shoulders and smile at the many people working so hard to make this day special...for her.

And they all depended on her to a certain degree.

She was to be the lady of this great townhouse, something that had been lacking for many years, and a duchess to all those under the Chastain Dukedom. It would be Ellie's responsibility to go forth into society and represent them all.

It was a task and duty she felt unworthy of.

But the hope and promise in every face that stared back at her told Ellie *they* believed in her—they'd assessed her and found her worthy.

More than worthy, and not only of being their duchess but also to be at their long-lost duke's side as his mate.

It was the exact thing she'd tried to force on the servants at Drake townhouse after her father had passed away, but these people...they were willing to accept her because Alex had. They hadn't seen him since he was a babe in swaddling cloth, but they trusted him nonetheless.

Their warm and welcoming smiles told Ellie they didn't care that her mother had earned a living as a strumpet.

Ellie only wished she possessed a fraction of the confidence they had in her, for she sensed she'd need it in the days and months to come. They didn't know her. In fact, she'd only begun moving her things to Alex's home the day before. But the servants trusted that her intentions were good and true—both toward them *and* their newly found master.

And every pore in Ellie shouted that her intentions toward Alex—and his many servants across the four estates—were true. The thought of hurting the man who'd taken such care with her since before her father's passing ate at her very core.

Even this morning, Alex had sought her out, taken her into his strong, capable, yet compassionate arms, and not only told her but also *showed* her everything was as it should be.

So why the uncertainty now?

Ellie smiled, hoping no one noticed the slight

wobble of it. "Good day to you all. Thank you for all your hard work to make this day special for my lord." She inclined her head, her chin dipping as she hid her watering eyes. "I know this means so much to him—all of you do."

If it were possible, all the smiles turned her way grew even wider at her words. Though Ellie had said very little, she'd spoken from her heart. It was something she wasn't accustomed to. In all truth, she'd spent her entire life hiding her heart, guarding it from the hurt and pain that had assaulted her all too frequently under her father's dubious care.

"We be happy ta have ye, m'lady," Mrs. Dutton gushed as she moved quickly to stand before Ellie. "Ye be all me boy eva needed ta realize he be so much more 'an all he be think'n."

Ellie closed her mouth tightly to keep her chin from trembling as she stared into the eyes of a woman whose compassion and selflessness was only rivaled by that of the man she'd raised since infancy, the man Ellie was to call husband. Every good trait Alex possessed was because of the woman before her. She was on the short side with a more rounded figure, but to Ellie, she stood ten feet tall—a pillar, a woman Ellie would do well to learn from.

"Thank you, Mrs. Dutton," Ellie said, her voice cracking on the last word.

She'd been surrounded by so many strong, fierce, and loving women all her life, yet she'd neglected to truly notice. It would have benefited her greatly to study these women, learn all she could from them, instead of trying— unsuccessfully—to gain her father's favor. She'd lived her life all wrong thus far. That ended today.

It *had* to end today, there was no other choice for her.

Or her future.

Ellie stared into the welcoming faces of the people surrounding her and all she saw was love and acceptance.

Maybe it was time she accepted herself—for who she was now and who she'd strive to be.

A woman worthy of all those around her. Worthy of their love, dedication, and unwavering support.

"My lady?" Daphne squeezed Ellie's hand where it had fallen to her side. "Lord Chastain, and the others, are awaiting you outside."

It was time.

Her hesitancy lingered as she walked through the grand dining hall and toward the double doors, thrown wide, that led to the terrace and the steps she'd take to the gardens below.

Her sister and Lady Haversham had forbidden her from seeing the gardens, saying it would make the moment more special if Ellie entered the gardens and saw not only the decorations for the first time but Alex, too.

"I am ready," Ellie whispered, squeezing Daphne's hand in return before releasing it and bringing her bouquet from her side to before her.

Mrs. Dutton gave her a quick peck on the cheek. "We all be overjoyed ta see this day finally come." Without another word, the older woman turned and hurried out the open doors, her movements shockingly agile for a woman of her years.

"Dear Daphne." Ellie turned to her trusted maid. "Please, go and take your place. I will be right behind you."

"You are a vision, my lady. My lord is going

to be so pleased with his bride." Daphne followed Mrs. Dutton's path out the open doors and disappeared from sight, leaving Ellie to her own thoughts once more.

Alex was what she wanted. To be his duchess was more than she could have hoped for.

Ellie took a deep breath and slowly walked toward the terrace doors—and her future.

The floor trembled beneath her feet, and it took her a moment to realize it was her legs shaking, not the ground beneath her.

Servants could be heard moving to and fro behind her in preparation for the wedding feast and the grand ball that evening. She'd requested only a scant few be included in the actual ceremony, which Alex had readily agreed to as they were both new to society, but all of London had received invitations to meet the newest Lord and Lady Chastain.

There would be no more hiding, no more secrecy.

And the most adequate way to satisfy the *ton's* interest in them was to present themselves to all of society properly. Allow the masses to view and assess the Duke and Duchess Chastain, allow the scandal of their pasts to be exposed, discussed, and put to rest. Once that part was over, it would be safe for Alex and her to start their life together, go where they chose to go and be whomever they wanted to be. To start a family. Possibly retire to the country. Live a life in London among the *beau monde*. It was up to them, as a pair, to determine their future happiness and life.

They'd decided to create their own destiny...make their own happily ever after. And with the support of their family and friends they'd attain everything their hearts desired.

The late morning sun shone brightly, blinding Ellie for a few seconds when she stepped through the doors. Her eyes adjusted, revealing a small gathering—all the people she held dear. All those who hadn't given up on her, no matter how much she'd pushed them away over the years.

Friends and family...new and old.

All in attendance to witness the vows between her and Alex.

Though there were only at most twenty people, the congregation was daunting.

Ellie's heart pounded loudly in her chest. So loud, she could see people's mouths moving as they spoke to the person next to them, but their words were drowned out by the sound of her heart and the blood pumping rapidly through her veins.

Suddenly, she was scared—terrified to her core—of walking forth. Of accepting all that Alex was offering her.

Her doubts, her fears, her hesitation...would they ever recede?

Would there be a day where Ellie was free from her past, able to put her father's misdeeds behind her and live the life she was meant to?

Every part of her wanted the freedom, craved the chance to leave it all in past—forget it all, and embrace the love being offered to her.

Ellie searched the crowd of smiling faces for the one that meant the most to her. The only one that mattered.

A moment of panic struck when Ellie didn't immediately see the man she was looking for.

The vicar stood proudly before the waiting crowd.

Ruby, Jude, Sam, and Lady Haversham stood to his left, looking back at her.

On the right side, Lord Haversham held baby Neill as he squirmed to be set down.

Marce, Daphne, Payton, and Mrs. Dutton sat proudly in the front row of seats, all looking expectantly over their shoulders at Ellie. Behind them sat all the servants from the Drake and Chastain townhouses, along with several servants from Lady Chastain's home. Ellie even spied Lady Aloria...now Lady Wolfeton with her husband.

It sparked a feeling of love so deep, Ellie's knees shook once more...but she quickly settled herself as she once again moved her eyes across the throng.

Finally, she saw him.

He took a step away from the vicar as if sensing her uneasiness and need for him.

Every doubt, fear, and uncertainly fled as Lord Chastain made his way to her, his steps sure and solid when he took the three steps and arrived next to her on the terrace.

Ellie was exactly where she was meant to be.

It was only with Alex at her side that she could fully recognize her place.

It was he who made her whole. And she did the same for him.

They'd lived their lives as two halves, never knowing what was missing—or who. They'd each had a void they'd tried to full—Ellie with her outlandish behavior, and Alex with his overgenerous nature.

Together, they were one.

It had taken Alex to show Ellie the woman she was destined to be. That all she needed was him at her side.

"My love," Alex whispered. "Are you ready to start our future? Are you ready to be my duchess?"

Ellie was ready and prepared to be that woman.

It was he—and only him—who not only told her, but also showed her, that she was worthy.

"There is no other place I belong, or desire to be, except by your side." They were the most honest and unabashed words she'd ever uttered to another.

"I have longed to hear this." His smile filled her with a sense of rightness. "Shall we entertain our guests? It is long past time you are presented as my love, my life, and finally, my duchess."

Ellie nodded, words escaping her at the look of love he sent her way.

She knew it to be an unconditional, unending, unbreakable love that would last until they drew their final breaths.

It was everything, and something she'd never known she wanted.

Yet, it was everything she needed.

"I have never been more ready."

With one final smile for each other, Ellie took the first step toward the rest of her life—Alex by her side, and everyone she held dear watching and supporting them.

It was the way things would be forever more—a future with an overabundance of love, family and friends who supported her every decision, and a husband who cherished her above all else.

There was nothing more she could ever wish for.

Ellie was loved. Ever more.

ABOUT THE AUTHOR

USA TODAY Bestselling Author Christina McKnight writes emotional and intricate Regency Romance with strong women and maverick heroes.

Her books combine romance and mystery, exploring themes of redemption and forgiveness. When she's not writing, Christina enjoys trying new coffeehouses, visiting wine bars, traveling the world, and watching television.

Email: Christina@ChristinaMcKnight.com
Follow her on Twitter: @CMcKnightWriter
Subscribe to her newsletter:
http://hyperurl.co/CMNL
Keep up to date on her releases:
www.christinamcknight.com
Like Christina's FB Author page:
ChristinaMcKnightWriter